FEAR THE REAPER

STRIKE FORCE (BOOK FOUR)

FIONA QUINN

FEAR THE REAPER

BOOK FOUR

FIONA QUINN

THE WORLD OF INIQUUS

Ubicumque, Quoties. Quidquid

Iniquus - /i'ni/kwus/ our strength is unequalled, our tactics unfair – we stretch the law to its breaking point. We do whatever is necessary to bring the enemy down.

THE LYNX SERIES

Weakest Lynx

Missing Lynx

Chain Lynx

Cuff Lynx

Gulf Lynx

Hyper Lynx

STRIKE FORCE

In Too DEEP

JACK Be Quick

InstiGATOR

F ear The REAPER

Uncommon Enemies

Wasp

Relic

Deadlock

Thorn

FBI Joint Task Force

Open Secret

Cold Red

Even Odds

Kate Hamilton Mysteries

Mine

Yours

Ours

Cerberus Tactical K9 Team Alpha

Survival Instinct

Protective Instinct

Defender's Instinct

Delta Force Echo

Danger Signs

Danger Zone

Danger Close

Cerberus Tactical K9 Team Bravo

Warrior's Instinct

Rescue Instinct

Hero Instinct

This book is dedicated to
Devin and Ivey Jane.
Every child deserves to be richly cherished.

THE GOOD GUYS

Strike Force

Striker – Commander (Fiancé, Lexi "Lynx" Sobado)
Jack – Second in command (Wife, Suz McCullen)
Lynx – Puzzler (Fiancé, Striker Rheas)
Deep – Computer support/logistics (Wife, Grace Del Toro)
Blaze – Operator (Fiancé, Faith)
Randy – Operator
Gator – Operator
Reaper – K9 handler (Wife, Kate and father to Zack)

FBI

Damian Prescott
Steve Finley

Silver Lake Neighbors

Dave and Cathy Murphy (Twin boys Fletcher and Colin)
Sarah (Children Mikey and Ruby)

1

Cyn

Friday afternoon

The clamor of humanity bumped and knocked against the slick glass walls of the airport departure hall. As the babbling volume swelled to overflowing, it swept upward into the rafters where it perched, staring down at the incoming passengers.

The din engulfed Cynthia Dimitrova as soon as the automatic doors mechanically slid wide.

Stepping away from the snow-muffled D.C. morning, boots damp with salty slush, a blast of artificial heat rushed past Cyn, pressing the frigid temperatures back away from the building's interior.

The gust ruffled through Cyn's collar-length brown wig, a strand caught in her freshly applied rose-colored lipstick. She stopped to brush the wayward tendril back behind her ear and adjust the strap of her purse higher onto her shoulder.

Cyn inhaled deeply.

To her, airports smelled like sunscreen-scented tourist escapism, the garlicky fatigue of families fulfilling emotional obligations, and the wet wool of business banality.

Banality was the category where she placed herself for today's flight. This certainly wasn't about fun. Though, Cyn's idea of a good time didn't necessarily line up with that of most people.

To her, fun was edgy, exciting, *dangerous*.

Mind games were fun.

Power was fun.

Winning was *everything*.

This? *This* was a losing situation.

No. Not fun by anyone's standards. Certainly not Cyn's. But a favor was a favor. And it would be repaid in time.

She'd make sure of it.

Cyn glanced back at Nia—nineteen, sullen, and much more problematic than Cyn had been led to understand.

Nia would fail today's test.

And Cyn couldn't care less. Cyn's psyche wasn't built to be nurturing, not even as tradecraft.

What happened to Nia fell heavily on Nia's shoulders.

Cyn wasn't responsible for what happened next in this teen's list of poor life choices.

Bright star? Hardly. Well, at least in this part of the job.

Cyn reached back to the teen's elbow and pulled her forward, so they walked side by side, and Cyn could keep an eye on her. She looked down at the girl.

Nia was pretty enough.

She liked to wear her hair in two buns on the top of her head, like kitten ears. Artificial lashes fringed Nia's dark doe eyes. Her lips were soft and full, accented by baby pink lip stain and glitter gloss. The kind of lips that men would fantasize about encircling their hard cocks.

Nia looked like she was just out of middle school—except for her ginormous breasts.

Yes, indeedy, Nia's most remarkable physical attribute was her enormous boobage that hovered over an otherwise toothpick of a body.

It made her look theatrically top-heavy like she needed the strong hand of a daddy figure to keep her from toppling over.

If a man had a pedophile fetish, Nia was someone to fantasize about and still keep things legal if push came to shove came to grunting orgasm.

Cyn could see why others in their organization might find Nia compelling as a tool. A "screw driver," Cyn thought with a smirk.

Depending on the guy's fantasy—with the right clothes, hair, and makeup—Nia could continue exploiting men who liked to think with their dicks. In Cyn's experience, that was a goodly portion of the male population—gullible when their egos and cocks were stroked, manipulatable when their johnsons thought they'd have an in.

In *this* circumstance, though, Nia *wasn't* using her assets to her advantage. The girl was blanched white, making her sparkle pink blush stand out like two circles of color painted on a discount store doll. Her hand clenched the pull handle of her bag. Unblinking eyes held too wide for too long. Her hostage-like behavior was going to attract attention, if not scrutiny.

Hardly the victim, Nia had *asked* to take the next step up the rungs of the Prokhorov Family ladder.

Dragging her carry-on bag behind her as she moved into the press of travelers, Cyn's voice was barely audible, pitched to reach Nia's ears only. "You're going to be fine. Complete your task, get on your plane, done."

"I have to pee," Nia announced.

"Can it wait until we get through the security check?"

Nia rubbed the flat palm of her free hand over her mouth, her eyes watery. "Probably not."

Cyn stepped around the guy who had stopped mid-stride, patting frantically at his pockets. She scanned the corridor ahead of them, looking for a sign, pointed, and headed in the direction of the blue triangle skirt icon, jutting out overhead.

Nia's anxiety was palpable, but Cyn wasn't going to worry about that. Cyn had a solution hiding in her coat pocket. She didn't get this far in life by not thinking ahead.

Besides, of all places to be agitated, Cyn reasoned, this was it.

At the airport, anxiety was par for the course.

The thing about airports, Cyn mused as she bustled along with the crowd, was that they were filled with navel-gazers. Everyone was busy with the act of moving from departure to arrival. Little worries felt big. Will the plane be on time? Will I make my connection? Will my bag get there when I do? Will my things be safe?

There were the bigger worries, too. For people who hated to travel, this was a time to confront the phobias that made their flight feel like a game of Russian roulette. Phobic travelers were easy to spot, checking the weather apps for information about turbulence, wringing their hands, and deep breathing—usually with no good effect.

Angling out of the stream of passengers, then rounding into the ladies' room, Nia jogged down the line of doors.

Cyn took advantage of a free stall that opened up next to her.

Pulling her carry-on in behind her, she locked the door and peeled off her coat.

Almost immediately, the sound of gag-puking came from her right.

Cyn was sure it was Nia.

Absolutely gross. *Craven little shit.*

Unzipping, Cyn dropped her jeans and panties to her knees.

She sat on the toilet seat, still warm from the last occupant. She might as well settle in and wait for Nia's stomach to empty. The less time spent out in the open where Cyn's face might be seen and remembered, the better.

Protecting herself from facial recognition was probably overkill for the banality of this drop. But tradecraft had become muscle memory, and best practices should always be applied. One never knew—shit hitting the fan was a truism. It was better to duck any blowback from the crap.

And this unexpected assignment was *total* crap. Cyn had been handed a coward to field test.

The bathroom walls echoed with the clacking shoes of women coming and going, the whir of the hand dryer, and running water. It sounded like the puking might be done.

Glancing at her watch, Cyn felt the pressure of their time-window narrowing. Cyn didn't know how long it would take to get through the security check.

Cyn pulled off a length of toilet paper and crumpled it into her hand.

She stood dragging her clothing back into place. Cyn adjusted the padded vest that hugged her under her turtleneck sweater. A costuming prop—good enough to fool the TSA machines and even a pat-down if it were required—added a good thirty pounds or so to her frame. With the majority of the cushioning just under her breasts, it created a menopausal redistribution of weight and aged her about fifteen to twenty years. Cyn was aiming for "early fifties," the oldest she thought she could get away with.

This was the persona Cyn used when she flew. The brown wig with a Jack Frost-like dusting of gray strands at the crown, the padding, and the proper application of high-tech makeup contouring meant that Cyn matched her fake driver's license. The license had a "good to go" star in the upper right-hand corner, saying that the department of motor vehicles had approved her identity.

With a last tug to her turtleneck sweater, a smoothing swipe of her hands, everything was in place. The automatic toilet flushed as Cyn reached for the lock, flecking her with bowl spittle.

Disgusting.

With a sigh, she moved out of the stall, pushing her carry-on bag—where she'd laid her coat and purse—out in front of her.

After a quick wash of her hands, Cyn slid past the bathroom attendant relining the trashcan.

Cyn turned her face away from the mirror. Habit. Though, her wig's long bangs did a "bang-up" job hiding her features.

Moving down the rows of stalls, Cyn peeked under the doors looking for Nia's shoes. There she was in the last stall, her white, thick-soled tennis shoe tapping the ground.

Cyn knocked. "Hey, you okay?"

"No."

"Are you ill?"

"Pretty much."

Teenagers. Miserable freaking creatures. "Come on out. Let's get your hands washed. I have something that will take the edge off."

A woman came out of the stall, startled that Cyn was standing right there. She sent Cyn a suspicious glance, then looked toward Nia's door, and then hard eyes back on Cyn.

The woman looked like she had something in her background. Cop maybe. FBI? It was in the way she squared off, the rigidity of her posture. *Crap.*

Cyn sniffed a deep breath as she stepped out of the woman's way. She talked to Nia's door. "Your therapist said that if you had a panic attack before we fly, you could take a pill. You won't feel the effects. It'll just take the edge off."

The woman moved away.

Nia's door swung open.

"Jeezis." Cyn grabbed Nia's wrist and hissed into her ear. "Get it together. Wash your face, rinse your mouth. This is unacceptable." Reaching into her pocket, Cyn pulled out a bottle. Pressing her palm into the top, she twisted it and felt annoyance rising when it didn't give. Cyn looked down at the bottle as Nia pushed past her.

"I don't want a pill."

"I didn't ask you what you wanted, dear."

The woman who smelled like law enforcement was slow washing her hands. Worried eyes. She'd pulled her lower lip into her mouth to chew on it, making a decision. She looked like she wanted to intervene. She looked like she was choosing her words.

For the most part, cops knew when to mind their own business because who wanted to miss their flight over something inconsequential? Or shoot even for something consequential? If they were off the beat, there was no reason to stretch their neck out to potentially get caught in an unexpected guillotine.

Cyn let her hair fall over her face as she slid a hand down Nia's arm and sent her a warm, maternal smile. Maternal-ish. Cyn wasn't mother material. Up until recently, she'd never considered it. Any baby fever she'd been experiencing, Cyn chalked up to hormones and ignored them. Estrogen wasn't going to crap up her life with diapers and puke. "We're going to trust your therapist. I want you to feel comfortable. It's a short flight. Up and then down, okay?" She looked at the childproof mechanism on the screwcap.

Cyn squeezed the sides, twisted, and picked a tiny white pill from the seven that rested inside.

Seven—the normal prescription quantity written for this highly addictive drug.

Seven, Cyn mused, was just enough pills—crushed to a fine powder and mixed into a high-dollar room service meal coupled with a stiff drink or four—that could suppress the respiratory system and make the death look like an accidental overdose.

But that wasn't necessary information for today.

Nia held out an open palm obediently. She seemed to realize she'd put her toe a little too close to the "you're screwed" line. Nia popped the pill into her mouth and flashed her hand under the faucet to collect a palmful of water, slurping it down. Nia turned to Cyn, opened her mouth, stuck out a rigid tongue. She swirled it from left to right and up to show that the pill wasn't being held in her cheek to spit out later.

While Nia was insolent, Cyn recognized that pill check was a practiced move. Cyn wasn't aware that the girl had ever been institutionalized in a nuthouse.

Someone needed to do better vetting. This was too dangerous a game to play with someone who was mentally unstable.

Who knew, maybe Nia hadn't learned that step in a psych ward; perhaps, she'd learned that move in juvie—juvie would be better.

Not great. But better.

2

Reaper

Friday Afternoon

Reaper Hamilton reached across the back bench of his buddy Striker's SUV to unbuckle the baby's car seat.

Fighting the straps, slush from the vehicle's roof sliding down his collar, Reaper angled the safety seat out.

His wife, Kate, stood out of the snow flurries on the sidewalk in front of the airport's departure doors. As he walked around the front of the vehicle, Reaper noted the stress tightening the muscles around her mouth as she jostled their ten-month-old son, Zach, in her arms.

Reaper knew that look on her face. The old adage "ignorance is bliss" was a phrase that Reaper often thought about when Kate got that look in her eyes. Kate was so damned smart, and he loved that about her. Far from the bliss of ignorance, Kate's level of smarts and her huge sack of factoids meant she was constantly processing…thinking about ramifications. Making a long list of outcomes—ways that things could go wrong. She'd always been that way. It just seemed to have magnified since Reaper's medical retirement from the military and all the crap he'd put her through these last few years.

Kate jostled baby Zack in one arm as she lifted the other to signal a porter over, then turned to Striker and called out, "Thanks for making the trek out here in this weather."

Striker—a SEAL buddy from back in the day, and now Reaper's temporary commander at Iniquus Security—hefted the bags from the cargo hold. "No problem." Slamming the back hatch down, Striker moved to set the two suitcases onto the sidewalk. "So Reaper's heading home Sunday, and you're staying in Boston a while longer?"

Reaper set the car seat with the luggage, then turned to unload Houston from the back.

"Man, that's a beautiful German shepherd," a woman crooned as Houston jumped to the sidewalk and shook her coat.

Reaper reached down, adjusted Houston's service dog vest, and checked the connection on her lead.

Houston ignored Reaper's efforts as she dragged over to Kate. Houston believed that her first and most important job was keeping baby Zack safe.

Kate and Reaper agreed that Houston had the right priorities.

A nose boop on the baby's bottom, a tactical sweep of the area, then Houston found her spot, on Reaper's left side, squatting rather than plunking her butt down on the wet cement.

"After the wedding," Kate explained to Striker, "all of us bridesmaids have a rental on the ocean for next week. The weather looks glacial up around Boston Harbor, but it's really about having a pretty view while we hang out, drink wine, and eat raw cookie dough out of the bowl. Girl talk." She looked at Reaper when she said, "No boys allowed." She tucked her head to kiss Zack. "Except for Little Guy, of course. He promised not to tattle on us." She sent a wink Reaper's way.

"Sounds like you're set up to have a good time." Striker turned to Reaper. "Safe travels. Someone will be here to pick you up on Sunday. We'll meet at baggage claim."

"Yeah, man, thanks." Reaper extended his hand for a shake. They had served together many years ago. But a brother was a brother. After they left the service—Striker for family reasons, Reaper for medical ones—Reaper appreciated their ongoing friendship and Striker's support.

Heck, Reaper was almost a hundred percent sure that the reason he even had his job at Iniquus Security had to do with Striker recommending him.

As Reaper made his way back into the workforce after years of physical and mental agony, and now a new lease on life after experimental interventions released him from the torture chamber inside his head, Reaper wasn't going to let anything he did tarnish Striker's golden reputation with Iniquus Command.

Everything was by the book and to SEAL level of perfection. No "I" was left undotted, no "T" left uncrossed.

Dressed in his Iniquus operator's uniform of a charcoal gray compression shirt and tactical pants, Striker slid back behind the wheel and angled into the slow-moving traffic, headed toward the Iniquus campus.

Reaper turned his focus to the porter. Pulling the printed tickets from his pocket, Reaper handed them over to the guy's outstretched hand.

Yes, Kate had told him just to put the tickets on his phone. And sure, it would make things more streamlined. But Reaper hated the idea of cell phones. Despised the concept. To him, they posed a clear security hazard. Unless he was ordered to carry one, Reaper had been old school in his communications. By contract with Iniquus, though, Reaper had to be within arm's reach of his cell phone—fully charged with audible volume—at all times. *All times.* Even when on R& R.

And by all times, it meant in a waterproof bag on a lanyard around his neck when he was swimming. And fully charged meant Reaper carried two extra batteries in his tactical pants' pocket.

Excessive?

For most jobs, maybe. Rules were rules, like it or not.

If the world were imploding, Iniquus would need a way to inform and command.

While the porter laced tags through the handles on their cases, Reaper slid his hand over the baby's damp curls, then tugged Little Guy's hat over his ears against the frigid wind.

Zack pushed it right back off, ratcheting up his displeasure with a bat of his tiny fist.

Kate sent Reaper the tightest of tight-lipped smiles. He could see that Kate had projected a shit show for their flight to Boston.

Heading north for their friend's wedding and some time with the old gang, this was supposed to be relaxing.

Kate deserved some fun. It had been a hell of a few years for her.

For them.

He wished he could make her feel safe and comfortable, wished she could Zen the hell out.

But then Kate wouldn't be Kate.

And Reaper *loved* Kate with every cell in his body.

If he were plotting their relationship on one of Kate's copious graphs she used when she was a biology teacher, Kate would be the crests and trough that kept their relationship interesting, the late-night debate part, the sobbing over a sad book part, the silky lace and ribbon panties part.

He saw his role more like a straight line (or "longitudinal

waves," as Kate would phrase it). For most of their relationship, he'd considered himself the solid and steady base.

What a crock of shit that was.

Kate didn't like that "wave" description, anyway. She said it made her sound like she was unstable.

"What would you prefer?" Reaper had asked.

Back when they were dating, back before...*everything*—younger, less beaten to a pulp—she'd smiled. "I'm not saying I disagree with the concept, just that particular visual... I think of us more as ballroom dancers. There you are—athletic, graceful, supportive. And there's me, feeling my way around the music with some kicks and twirls."

He'd laughed and hurt her feelings.

But it had been the idea of him as a graceful dancer that was ridiculous. For a man who had risen to top-tier special ops, SEAL Team Six, he was miserable at trying to find and keep a beat outside of a marching cadence.

And he'd learned over the last few years of hell that it was, in fact, Kate who was the rock, the steadiness.

Reaper just had to make sure that her rock-solid tenacity, her unwavering belief in him—in *them*—was justified.

3

Cyn

FRIDAY AFTERNOON

THE LONG LINE at airport security gave the meds enough time to soothe Nia's craven nerves.

The two women walked in the direction of their gate within arm's reach of each other, but they did it as strangers, each ignoring the other.

Despite their rough start, they'd made it to their tactical position a few minutes ahead of time.

Nia stood by a magazine kiosk, her back to the wall, seeming to focus on her phone, waiting.

The airline staff closed the door on the last of the passengers boarding from that gate and were now changing the signage over from the departing Chicago flight to the boarding Boston flight.

The timing was perfect. The holding area had to be cleared out so Nia could choose the exact seat in their mission file. Soon the chairs would fill again.

The flight to Boston was in an hour.

Cyn stopped to grab a bottle of water and a bar of chocolate at the coffee joint while she kept a surreptitious eye on Nia's behavior.

Nia dragged her carry-on to the required seat—third row, the end closest to the window bank. There she plunked down and scrolled on her phone some more. After a few minutes, she opened her carry-on.

Admittedly, the assigned task was ridiculously easy.

Still, if Nia looked around furtively, if her body was too tight or robotic, if she were anything but casual, it could call attention. Curiosity.

But she did fine.

It was only because Cyn knew exactly what Nia was up to that she could decipher Nia's next moves.

Nia retrieved the drop box—a small plastic container that held a micro thumb drive—from the side pocket of her bag. She peeled away the adhesive backing and palmed the device. Pretending to pop a piece of gum in her mouth, Nia hid the purpose of her gestures.

Cyn would point out that Nia should palm a piece of gum next time because she only remembered to fake chew a few times.

Someone with a trained eye would remark on that.

On this operation, though, that wasn't a concern. The Family had hacked into the security cameras. This corridor's CTV would be nothing but static until the Boston flight took off. An hour was enough time for the security guards to see that there was an issue and call for technical support. It wasn't enough time for anyone to discover the breach. And, once the flight took off and everything came back online, everyone would chalk the event up to a random glitch.

As Nia palmed the box, she pulled a college hoody from her case, thrashing a bit as she tugged it on.

That flail covered her actions.

Slightly larger than a postage stamp, Nia pressed the box against the underside of her chair's seat. The act was easily concealed behind her luggage.

Yes, indeedy, while the documents and photographs on the thumb drive were explosive to someone's life, the act of getting it into the right person's hands was rather banal.

A newbie test.

Nia zipped her case closed. Dragging her empty water bottle from her oversized purse, Nia

glanced around. Neck craned, her gaze lit on a water fountain with a bottling spigot. She dragged her case over there, filled the bottle, then window shopped at the sandwich kiosk.

Cyn made her way to the gate, waiting for her flight to Boston where she'd fulfill another Family directive. Cyn kept Nia in her peripheral vision as Nia wheeled her things to the line at a gate cattycorner.

Nia was flying to North Carolina to meet another one of her soldier pen pals, home on leave.

Garbled words from Nia's boarding call projected from the speakers.

And there she went…

Buh-bye. Bye now. Buh-bye.

Cyn took a well-deserved bite from her chocolate bar.

Nia didn't do badly with this last step; Cyn thought without any emotion attached, just mental notes.

The Family would want Cyn's assessment of Nia's work. She wasn't quite sure what she was going to say. The first time doing an assignment could be a bitch. Nerves could be surprising. On the other hand, Nia might actually have a stomach bug, and Cyn was misunderstanding the situation. Nia had been given little in the way of training to make her more sure-footed. But lives and freedoms were on the line.

Cyn wasn't going to jail because someone was sloppy or gutless.

Cyn thought it was probably better that Nia had a strong handler and that she stick to writing her, "I want nothing more than to sit on your face," letters to the lonely soldiers far from home. For now, anyway.

Maybe offer her some other honey pot duties and see how that went.

Nia's role thus far in The Family was simple.

The Prokhorov Family recruiter looked for young American women, like Nia. There were criteria, of course. Eighteen years old was the minimum. Attractive. Dysfunctional families who wouldn't give a rat's ass about the girl's welfare. Non-conformists. Rebels. Clean from both street drugs, police records, and communicable diseases. Unfazed by authority figures, except when those authority figures applied pain pressure to set limits within The Family's business.

Once spotted, these girls were recruited to Vienna, Austria, for a "job interview" that included a thorough physical of both the medical and bed-tumbling kind. They were then either hired by The Family or sold to traffickers.

Once the girls had been found and recruited, they were moved to a complex at the junction of Europe and Asia. Where exactly, Cyn hadn't a clue. It was need-to-know, and, honestly, Cyn couldn't care less. At the complex, the girls were given the names and profiles of vulnerable U.S. soldiers, horny men who were far from home and longing for female attention.

The girls became their lascivious, ego-stroking pen pals, tasked with befriending the soldiers stationed in places of interest to the Prokhorovs.

Letters sailed back and forth.

Those letters were usually sexual fantasies they shared with each other. The men shared theirs; the girls would follow a script created by their supervisor. More of a list, really. Tell him this, tell him that. Porn on pink perfumed paper scrawled in curly-girly lettering. And, of course, the intimate pictures that were tucked inside. "For your eyes only." "I trust you with this because we have something special." "I'm willing to be vulnerable for you. Be gentle with me."

Men weren't trustworthy when they swaggered. Some random Idaho farm boy, who registered a solid three on the attractiveness scale, sure as heck wasn't going to protect the woman's photos when she was a nine/ten on that scale, hugging a teddy bear and playing with herself. Big heart with "Hot for you, Leo" proved this chick was rubbing it out thinking of him.

The software programs kept track of *everything*. Most significantly, it ensured that the girl's images never overlapped by having the same gal write to more than one person at a single location. Since the areas where these guys deployed were often fluid, it took a computer to keep it all straight, especially since each girl might be flirting with maybe a hundred lonely military men.

The goal?

Simple. The Family wanted every piece of information they could gather on the U.S. military. A sentence here or there? Innocent. Innocuous. But sixty girls? Six *thousand* active targets? Priceless information came through the post—those details accumulated like pixels on a photograph to bring the image into clear focus.

And then The Family could act.

Nia was good at writing seduction and twisting men around her little finger.

When the targeted soldier went home on leave, the girls who had proven themselves could fly home to the United States. They'd land in Washington D.C., where there was an apartment that the girls could claim as their home.

The soldiers wouldn't be pen pals with someone in, say, Romania now, would they?

A Family member took in the correspondence each day, boxed the letters up, and shipped them to Vienna overnight. In Vienna, there were runners who took turns driving the box of letters to the girls. While the courier slept, the girls would respond. In the morning, the courier would return to Austria. In Vienna, they were same day shipped to Washington D.C. The D.C. manager would put American stamps on the letters and take them to the post office for shipping back to the soldiers.

Cyn thought of it like the American Pony Express.

From one hand to the next with machine-like efficiency.

It was an impressive operation.

This had gone remarkably well until last May when one of their girls who had swung the grand slam and married a Delta Force operator was discovered living and spying at the fort. The Family had to move their apartment to location B.

As planned, that move took less than three hours once the emergency button the gal wore around her neck as a "favorite necklace" was pressed. Before she could spill the beans, before the feds could bang on the door, they were gone.

Now that chick was locked up in a federal pen for life—stupid girl. Her Delta Force husband divorced her immediately, bowing his *mia culpas* to the powers that be for not recognizing the danger and bringing a deadly snake into the fort.

Nia was one of those correspondence girls. But she had ambition.

Shuffling through the door onto the boarding bridge, Nia was flying to meet up with another one of her pen pals home on leave.

This was allowed after the girls showed both success and loyalty. The girls' home visits—where they pretended to be living a normal life in the D.C. suburbs—allowed the men to see that the girls were real and "truly cared for them." Typically, when the girls flew back to the compound after their hook up, they had earned a healthy-sized diamond on their left ring finger—the girls got to keep any engagement rings as a "bonus" for a job well done. In her year and a half with The Family, Nia had accumulated a record five engagement rings that she stored in a safety deposit box, or so Cyn was told.

On this trip, Nia had shown up to meet another of her secret-sharing horn-dogs, boffed him, received her diamond engagement ring—ring number six—and when her handler offered her praise, Nia said, "I'd like to move up in the org."

No, she didn't. She didn't have the balls.

She had a weak gag reflex was what she had.

Fairly new to the game, Nia was only offered *this* opportunity because she'd been a star. She'd convinced her marks to share important information. Information that thwarted the European Union from locking down a sizable chunk of Family assets. Another that won The Family a useful political chit from a guy who had been part of a security detail with Senator Belincraft and his overheard seditious money-grubbing conversations. Even though The Family didn't have proof, it could threaten. There were enough details that Senator Belincraft *believed* he'd been caught red-handed. When pressure was applied, The Family felt sure that Belincraft would vote the way he was told to vote. Perhaps more importantly, he'd say what he was told to say on the news channels.

Excellent propaganda.

Papa Prokhorov was delighted.

Everyone was delighted.

Well, not everyone.

The senator was pissed.

The enemies of my enemies are my friends. Cyn broke off another piece of chocolate and popped it into her mouth, a wicked smile lighting her features.

4

Reaper

Friday Afternoon

As they arrived at their gate with less than an hour before boarding, Reaper found a spot at the end of the row near the plate glass window. Reaper thought the bustle of the neon-clad workers buzzing around outside and the excitement of planes taking off might keep Zack's attention.

Houston's attention, too.

Houston was an amazing dog. But she was also curious and high energy and still considered an adolescent.

This wasn't her first flight. The echoing noises, smells, and sights were routine for Reaper and Houston.

Reaper had been involved in a number of experimental treatments trying to pull him back from the abyss of a series of profound head injuries.

Just over a year ago, all Reaper could do with his day was lay flat on his back and grit through the pain.

While Reaper had been willing to try just about anything, outside of actual snake oil, to get his life back, nothing worked. Except for Houston. Yeah, Houston had been a big help in so many ways.

As Reaper thought that, Houston turned and caught his eye. Held. Reaper knew she was picking up on his thoughts and was checking to see if the monsters were back and things were getting too dark.

But that time in his life was over. A miracle shined its light on him. Research out in California offered him a ticket out of his hellscape.

But, it meant flying out and flying back each week.

Expensive as hell. Impossibly pricey on his disability pay and Kate's teaching salary. Good thing for study grants that helped cover all that. The only reason the scientists spent that kind of money on Reaper as he was one of the few who qualified for that elite program—Phase One, the experiments were only being conducted on those who had earned a SEAL trident.

Yeah, it would have been easier to just live out there on the West Coast, but Kate was here. Zack was here. After all Kate had gone through to navigate Reaper's floundering ship to safe harbor, Reaper would never ask her to leave the circle of support that she'd created in D.C.

Reaper and Houston made the weekly trek until it became every two weeks, then once a month, then he'd been handed his papers, graduating him from the interventions. Though, he'd agreed that as long as the trials were running, Reaper would present himself for testing every six months to make sure that the new neural pathways held.

"Good enough. Glad to lend a hand," he'd said on his way out the door. But if this worked for him, and his original level of pounding pain pudding brain, Reaper saw good things for other soldiers down the road.

Civilians, too.

As Reaper settled into the seat by the window, Kate handed off a fussy Zack then bent to dig in the diaper bag.

Reaper folded Zack over his shoulder and with a pat-pat on Little Guy's back, the baby farted long enough and loud enough that the passengers in the seating area tipped their chins down and chuckled.

Yeah, farts were funny. Always would be.

Then, Reaper felt the slow trickle of warm slime skating under his shirt and down his back. "Kate," Reaper said. Just his tone gave Kate the information she needed.

She came up from the bag with a cloth in her hand and unceremoniously wiped the baby's mouth, tugged Reaper's shirt out, and cleaned down his back. If Kate had a complaint about motherhood, it was that she was never clean; she always stank like sour milk puke. It was true. But for some reason, that smell on Kate was wholesome and good. It meant the family was doing what a family did.

And a year ago, that was unimaginable.

"Thanks." He made sure to catch her eye, so she'd register his gratitude.

Kate leaned forward, sniffing at Zack's diaper. "Yup. That needs to be changed."

Reaper stood, reaching for the diaper bag.

"Men's public bathrooms rarely have baby changing stations, Ryan. I'll handle it."

Kate was right.

Reaper didn't mind doing his share of diaper duty, but for some reason, bathroom designs hadn't kept up with the times. To change Zack's diaper, Reaper had to sit on the crapper and balance the baby on his knees. That was all fine and well until Zack was around five months old and he got into the squirming "ha-ha-ha I can get away from you" stage of diaper changes. And now, Zack was getting too long to use that strategy.

Pulling the diaper bag over her shoulder, Kate reached for Zack and draped him over her arm in such a way that any leakage wouldn't get on her.

Reaper clocked that move. It was a good one to remember.

Kate hustled away.

Reaper kept his gaze on Kate as she made her way through the gauntlet of waiting passengers. Zack fretted in Kate's arms as she wound around the other passenger's knees and rolling bags toward the bathroom.

Houston had her gaze on them, too.

Protecto-pup.

Reaper reached down to put a reassuring hand on Houston's head. For better or worse, Reaper took a lot of his own parenting skills from his decades of work with military war dogs. Emotions run up and down the leash. If he was stressed, his dog was stressed.

Steady and calm, that's what was needed.

Reaper thought some of Zack's agitation was just a response to Kate's stress.

If she'd just calm down some of the scenarios her mind was projecting out in front of them, the bad stuff would have a lower probability of manifesting.

Granted, when Reaper was still with the Teams, they'd look over a situation, plan, contingency plan. They'd tried to figure out all the bad that could happen and prepared for it. The *difference* was that once they'd visited the pros and cons and wrote their playbook, they kind of packaged up the worst-case scenarios and let them sit on a shelf. After all, no plan survives the first contact with the enemy. No point in expending energy on fear and nerves.

Kate had the SEAL planning phase down. What she lacked was the ability to just go with the flow once things went kinetic.

Would Reaper tell his wife to calm down?

Hell no, he wouldn't. He wasn't stupid.

Reaper focused his attention on Houston. She was lying to his right side, out of the way where her tail was safe from accidentally getting trod upon. With Kate and Zack gone, Houston stretched her nose forward, her attention was now fixed on the chair directly in front of Reaper. Her noisy nose was sucking in and puffing out the air, deciphering the particulate smells.

Houston had been trained on a variety of scents.

Could be anything.

Maybe a security guard had sat there to tie their shoe and left a trace of gun powder residue on the seat.

Houston was focused so hard on the chair, and Reaper was focused so hard on her behavior that Reaper didn't immediately see Kate returning to their space in the boarding area. Kate drew Reaper's attention away from Houston when she dropped the diaper bag onto the floor beside him.

"Okay?" Reaper checked in as he pulled Zack into his arms while Kate took her seat.

Zack pressed his toes between Reaper's ribs and with a wail of desperation, launched himself back into his mother's arms.

"He doesn't want me." Reaper relinquished the baby, both relieved and a little chaffed that Dad was second fiddle to Mom.

"He thinks I have a bottle for him." Kate pulled a pacifier from her breast pocket. "I'm trying to hold off until the flight. I figure, drinking will help calm him and swallowing will help with the change of air pressure hurting his little ears." She pulled in a long breath as her gaze scanned the waiting room.

Reaper got it. *Nobody* on the plane was interested in an hour and fifteen minutes of screaming infant. Sure, they'd try to be understanding. It was a miserable experience for everyone involved.

Kate would take the burden of the guilt trip onto her own shoulders.

Reaper had offered to drive through the night last night while Kate and Zack slept, then she'd have her own car up there for the length of her stay, all the things that she needed. He'd fly back to D.C. then fly back up to drive them home.

Kate had nixed the idea. She didn't say why. Just, "No, that's not going to work."

As a first-time mother, Kate felt the pricks and daggers of people's judgment about her parenting. When everything was chunky baby thighs and giggles, they'd nod their approval.

But how often did that happen with a baby?

The flip side of the indulgent smiles was the pursed-lipped scowls that came whenever the baby was upset in public.

Kate didn't want anyone scowling at Zack, she only wanted him to be adored—perceived as the miracle he was. Reaper thought that was the way a mother *should* feel about her kid.

Frowning down at the bright pink patches splotching Zack's cheeks, Kate focused on Zack's eyes. Even to Reaper with his limited experience, they looked glassy and feverish.

The doctor had given Zack a once over yesterday, in preparation for their trip, and pronounced that two teeth wanted to push through the gums. "Nothing catching or dangerous. Keep a close eye on that ear he kept tugging."

She dropped her voice. "We're going to piss people off. He's going to scream the whole way."

"Let them be pissed. He's a baby. This is what babies do."

"Still, Ryan."

"Not 'still, Ryan'. Let it roll off your back. You'll never see these people again. They all know this happens. Yeah, they might not like it, but they can speak to me if they have a problem." Reaper puffed himself up.

"Ryan, stop."

"Serious."

"I know you're serious. And that's why I'm telling you to stop." She lifted her chin toward Houston who was inching forward.

Houston's back legs stayed glued to the spot where Reaper had commanded, "Place." She looked like a rubber band dog.

"What's up with Houston?"

5

Cyn

Friday Afternoon

She watched the whole thing.

From the point where that man had rounded into sight, Cyn had trained her attention on him.

Like the authority figure in the bathroom giving Cyn the stink eye when Cyn was medicating Nia, this guy had *that* vibe.

If someone knew what to look for, they'd see it, too. This guy was dangerous as hell.

Lethal.

And, apparently, heading to Boston.

If anyone asked Cyn how she came to that conclusion even before she saw the German shepherd with its service dog vest, Cyn wouldn't be able to put a finger on the exact tell.

The guy was tall-ish. He had an athletically muscular build. Soccer body, mmm…maybe rugby. Yes, he looked like he liked to go at it fast and hard. The kind of man who became sharp-edged as soon as things got physical, his abilities becoming focused and amplified by pain.

If all she knew about him was his take-no-crap gait or his rugged frame, she might wipe a bit of drool from the side of her mouth and conjure his image in bed that night, when she took out the portable "boyfriend" she kept in her cosmetic bag when she traveled.

But Cyn lived in the world of latent violence.

Pain—financial, emotional, physical—was typically understood to be a potentiality in all of her undertakings. For her victims that was, not for her. She floated above the fray.

In her line of business, Cyn had found that the actual use of pain pressure was usually unnecessary. The mere threat of unwanted consequences was typically enough of a lever. A switch that could flip a cordial meeting to a life-threatening one.

Unspoken, but, nevertheless, understood.

The actors Cyn usually dealt with were the power brokers. The cigar smokers. The men who got felt up by their tailors, standing in front of three-way mirrors. They'd sip scotch from cut crystal as their ten-thousand-dollar suits were fitted to perfection.

Those men crooked their fingers at men like that one with his tactical pants.

That man was someone's weapon of choice.

If Cyn could guess from looking at the Navy veteran patch on the dog's service vest, the guy was a SEAL.

Cyn had been around too many elite operators not to feel his capacity for violence in her bones. She'd lived through it too many times not to have a visceral response. In those instances, caught in rooms that were the focus of a raid, she played the role of victim so as not to get rolled up in their mission.

Pop. Pop. Pop. "Women over there. Lay down flat." *Pop. Pop. Pop.* "Moving." "Clear."

They'd step over the bodies they left behind as they finished their task—pick up the hard drive or whatever the heck they'd been ordered to capture—and disappear into the night.

Movies weren't even close to depicting the sheer terror special operators engendered when the door suddenly blasted from the hinges, and the pack swarmed in. Their green laser lights searched the corners. Their rucks and equipment jutted out, turning them into alien beings.

Gods of the underworld.

Cyn was sure that guy could kill a village of enemies at lunch, shower, and go home to play peekaboo with that baby over his wife's shoulder.

As she observed them come into the boarding area, Cyn thought that the family didn't fit together in a cohesive picture.

The woman walking next to the guy was flaccid in comparison.

How in the heck did a warrior of that guy's magnitude end up with…*her*?

Probably took his marriage vows as a snivel-nosed recruit, Cyn thought as he took a place across from Nia's drop point.

Cyn lifted her lip with derision. A man like *that* needed a woman more like *her*. A woman who knew how to manipulate and dominate.

For a moment Cyn imagined herself by his side.

Minus the offspring for sure, she thought as the kid projectile puked white slime that drained down the warrior's neck.

That scene would never happen if she and the man were together. "Ryan." The wifey was calling him Ryan, as she snagged the baby back out of his arms and headed for a diaper change.

Cyn enjoyed a momentary daydream of what domestic bliss looked like with Ryan and Cyn as a power couple. She would enjoy playing that through her imagination that night when she stretched naked under her hotel sheets.

She'd tuck Ryan's image away and pull it back out when she had to screw some mark for some piece of power that was typically handed to Cyn in the form of paper—whether that was cash or intelligence depended on which was worth more to her at the time.

As Cyn contemplated the guy, his wife took the baby away.

Soon enough, his wife brought the baby back.

But right now, Cyn was done with the speculation and fantasy that she'd been indulging in to pass the time. Now, Cyn struggled to overrule her nervous system as she took an adrenaline hit.

Straight in front of her, Ryan's dog was focused on Nia's drop chair.

Cyn had been around a lot of working dogs in her career. Heck, it was part of their training rotations to learn how to take down an attacking K9. She'd seen scent-trained dogs find crazy things in improbable places. Always impressive. But this dog…

"Houston" the guy called her, and "good girl." Houston was a weird name for a girl dog.

When she saw the dog, she'd assumed it was a PTSD support dog.

But the dog seemed to be more than a service dog.

Houston had her gaze trained on the drop seat.

From her angle, Cyn could see the dog chuff air. The expanding nostrils, the intensity of focus, these were traits she had seen in scent trained dogs—drugs, explosives…

Cyn had read how a dog could discern a drop of gasoline in a pool full of water. Researchers were using their noses to detect all kinds of medical issues from diabetic glucose numbers to hard-to-find cancers. She'd also read how there was a dog who had been trained to find electronic scents, specifically for use in finding hidden thumb drives on child porn raids. But that was really new. Something to be concerned about on the horizon.

And since Cyn had nothing to do with pornography of any

type, it had been a blip on her radar screen then dismissed. But it pinged back up in her awareness now because Houston was hard focused on the exact spot where Nia had placed the box.

What were the chances that a trained electronic search dog would be flying to Boston today of all days?

That she would sit near *that* seat?

The K9 was a twist that Cyn hadn't anticipated.

6

Reaper

Friday Afternoon

Houston was definitely alerting on something to do with that seat.

Reaper put a fist to his chin, stretching his thumb to paint along his jawline as he considered. He reached out and squeezed Kate's knee to signal her not to pay attention. She could read his mind. Kate swung her interest to the baby.

Reaper walked the two steps to stand next to the seat giving a surreptitious hand signal to Houston, "Find it."

Houston stood, tail wagging furiously. She walked over to the chair as if she were relieved to finally be allowed to show Dad what she'd found. Sitting, she placed a delicate paw on the seat. That was a signal Houston used for a hit on an electronic scent.

One of Reaper's first assignments with Iniquus was to train a military K9, Digger, for the Asymmetric Warfare Group to find electronic signals.

When Digger and his handler Scott took off on an overseas assignment, Reaper trained Houston as a way to demonstrate the potential to future Iniquus clients.

Reaper had taught Houston different signals for different scents that she could trace.

Explosives? She'd claw and bark.

Drugs? She'd lie down with a fixed stare—that protected her from inhaling the possibly lethal chemicals.

For electronics, since they were often hidden within something else, she'd place her paw where Reaper should look.

Something was under that seat. 100%.

Reaper's internal debate was momentary. Yes, this was probably going to mess up his day… But Reaper had three FBI dogs that were coming in next month to train specifically to help find child pornographers by scent searching electronics. That was a potential here. If there was a chance that there was something under the seat that would exploit children, it wasn't something that Reaper would abide.

And certainly not something that Reaper would leave unchecked.

Kate leaned forward and whispered, "What's she doing, Ryan?"

"Oh, she just wants me to sit here so she can keep an eye on you and the baby." Houston rounded in front of Reaper and sat tall between his knees, responding to Reaper's hand signal. "I let her break rank when she's in protective mode. I don't want to train that out of her."

Houston had saved Kate from a knife-wielding lunatic when Kate was eight months pregnant. Houston had yanked herself free of her lead and flown through the house full-on fur missile, launching herself into the air and biting down on the guy before he had time to realize she was there. Houston bit down so hard that she pulverized the guy's bones. He ended up needing that arm to be amputated.

"No, we don't want to train that out of her." Kate's focus was on Houston. "Because she's my best girl. Aren't you, sweet hero girl?"

Kate bought it.

Ryan took out his phone and pretended to scroll and read. Hiding his moves behind Houston's back, Reaper held the camera under the chair, taking a surreptitious video. He pulled it out, letting his phone dangle between his knees while he looked at the footage. "Son of a gun," he muttered under his breath.

"Ryan James Hamilton, what are you doing over there?" Kate's voice took on that edge she'd developed as a science teacher for teens. It had a controlling quality, especially when his whole name was slipped into the sentence. It recalled the oh-shit sensation he used to get when he was called down to the principal's office. Rare but not unheard of.

Ryan held up a finger. "Give me a second, will you? I just got a concerning text in from work." He lied to her. Man, he *hated* to lie to her. But if someone were watching this drop box, he couldn't let them know that their drive had been discovered. He had no idea what kind of reaction that might illicit. If it might put Kate and Zack in danger.

Standing, Ryan shifted over to the plate glassed windows with Houston at his side.

He quick dialed into Strike Force war room at Iniquus, someone was always there and ready to start moving pieces into place.

The phone rang once. "Striker."

"Reaper here." He leaned his broad shoulder against the metal rib of the window. Finger in the other ear to diminish ambient noise and focus. Eyes scanning for anyone who might look interested in his doings. "Striker, man, I think Houston stumbled on a situation . I'm still at the boarding gate. Houston signaled an electrical alert. I'm sending you a video." His eyes landed on Houston, who was focused on Kate and Zack, making sure they were safe. "It's definitely an electronics drop. I need marching orders."

7

Cyn

FRIDAY AFTERNOON

AS THE EVENT UNSPOOLED, Cyn wasn't sure what she should do.

She could move over to sit in the drop seat…

For what reason?

Block it from further investigation? Stay there until this Ryan guy had gotten on the plane?

The thought came and was instantly rejected. First, it would put her face right in front of Ryan's.

If she were right about Ryan's background, he would have been trained to spot a counterfeit—to see her hair was a wig, her makeup thick, her contacts colored, her bodysuit not quite right the way it shifted under her clothes.

If she were right about Ryan, he would be trained to memorize the people around him. And Cyn most certainly didn't want her image retained. She especially didn't want to be remembered as someone who had been sitting in a seat where a thumb drive held life-destroying information.

Ryan had images of it. He'd sent them on to someone as he muttered into his phone with studied nonchalance.

Sitting in that seat now would do nothing to help the situation. And if she extracted the thumb drive and fled, well her name was on the passenger list. Not *her* name. An alias. But still. Her alias had a second life running, and Cyn didn't want to have to start a new persona all over again. It was just too darned much work.

This task had been stupidly pedestrian.

While it was Nia's plant, Cyn was there for oversight. The collector should be arriving soon and sit in that seat. They were scheduled for the next plane heading out of this gate.

Maybe Cyn was contriving too much in her imagination. Maybe she was seeing spycraft where none existed. Had this guy not been as conspicuously lethal and trained as he was, would her mind have seen what she thought she had seen?

Maybe they were just a retired military family.

Maybe the dog was just being a dog… Someone spilled food on the chair and didn't wipe it up.

Cyn sat with those thoughts for a moment. She tried to bring down her temperature and restore her *sang froid.*

She wasn't wrong. Cyn knew it in her gut.

She just didn't know what to do about it.

Sticking an earbud in her ear, Cyn pulled up an app that would amplify the conversations around her. Luckily, most people sat in silence waiting for boarding to be called.

"Ryan James Hamilton," his wife had said with a sharp tone that carried the name to Cyn's ear. Cyn typed that name into a text message, sending it on to a colleague who worked for Omega, a security firm that The Family contracted with for just this kind of thing.

Not waiting for a text back, Cyn stood. She had to stay one step ahead of the game.

Moseying over to the attendant's desk, Cyn waited behind the elderly woman who wanted to check that a wheelchair would be meeting her when they landed.

Ryan moved to the window, out of earshot. He was calling it in. He definitely found the thumb drive. "Reaper," he said into the phone.

Yeah, that seemed to be the right name for this guy. Not some wimpy "Ryan" crap.

Cyn made sure that she continued to call the guy "Ryan" in her mind so she didn't mess up should she have to interact with the guy.

Right now, Cyn needed to pull this mission out of the sewer pipe.

Things were definitely turning to shit.

Her phone pinged, Omega: **Iniquus Security. Strike Force. Newby. Medically retired SEAL.**

It was of little comfort that her instincts were sharp enough to have identified him correctly.

Iniquus was a security group that provided both private institutions and the gamut of governmental alphabets support and expertise. They hired the best there was in applied fields like AI and computer sciences, lawyers, and forensic CPAs. They also hired their task force operators from amongst the US military elite, Delta Force, Marine Raiders, Green Berets, SEALs…

Elite pedigrees and field success along with impeccable ethics were required to get the golden ticket onto an Iniquus roster.

Reaper sent a quick glance at his wife, then his gaze once again swept the area. The move didn't seem to split his attention. He was processing, analyzing, searching, and rejecting.

Could she get the data back?

Ryan "Reaper" Hamilton from Iniquus with a trained electronics detections K9.

This was catastrophic and… As the situation was sifted through for an off-ramp, Cyn smelled an opening. Potential.

Could she exploit this situation?

8

Reaper

FRIDAY AFTERNOON

"DID you see anyone in the area before you sat down?" FBI Special Agent in Charge Damian Prescott had been meeting with Tidal Force down the hall at Iniquus when Striker snagged him for this conversation.

Reaper's voice projected into the Tidal Force war room over speakerphone. "No, sir."

"No need for formalities, Reaper." Prescott said. "Did anyone see you make the find?"

Using the reflection of the massive plate glass windows as a mirror to scan the room, Reaper tried to make it look like he was focused on the workers below. "Hard to tell. I tried to be circumspect."

"Can you watch the area while we get someone in place?" Prescott's voice was tight and soft. It wouldn't carry out into the loading area to be accidentally overheard.

Striker cut in, "He's with his wife and baby. Iniquus policy states that's a no-go. Come up with a different plan."

Reaper was glad it was Striker who said it. For sure, Reaper wasn't dragging Zack and Kate into anything that even had a whiff of danger tied to it.

"Okay. Thinking." That was Prescott.

Reaper took advantage of the pause to turn, looking for any curious eyes, or people who were a little too theatrically engaged in something else.

The drop chair remained empty. What would he do if someone were to go sit there?

"The thumb drive can't be abandoned," Prescott said.

"Airport security?" Reaper offered.

"I don't want them involved," Prescott said. "It'll land on someone's social media and conspiracies will spread like wildfire. It's happened to us too many times. Where are you flying?"

"Boston." Reaper's gaze rested on the boarding information. The flight was on time. The *one* time when he'd welcome a couple hours' delay.

"How do you feel about gathering that thumb drive? I can have an agent meet you in Boston."

"I don't know, man…my family." Reaper glanced toward Kate.

Reaper would be a lot more concerned about this situation if Houston wasn't a fur missile always ready to launch. She was Reaper's weapon of choice when it came to protecting his family in public.

"You can collect the drive quietly," Prescott suggested. "We can make a show of you handing it over to the FBI, lots of badge flashes. Put together, you should be safe."

Reaper wasn't sure. It sounded like a reasonable solution, but he didn't understand the situation, so he wasn't in a good position to tell if that was accurate or not. "Striker?"

"Your call, Reaper. Running with only the information that you shared, being in D.C… could be a prank. Could be…well, no point in conjecture. It's improbable that it's something innocuous. We don't know the ramifications of that drive moving forward to the next hands. One suggestion, we could just put a camera on it and monitor who goes near the seat."

Nutsbe, Panther Force's comms and logistics guy, called out, "No go. I have access to the CTV there and that particular seat is out of view. That speaks to insider information. There are literally two seats at that departure gate that are outside of the camera's view. I'm looking at Kate and Little Guy. Man, she looks stressed."

"First time flying with the baby," Reaper said. "Which seats can't you see?"

"The one next to Kate," Nutsbe said.

"That was the seat I was sitting in," Reaper explained.

"And the one across from it. I can see the corner, and that's it. So if someone leaned toward the windows, they wouldn't be picked up on tape."

"Thanks, Nutsbe, that's good information," Prescott said. "The chances that the person who left the drive didn't know that was a safe seat is, I'd say, around zero percent. That moves the level of concern higher on my threat meter. Maybe put Kate and the baby on the plane and send Reaper on the next?"

"I checked," Nutsbe said. "Next flight is tomorrow."

"Okay." Prescott tugged the elasticity of the word out as long as his breath and left the conversation open-ended. He was waiting for a decision from the boots-on-the-ground, Reaper.

Reaper wrapped his hand around the back of his neck feeling the tension in his muscles as he committed to the mission. "I want at least three special agents with badges out and as conspicuous as possible waiting for me as I exit the plane. I mean full-on G-man."

"Great!" There was relief in Prescott's voice. "If you can pull off the whole apparatus, do. If not, then just collect the thumb drive. Obviously, you need to treat this with the normal protocol that Iniquus applies to evidence. I'll have a team of the foggiest of Foggy Bottom-looking agents that I can wrestle up waiting for you."

"Wilco. Out."

Reaper thrust his phone into his left thigh pocket. He wanted to get this done. They'd be calling seating soon. And with the dog and the baby, his family would be first on.

Their tickets were the three seats on the right-hand side at the bulkhead, where Reaper would have more legroom, and Houston could stand out of the way.

When Reaper was flying back and forth for his treatments this was their routine. The researchers had paid for Houston to have a seat, and it really made all the difference.

Reaper decided to put Kate and Little Guy in the window seat. He'd take the middle seat. And if anyone wanted to get to them? Well, they'd have to make it past Houston's biters first.

Then, they'd have to get past *him*.

While still at the window, Reaper adjusted Houston's vest, reaching into the side pocket to get a poop bag. Reaper then turned to the window using the cover of his jacket to get his hand into the bag and prep it for quickly accessing and storing the drive without his getting his prints on it or wipe it of any residual DNA that would help them track the owner.

Reaper strolled to the drop seat and signaled Houston to sit tall between his legs.

"Is everything all right at work?" Kate's brows drew together in a scowl. She knew that Reaper was always on call—just like when he was a SEAL—and that he could get the signal at any time, drop everything, and hustle to join his forces.

"Yeah, it's fine. Someone's meeting me in Boston when we deplane is all."

"Can I ask?"

"Just need to share some information. It won't interrupt us at all. Two minutes, tops."

As they spoke, hiding behind Houston's body, Reaper had tugged at the casing.

Whatever adhesive the bad guy had used, the plastic box was cemented to the chair. It reminded him of the glue pads that were used to trap rodents in people's kitchens. Once one of his military K9 got the rodent trap stuck on his fur. They ended up having to shave the dog's fur off.

Maybe it was a permanent drop site, Reaper speculated. It was a shame, in a way, that they were ordering him to collect the evidence. He understood the thought process connected to these circumstances. But the best way for them to handle the situation was to let it be and put a set of eyes on the issue. Track and trap the person with the intel, cuff them, and ask some pointed questions in an austere room.

Reaper gave the box another yank.

It didn't budge. Maybe they bonded this box in place and filled it from time to time.

Nah, that didn't make sense. A bored kid crawling around on the floor during a pre-flight wait could find the cache.

Reaper wondered if that scenario didn't come up in a planning meeting. They'd need to know the product was safe. They'd put someone in the room to watch and report.

Typically, when someone had their eyes on him—be it from behind a curtain in an upstairs window or through the sights on a sniper rifle—the tiny hairs on the back of his neck tickled to life. "Pay attention." He didn't feel that here. Granted, his brain had been rewired by the researchers in California, so his survival reflexes might not be the same as they were when he was on the battlefield.

Genius, Reaper thought as his fingernail caught under the lip of the closure and he popped it open. Someone flies in, sits here, places the drive, gets on a plane, flies out. Later, someone flies in, comes here to gather the tiny drive, gets on the connecting flight and powers away to another state. The airport wouldn't care. The state wouldn't have much incentive to chase this down.

Feds…? Yeah, maybe. It depended on what was on this thing.

This being Washington D.C., could be anything from whistle-blower files to child porn.

Kate stood up, Zack dangling from her outstretched arms.

Please don't be kiddie porn, Reaper thought as the drive dropped into the dog shit bag. Reaper put the bag into the zippered pocket on Houston's service dog vest, then leaned seamlessly forward to gather the baby from Kate's arms.

"I think I have time to run to the ladies' room," she was saying.

Perfection. Reaper thought that had gone as smoothly as possible.

There was no safer place to stash the damned thing than on a trained attack dog like Houston.

Bouncing the baby on his knee, Reaper wondered why such a complicated scenario was contrived.

What was on that thumb drive?

Did Reaper really want to know?

9

Cyn

Friday Afternoon

Ryan Hamilton... tsk tsk tsk, taking things that don't belong to you. Such a naughty boy.

Cyn stepped forward now that the old lady had her wheelchair situation squared away.

The attendant looked up with lifeless eyes. Yeah, the job was probably soul-sucking. Cyn decided the best approach was to get the woman on her side as a co-conspirator.

And to that end, wasn't it lucky that a note slipped from the corner of her counter?

Cyn stooped to retrieve the paper—careful to angle her face away from Reaper.

She had to assume that he'd snagged the data. She'd tried to watch where he put it. She assumed it went into his right thigh pocket when he slid his hand in then secured the hook and loop fastener. As he tugged the flap open, the noise had been written large across the room. It meant that if she was deploying her sticky fingers, he'd hear it.

She was going to try anyway. This was a Hail Mary if ever there was one. The Family would be appreciative.

"Excuse me," Cyn said under her breath with a warm smile to the woman. Cyn lifted the paper that had fluttered to the ground. "Is this important?" In black magic marker it said "Ben" and there was a phone number. In loopy, blue-inked cursive, Cyn read out, "The nice guy that jump-started my car." Cyn popped her eyebrows conspiratorially. "That sounds promising."

This woman was about the same age as Cyn's current persona, the same level of medium middle-aged attractiveness. Presenting as a solid five on the attractiveness scale meant Cyn was neither pretty enough nor ugly enough to catch anyone's attention. And to this woman—based on Cyn's "Mary Wise" clothing choices and the cut of her wig—Cyn would be seen as accessibly suburban middle class.

The woman with her "Brenda" name badge glanced down at the note before accepting it. "Thank you." She offered up a smile, and her eyes took on a bit of excitement. "I hope it's something good." She slid the number into her pocket.

Cyn leaned in. "Hey, I'm wondering if you can help me. Do you see that man over my shoulder? The one with the dog?" Cyn moved her body to the left so when the woman looked over toward Ryan sitting there with the baby on his shoulder, it would look like the attendant was just looking at Cyn.

"Cute!"

"Yeah? I guess he is." Cyn sent her new friend a big old conspiratorial smile. "His name is Ryan Hamilton. He's a disabled veteran. He wouldn't know me because we've never met. But I recognize him from my brother's letters home. They served together, in the Navy, Ryan and my brother Jimmy." Cyn sucked in a stuttering breath as she fabricated on the fly. "Yeah… Jimmy was off his ship on some mission when his convoy hit a roadside bomb. He died on the medivac flight." She paused to put a hand over her heart and let her gaze slide to the window as she froze for the count of five.

Refocusing on the attended and offering her a flat-lipped smile, Cyn received the woman's "Oh, I'm so sorry. Thank you and, and, and your family for your sacrifice. My brother is a retired Marine. He tells me stories." The woman frowned down at the countertop.

Cyn waited for the woman's thought to pass and for her to focus back on their conversation. "I was wondering if you had any empty seats in first class, I'd like to upgrade his ticket. He's got a lot of pain issues. He'd be more comfortable with a little extra space. I'm paying it forward. He did a lot of good for my brother."

"Oh, that… yes, let me look." As she clicked around the computer the attendant said, "I'm sure he'll be happy to meet the sister of a fallen brother."

Agh! Yeah, that was the danger. If she hadn't used his first and last name, Cyn could have just pretended that she'd been mistaken. She saw the trap she'd put herself in should any of this go awry. She hadn't taken the time to think this all the way through.

Granted they had her fake name and PO box should anyone look her up.

And surely, they'd look her up once Ryan-Reaper got to his destination and made a report.

Why did I offer to upgrade Ryan? Cyn rebuked herself.

They'd interview the attendant. The attendant would tell this story…

Who knew, maybe there was a Jimmy somewhere in Reaper's backstory and he wouldn't blink.

Either way, she'd bring this to The Family and see what they could do with the computer records from this flight. It shouldn't be but so hard to wipe this flight from the hard drive.

She hoped that was true.

With the CTV cameras hacked, her image shouldn't be on any D.C. camera spools. In Boston, she'd need to tuck her face down hard all the way out to the cab.

"If it's okay, not against your policy or anything." Cyn exercised exquisite control, stopping herself from looking over at Ryan. She knew that that would make the hairs tickle on the back of his neck—the early warning system that all operators developed in the field.

If not? They were dead.

"I'd rather he not know that someone upgraded him. I… yeah…It's still too fresh for me, the loss. I'm not up to talking about my brother in public, yet. And I certainly don't want Ryan to think this is charity or pity on my part. You said you have a Marine brother. You know how they hate to be seen as weak or needy." Cyn tipped her head. "I was hoping you could just say that the airline upgraded him?"

"Let me see what I can do here." The woman's fingers danced over the keys. "What's your name?"

"Mary Wise."

"Uh-huh, there's a seat across from you in business class. Both aisle seats. But he looks like he's traveling with his dog." Brenda looked toward Reaper, and Cyn did a quick look see to make sure he was occupied with the kid while the mom went off somewhere else. "The dog tucks in under his feet in a little ball. See?"

Brenda gave a tiny head bobble then looked back at the computer screen. "I only have the one upgrade seat. If he's traveling with his family…"

"Sadly, I can just afford the one upgrade. Surely, his wife

would want him to be comfortable. The shrapnel embedded by his spine and all."

Brenda nodded as she tapped at her keyboard. "Okay. I've got that all set. It's four hundred to upgrade."

Cyn reached into her wallet to pull out the cash.

Yes, it was a lot of cash.

Yes, it might be suspicious.

But Cyn didn't want a record of "Mary" being the one to upgrade him. With cash, it would just be Brenda's memory of the incident. "So worth it. I'm so happy to do this. I know he lives with a lot of pain." She slipped her wallet back into her hobo bag.

Now, her skills would be put to the test. Could she retrieve the flash drive?

10

Cyn

Saturday Evening

"Tell me." Borka Prokhorov sat in a high-backed, oxblood leather chair. His hands rested on the surface of his desk in a relaxed open manner. It was a consciously developed habit that was supposed to make the person sitting on the other side of the intricately carved mahogany desk feel at ease that there wasn't a pistol pointed at them under the surface with a twitchy finger on the trigger.

When Cyn was around Borka, she was *never* at ease.

Even in his uncharacteristically informal pink polo shirt, Borka exuded power.

Cyn would guess that he was in his mid-sixties. With a thick crop of steel-gray hair, he kept himself trim and fit—running, lifting, grappling, and ARB (the martial arts that he practiced as a Russian special forces operator back in the day). Borka could kill with his bare hands if necessary. But his weapon of choice was a finger that lifted from his desk to point at his worker bee, then at the door.

Orders issued, Borka allowed others to do his dirty work. The paid hire could take the chances. If they weren't good enough to succeed, they could take the hit. Borka didn't abide people who had poor outcomes associating with The Family.

Sitting on the edge of the visitor chair, feet pressed into the oriental carpet, Cyn's lashes shielded her gaze, showing Borka the deference he was do. This posture helped Cyn hide from the slick cold fear the man induced in her when he caught her eye.

Borka had found and recruited Cyn to The Family and overseen her training into their methodologies himself. Though he tried to impose a father-daughter feel to their relationship, it was a veneer that both of them acted out but neither of them believed.

Borka didn't care about anyone but himself. Not a narcissist. Narcissism, Cyn had learned in training at the CIA Farm—way back another life ago—was a mentally unsound coping mechanism. A means for surviving childhood trauma.

No, that wasn't Borka.

Nor was he a sociopath driven by early wounds to his psyche, needing to hurt others to feel better about his own loveless state.

Borka was a true psychopath, born without feelings—not emotional, not physical, nothing.

A void.

Though, he tried to find pleasure in the quality of the items that touched and surrounded him, from exceptionally crafted foods, from his orgasms, and from power.

Power meant he decided who lived, who thrived, and who died.

He once told Cyn—as he was inviting her into the inner circle—that The Family labor force reminded Borka of that silly American game called bowling. The pins were knocked down, the engine whirled…the next group of pins was reset for another go.

Clean. Mechanical. And most importantly at a long distance from the man rolling the ball.

Borka was a dangerous game to play.

Cyn had to prove her loyalty along the way, to make crystal clear that she played for the Prokhorov Family team alone.

She most *certainly* was no double agent.

Why would she want to associate with Borka when he scared the hell out of her?

Because his organization gave Cyn the pockets, the technology, and the manpower to do what she wanted.

What did she want?

To *destroy* the CIA… and, if possible, the American government as a whole.

Lofty? Idealistic? Maybe.

Unlike Borka, Cyn felt acutely. And what she felt most was her brother calling from the grave, "*avenge me*."

Borka pressed the pads of his fingers together, tenting his hands as he prepared to listen.

"Tell me," he repeated, his voice ratcheting up a notch. "Nia was a mess before you medicated her…" Borka offered a leading statement.

While Borka stressed her out, Cyn was grateful that she was out of her Mary Wise get up and was back to looking like her own self, unincumbered. Blue eyes, long blonde hair, a tight athletic body that she trained hard for combat, be that a physical fight or a necessary seduction.

Cyn leaned forward. The cold from the leather seat back had seeped through her silk blouse. Being uncomfortable was the least of her worries, she didn't want to quake, making Borka think she was nervous. "Nia was puking in the bathroom."

"Her performance on task?"

"Beautiful. Medicated, she was seamless." Cyn crossed her legs at the ankles to hold her feet still from tapping the ground.

"Which isn't surprising. Thus far she's hit every nail squarely on the head."

Cyn dipped her head to the side. "Maybe it was first-time jitters. Maybe let her focus her skills on her sexual appeal until she has a little more maturity under her belt."

"But she succeeded with the plan. She placed the drive where she was told."

"I'll admit, when Nia was puking in the bathroom stall, I thought she was going to crash and burn. Paint me surprised at her performance getting the drive in place. No, the problem had nothing to do with her."

Borka grunted. "I've called Nia in for a chat. She's done screwing her soldier and is on a flight back to D.C." He glanced at the desk clock. "I expect her any minute."

A cigar burned forgotten in the heavy glass ashtray on the right-hand side of the desk. A tube of ash looked solid, but Cyn knew it was an illusion. It could all be blown away with one focused breath. A metaphor for…well everything, really.

Shit, Nia was called in. That didn't bode well for Nia's health and wellbeing. Cyn wasn't willing to go out on a limb for the girl, but she could try an olive branch. "Nia was on her own plane when the dog alerted on the drive." The danger here was that Nia had succeeded in placing the drive and flying out. Would Borka perceive that the failure belonged to Cyn?

Was that what Nia would say when she walked through the office door?

"I was unable to see the man retrieve the flash drive. I assumed he had it. I did what I could under the circumstances."

"Yes. What exactly?" Borka waggled his hand wanting Cyn to get to the point.

"I upgraded his seat, so we would be seated together. The man's name is Ryan Hamilton. Call sign Reaper."

"Call sign?"

"Yes. Reaper didn't accept the upgrade. He said he needed the added space of the bulkhead for his service dog. Apparently, the dog had her own ticket and her own seat. Noble knight that he was," she let the sarcasm lay heavy on her lips, "he let his wife Kate take the upgrade, and he also took the baby back with him."

The baby had screamed at the top of his lungs the *whole* flight.

Originally, Kate moved back to help, but Warrior Ryan must have shooed her away because there she sat to Cyn's left, trying not to freak out about her baby crying.

"The FBI met the plane," Cyn explained. "They made a big show of accepting the handoff. One assumes so that if anyone were watching, they would know Reaper didn't have the drive anymore and following him would be futile. They filmed everyone's exit. Granted, I only saw the end of the display. I was one of the last ones off. I was concerned that if they took me in for questioning, my disguise would have made me a prime suspect."

"Agreed."

Cyn had followed through on her own mission by whispering a message into the proper Bostonian ear. She'd slept a few hours at a hotel, then Cyn rented a car to drive back to D.C. Here, she handed the keys off to a low-level runner—dressed in Cyn's Mary Wise disguise—to drive the sedan down to Florida where the worker bee would turn the keys in at the Orlando airport.

Just a little spycraft to throw anyone off the scent, should anyone be looking.

And why would they be looking for Mary Wise? Other than the upgrade…

Yeah, after she bought that upgrade, the Mary Wise persona was burned. Cyn would have to develop another working identity.

That sucked.

"Out of curiosity," Cyn shuffled her hips forward so she could lean her crossed arms on the desk, "and you can certainly tell me it's none of my business—"

"What was on the drive?" Borka asked. "We were able to get a girl in with a heavy hitter in the political realm, married to a dissatisfied wife who wields power of her own. During their interlude, she was able to download the contents of his laptop and phone. It was destined for our intelligence operations to cull through the data."

"By girl, are we talking female or are we talking age?"

"Both. Seventeen with daddy issues. She loves to go down on older men."

"Gross."

"Thank you."

"Just saying." Cyn shot Borka a playful smile. It was that father-daughter veneer thing. "So seventeen…"

"Seventeen on a private jet with a group of politicians. We have pictures of her mile-high club aerobic exercises. Apparently, orgies on a plane are a thing because turbulence makes for a fun ride."

Cyn lifted a nostril in disdain.

"To which is your derision applied? The orgy or are we back to censure for the age difference?" Barka pressed into his feet, rocking himself back in his chair. "He was more than twice her age, but she has *daddy* issues, not granddaddy issues."

"So not an old man?"

"Not really, late thirties politician." Barka let his hands rest lazily on his chest. "He just looks like he's been ridden hard and put up wet too many times. It's aged him to look like he's fifty."

"Ancient by teen standards. That drive wasn't the only one?"

"No. We would never let the original out of our house." Borka tsk tsked. "It seems that along with statutory rape laws, there are American laws about trafficking girls across state and international lines. Accessories all." Borka smiled his poison smile.

"Do what we want or it's the slammer for you." Cyn laughed to show she was aligned with Borka's pleasure in the incident.

"So, now that the FBI has the drive, it's easy enough." Cyn shrugged. "Contact the political donor, tell him he's about to get a fed knocking on his door. Tell him to call whoever you have on the payroll who can make this disappear."

"Already done. If he weren't such a connected and influential man, we would not have had to go through the cloak and dagger hand-off. But no trail should have been laid for his hounds to track back to us. Anonymity is key." He pulled his brows together. "But here is what I wish to know. How was the drive found? We'd been mildly concerned about a child crawling around on the floor, looking under the seats. Given that it was a workday when few parents would be flying with their families, we ruled that concern out."

"Dog not child."

"Repeat this?"

"It was a dog. Reaper's service dog, Houston. And while the operation didn't go as smoothly as one would have assumed, this actually might be a good break for us. Better even than if we gained leverage over the heavy hitter."

Borka tipped his head, a look of curiosity on his face. Hunger glinted in his eyes. "I'm listening."

11

Cyn

Saturday Evening

"Reaper," Cyn licked her lips, "was traveling with his wife Kate, son Zack, and service dog Houston. Houston isn't *just* a service dog. From an overheard conversation on the plane, Reaper was a K9 handler when he was in the Navy."

"K9 and Navy?" Borka drew his brows together. "What does the Navy need with dogs on the ship?"

"Omega believes he was a SEAL—I'll get to that in a minute. The point is, Reaper's K9 alerted on the chair. And Ryan extracted the drive." She uncrossed her legs and recrossed them in the opposite direction. Cyn was having trouble sitting still. Having trouble keeping her foot from wiggling nervously.

Excitement.

Her muscles bunched and ached. She wanted out of the office, away from Borka's scrutiny and onto the mission.

"As I was explaining, I upgraded Reaper's ticket so that he

was sitting across the aisle from me. I had hopes of recouping the drive during the deplaning."

"He sat elsewhere, your plan failed. Or are you playing games?" Borka leaned forward. "Do you have the drive or no?"

"No, I'm—I don't have the drive. And was never near the drive."

His scowl deepened. "Your skills, they are faltering, yes?"

She took a moment before she responded. Cyn knew Borka was trying to scratch her ego, hoping the wound would fester. It wasn't about her personally. Cyn speculated Borka had been dropped on his head too many times as an infant. His moral compass lost its magnetic spin and pointed nowhere near true north. "This wasn't a test of my skills. I spoke to no one except for the desk person. As I was explaining, Reaper sat in the bulkhead seat with his dog—"

"Houston."

"Exactly. His dog had her own ticketed seat. Reaper even took the baby back with him to give his wife the upgrade so she had a break from the kid since Kate—note this—will be in Boston for the week."

"I'm listening."

"I chose *not* to speak with Kate."

Borka laced his fingers and pressed his extended index fingers together. It was the way he held his hands when he was processing information. This gesture reminded Cyn of the childhood rhyme, "Here is the church and here is the steeple, Open the doors and see all the people." Only Cyn was afraid to see what Borka had behind his closed doors.

"Was she nervous?" he asked. "Scared about her husband's actions?"

"Not at all. Either she's cool under pressure, or Reaper didn't tell her what was going on. I'm assuming the great gladiator was protecting his sweet wifey from the big bad world."

Borka's features hardened. "Why are you subjecting me to this conversation?"

"Because the woman who sat next to Kate was an enormous fan of service animals and veterans. She was an interrogation phenom. I honestly couldn't have done better myself. It was the pure joy on this woman's face that made Kate comfortable enough to tell her story. And I, of course, was taking notes."

Borka drummed his long fingers on the desktop, clearly projecting "get on with it."

"Kate and Reaper Hamilton flew to Boston to be in a friend's wedding. Kate will stay up north to have a girl's week with her old friends. She will have the baby with her. Reaper will fly back to D.C. this Sunday, tomorrow. He has to get back to work."

Borka's gaze moved toward the reflection in his window.

Cyn knew that was a bad sign. She'd better cut to the chase. "He's training—ready for this?—at *Iniquus* with one of their security forces. He's just getting a feel for the kinds of assignments they train and execute so he'll understand what the K9s need to do on the job."

"*Iniquus*?" Borka jutted forward.

Iniquus had been a thorn in their side for years. They had destroyed two major Family missions that had been years in the planning and execution. First, they'd taken down a cell of imported jihadists that had aimed for a major terror hit on a Bethesda school, then they found their Delta Force mole and sent her to prison, ending their reign of terror on the Delta Force wives.

If Cyn could take down Iniquus, she'd be golden within the Prokhorov family, but also leaps and bounds closer to destroying the CIA. "Because Reaper has a disability from his time in the Navy, he won't be assigned to a tactical force. No jumping out of airplanes to save hostages or what have you. Iniquus wants him to get his sea legs—Kate's word choice—then, Reaper will be a full-time K9 trainer with their Cerberus Tactical K9 division."

Borka focused back on her.

"When Reaper found the drive, he didn't touch it at first. He called it in. And he started the conversation with 'Striker, man, I think Houston stumbled on a situation.'"

"Striker?" Borka jutted forward.

Now she had his full attention. Cyn didn't let even a soupcon of smug reach her expression.

"Striker Rheas? Striker, commander of Strike Force?"

"Omega believes so, yes." Cyn filled her lungs while she read the hunger in Borka's gaze. "Reaper was speaking while I was standing in line to do the upgrade. I had an earbud for my sound amplifier in one ear. I'm 100% sure it was Iniquus. I'm 100% sure he said, 'Striker'." Cyn lifted her brows. "How many Strikers could there be in one organization?"

Borka turned bored eyes on Cyn. His palms up, with a shrug of his shoulders, he asked, "And how does this help us?"

"For years The Family has been trying to get someone planted at Iniquus. Iniquus has thwarted our every attempt to get through their vetting system. What if we developed Reaper? He's already been vetted. He's already in."

Borka gripped at the desk as he threw back his head, letting his laughter boom. He stopped abruptly when he saw that Cyn was stone-faced. "How?"

"His body…" Cyn considered her adjectives. Magnificent? Hot? Powerful? "Is strong. His range of motion and gait seem intact. I'm assuming the disabled veteran patch on his dog means his brain is mush. That Iniquus hired him, and allowed him to shadow a force, probably means Reaper was special forces, too. That's why I suggested that he was a SEAL. It's conjecture on my part. But Iniquus picks from the cream of the crop. Omega texted me that information as well, but I always receive Omega intelligence with a grain of salt."

"Iniquus only hires people with sterling reputations. They scrutinize their psychological makeup to make absolutely sure that none of their employees will do anything that would cast a shadow on their shine."

"And?" Cyn lifted her brows with the open-ended question.

"And their people are not corruptible. We've tried."

"Oh, I'm not planning on corrupting the man. I'm going to exploit him. There's a difference. That it will be through Strike Force that we bring down Iniquus—and possibly, hopefully, the government alphabet agencies who put their trust in their organization—will be a beautiful thing for the Prokhorov family."

Borka lifted his tumbler, peering into the amber liquid as he swirled the ice around his scotch. Without looking up, he said, "Go on."

"My idea is a little complicated. Anticipating this talk with you, I've already started moving pieces into place. If we act fast, we can get everything in motion well ahead of when the wife comes home. Somehow, I think she's going to be the Achille's heel."

"If that happens, we take her out of the picture." He tipped his head back and forth as if weighing scenarios.

"The baby, then, becomes a liability to the father's work. We'd have to kill them both." Cyn shrugged. "Honestly, I don't think it will come to that. With your permission, I'll continue laying the groundwork."

Borka peered at her through the prisms of his tumbler. "You know as well as I do that speed can be the enemy of a good outcome. Patience. The long game." He took a sip.

"In general. However, for this, there's *no* time. We have until the end of the month. That's when Reaper finishes with his force training."

"And so the end-of-month timeframe will see Reaper moved from a force operator to Cerberus, out of the main building and away from what you intend to accomplish. Yes, I see the reason for haste. However, it is The Family's way to strategize and move with planning around the chessboard."

She inhaled a slow deep breath through her nostrils, trying to grab hold of her tongue and say the words that would make Borka agree to this mission. It was low-hanging fruit, ripe for the picking. A gift from the universe. The answer to tear-stained prayers to whatever force—good or evil—that would hear her. "I need Reaper to be working for Strike Force so we can get our spyware into the Iniquus computer. We set up a back door to go in and gather what we want."

"And you can't make a play from Cerberus?"

"I can't imagine that I could. They don't do what the Iniquus Forces do. I mean, sure, they show up as force multipliers when needed. That group mostly does goodwill shit. When natural disasters hit, they send out their tactical search and rescue. Reaper will be in the field with the dogs teaching them to find missing people under avalanches and what have you. From Omega's experience with them, Cerberus can request information from the headquarters proper, but they don't maintain a connection to the main computer system for security's sake."

"Omega knows this, how?"

"They sent in a drone to sniff the cell phone conversation during the Beirut explosion last summer. Cerberus was in the area training, so they flew in to search the rubble. The point was that Cerberus didn't have the information they needed and would send a request to Iniquus Headquarters."

Borka shook his head. "There's more to that Cerberus group than search and rescue. I would like to know what it is. It's too costly to undertake without a get."

"The get, from what I've read, is twofold. One, when Iniquus has a security contract, they go out and look for a specific group. Like, say a university sent a group of kids over to study Italian and there was a mudslide, or what have you, in their area, and now no one can contact the students. Iniquus goes in and finds them, gets them medical help, stabilizes their situation, then hangs out to do more goodwill shit. Iniquus gets international publicity and their reputation as the good guys shines bright. I'd imagine it ingratiates Iniquus not only with the locals but with the government. It probably means that when Iniquus makes an 'ask' that they get what they want. A tear in the red tape, a blind eye turned."

Borka offered a half-laugh as he raised his glass to his mouth. "Cynical much?" He took a studied sip. Staring at her through the crystal, he added, "You know I think that's why we call you Cyn."

"*Cynthia*." He wanted her riled; she knew him well. Borka liked the idea of torture with a thousand tiny cuts, nothing deep or deadly.

A thousand tiny cuts that didn't even draw blood.

Only irritating as a single strike, his words and actions became torturous as the number of slits increased; a little salt rubbed in for good measure.

Yes, indeed.

Borka kept looking for ways to become an infection that weakened her.

Not that Borka wanted *her* weak. This was just his way of moving through the world and interacting with people.

This was how he treated his allies.

Others looking in read the situation clearly: If this is how he treats his own, think how he treats those who come against him.

One could well imagine their punishment would be ruthless and long.

And that it would be gleeful for him to execute.

"Execute" was the wrong word. Executions usually happened with a quick bullet to the back of the head.

A last boat ride out into the sunset.

Chum for any circling sharks.

"Execution" was too gentle of an image.

To Cyn, psychopaths were like a gun in the hand. In the right hand, doing the correct thing, they were a useful tool. But in the wrong hands, they were often indiscriminately deadly.

And just like with a gun, when around Borka, one had to practice safety skills, ever mindful that he could go off without warning.

Cyn had learned, for self-preservations' sake, to act unflappable in Borka's presence.

No joy to be had here with your paper cuts, Mr. Psycho; move on to a more interesting target. "Cynthia was my grandmother's name," Cyn said sweetly. "She was dead before I was born. But more to your point, I don't think it's cynical at all for Iniquus to make those calculations. It's a pragmatic win-win. I actually think our organization could take a page from their book. The do-gooder Prokhorovs." Cyn laughed as she lifted her glass of water and stretched across the desk to clink with Borka's extended tumbler.

"Okay." Borka settled back against the tufted leather of his chair. "Talk me through your plan."

12

Cyn

SATURDAY EVENING

THERE WAS an exuberant knock at the door that spun Cyn around.

Without waiting for a response from Borka, the door flew open, and there stood Nia. Her hand was held over her head with a piece of white plastic that she waved about as she slut strut her way into the room.

"Yes?" Borka asked.

"Positive!" Nia swept, uninvited, around the desk where she laid a pregnancy pee test in front of Borka, the germaphobe.

He looked at it, an odd mishmash of wicked glee and disgust. "Yes. Yes. Two pink stripes." He looked pointedly over Cyn's shoulder.

A man rushed forward, sycophantic in his bumbling effort to get the pregnancy test into a clean envelope. Holding his cuff down with his fingertips, he rubbed the surface of the desk with his suit coat to remove any vestiges of bacteria, then placed the envelope in front of Borka. "Sir." He melted into a shadow.

Nia wrapped herself in a hug, spinning and laughing. "I'm preggers! I'm going to be a mommy!" When she finally collapsed into a chair, she grabbed her stomach, looking green.

The sycophant snatched up a trash can and raced over.

Holding the bin and puffing a breath, Nia looked much like she had on the way into the airport before she raced for a stall to puke.

Cyn had interpreted the airport dry heaves as nerves. She hadn't considered morning sickness. Obviously, planned and strategized morning sickness. Cyn was mildly curious but mostly irritated that her grand plan was being interrupted by the trollop.

Borka thrust his head forward. "You're sure that it's Greg's? He will insist on a paternity test. Those can be done in the first trimester. We will hold minimal sway over him until he is assured."

Nia wrinkled her nose. And with a deep breath, she set the can between her feet. "It's his. He's the only guy I screwed since my last period—well barring the last three days. But my period is late. I just wanted to wait until I got here to show you." She sent a curious glance toward Cyn then focused back on Borka. "Even, if say, I were to miscarry—which why should I? I'm young and healthy—"

Cyn didn't interrupt to explain that it didn't work that way but decided the sooner this girl was done, the sooner Cyn could get her okay to make her run at Iniquus.

"I have the videos," Nia explained.

"Videos can be denied," Cyn pointed out. "He simply needs to present an authority figure who tells his wife that this is the new technology. That the video was of someone else and was computer altered. DNA, on the other hand, is incontrovertible. A child is a lifelong shackle."

Nia gave a one-shouldered shrug.

She didn't seem like she was interested in thinking about the commitment of bearing a child.

Then, Cyn remembered her little airport fantasy when Reaper rounded into sight, and Cyn speculated about them together as a power couple. Cyn had projected children into their coupledom—and promptly handed the screaming brood over to a team of nannies and then boarding schools. Out of sight, out of mind.

But then, Reaper's dog found the flash drive and burst the little daydream bubble that had momentarily amused her.

With Nia as the mother, surely, this child's future was bleak. Unwanted. Uncared for. Loveless. Imagine what that child's life will be like, born as a pawn.

Another generation of sociopaths.

"Who's this?" Cyn asked.

Nia rolled her lips inward sealing away the name as if it was her treasure that she needed to keep safe.

"Berry Greg," Borka said.

"Ha! The news anchor. You're knocked up with his baby?" Okay, Cyn was impressed. That was a big get. "He's not the only one who is high profile. His wife, Bunny, works with some pretty heavy hitters in the think tank crowd."

"I *know*." Nia grinned.

"How did you end up in his sphere?" Cyn asked.

Nia sent Cyn a curious look. She obviously didn't put Mary Wise—the woman who monitored the drop at the airport—with Cyn, sitting here as a high-level Family operative. Nia decided to cast her answer toward Borka and not her. "He was getting on my plane, heading from Paris to D.C. When I recognized him, I upgraded my ticket to sit next to him. Well, there was already someone in the seat next to Berry." She glanced toward Cyn, then back to Borka. "I upgraded to first-class then boarded with enough time to ask the person assigned to that row to switch seats. They were cool with that."

Well played. Cyn was actually surprised by the girl's initiative. And also surprised that it paralleled, in some ways, what Cyn herself did on her way to Boston. Nia obviously had good instincts. She just lacked refinement. Cyn decided she needed to keep this chick on her radar.

To Cyn, Nia's aspirations were reading like the Russian chick with her long red hair and her passion for power. The one who laughed and flirted her way into all of the politician's photographs. The old men who thought their power made them desirable. Sadly, for her, that woman was arrested on charges of functioning as a spy—well, an unregistered foreign agent—and got eighteen months in a federal pen before getting placed onto a flight and sent back to the motherland.

Nia's brazen ego and naivetée were dangerous.

Why didn't Borka address that?

"We had a long talk on the flight," Nia said. "I showed him my social media pictures. He like the ones when I was dressed up in my Catholic school girl outfit with the pigtails. And the Lolita pictures with stuffed animals. He likes my feet."

"I'm sure he does," Cyn muttered under her breath before saying louder, "And you did this all on your own, without contacting your handler for instructions?"

"No one saw us out and about. It's not like we went to a hotel and got caught on cameras. I used the correspondents' apartment. I wanted him to see that I was just a gal working in the area. And I wanted him to know that things could continue." She shot another glance toward Cyn, as if Cyn were a dog that might want to get a bite in. Nia was wary of her, as well she should be. "His wife lives in New York for her job. They take turns visiting each other on the weekends. I figured that if I didn't get pregnant right away, I might need to use those little ovulation predictor kits at the drug store and time my visit."

"Wait. You asked Family management if you could use the apartment?" Cyn wanted Borka to see the level of Nia's rogue behavior. Hierarchy and control were paramount with The Family. "You brought the location to this guy's attention. That endangers the correspondents' program."

Nia glowered at Cyn. "It was only *one* night. I told him that my lease was up, and I was moving because my neighbors were too loud."

No one spoke as that information swelled like fog into the room.

The spell was broken when Borka leaned forward and pressed a button on his desk phone. "Tell Ján to relocate the correspondents' apartment immediately. I want it cleared out now. He has two hours."

Nia was shallow breathing and licking her lips. Yes, she'd messed up. Lucky for her, she was pregnant with a useful plan. They couldn't be but so punitive toward her.

"It's what had to happen to make this go forward," Nia stammered. "Berry asked if I'd tell him when I moved. I agreed that I'd invite him over so he could see my new place himself." She batted her thick fake lashes at Borka. "I'll need my own apartment."

Cyn's eyebrow flew up to her hairline. Did this pawn just make a demand of Borka? And did she really just do it after exposing a major breach of protocol?

"Somewhere nice where Berry will feel comfortable visiting me. You know, he's used to being in places where designers make things look good." She paused and scratched at her head. "Maybe find out where he lives and move within walking distance?"

"His mansion is near the embassy district," Cyn said. Yes, she knew the man. He wasn't on her quick dial, but his number was in her contacts. They had charities and social circles in common. No, she'd never slept with him. But he liked to play with the influential. And so did Cyn. "Real estate is pricey there. You'd have to have a backstory that made sense to live in that area of D.C."

Cyn decided on being practical. Solve some problems, get Nia headed out the door. Cyn had her own mission to develop. And she needed every possible second to get herself organized. "Any apartment would have to be secure but also protect the privacy of those coming and going." Cyn turned to Borka. "Is the Klomar home occupied? They have that lovely 1800s stable that was converted. Two stories, the upstairs views are nice, private garden entrance. Off-street parking. He should feel safe there."

"The occupants are in Europe for the foreseeable time." Borka steepled his fingers. "That location is a good one. Well thought out. Turnkey."

"I can see that with the right coaching," Cyn tipped an ear toward Nia, "that this could be quite excellent for The Family. Since Berry Greg does commentary, we can slip anything we want into the news cycle. He'll be a propaganda machine." She cast a disparaging eye toward Nia.

It wasn't like lying on your back took a lot of skill. Yup, Cyn was going to take some wind out of Nia's sails and orient this as luck of the draw by saying, "Good thing Nia was ovulating that week."

The glower of Nia's anger rose red and hot from her collar up to her hairline. "If I didn't get knocked up, I'd just go find him and screw him some more. I rocked his world."

"I'm sure you did." Cyn waved a bored and dismissive hand. *Lesson time, little girl.* "And you checked that he hadn't had a vasectomy?"

"I'm knocked up. So, duh, he obviously didn't get his balls clipped."

"That's not what… Okay, I'm trying to help you understand that research and questions are important. You spent your money, time, and blew a major Family cover site, possibly putting that program at risk. That's not a small issue. Do you know anything about his marriage? Did they come to an open marriage agreement?"

Nia stared at her wide-eyed. Obviously, she'd thought she'd walked in as a victor. Here she was being scolded.

"You have to think things through and gather data." Cyn added "deary" to the sentence to further erode Nia's pride.

"Listen and learn, young lady," Borka said then with a shake of his head. "It really is a stupid time we live in." Up came his finger, pointing at Nia. "Get this Berry Greg on the speakerphone."

"Now?" She pulled her phone from her pocket with trembling fingers.

"Now," Borka commanded. "You're excited and happy to have succeeded. We want him to think you're thrilled to be pregnant with *his* baby. Be prepared, he's going to offer you the moon and the stars to make this problem go away."

"Why would I do something like that?" She rubbed a hand over her abdomen. "This is my treasure chest."

"Exactly," Cyn said, trying to move this along. "Call the guy up. You're bubbling with pride, little mama. He's going to be the *perfect* daddy for your bundle of joy."

She tapped at the screen. Over the speaker, they heard the rings. "Berry, it's Nia."

"I know." The voice that answered was smooth and warm. "Funny, I was just thinking about you. I miss you. I thought you might like to play."

"Oh, I would! Yes, please. But first, Berry, I wanted to tell you the *best* news!"

13

Reaper

SUNDAY EVENING

"SORRY TO CALL you all in on a Sunday." Striker stood at the head of the conference table in the Strike Force war room. A speaker rested in front of him; the green light verified it was on. "Lynx, can you hear all right?"

"Yes, thank you."

"You're on speakerphone. In the room, we have the team: Jack, Deep, Blaze, Randy, Gator, and Reaper."

"And Houston?"

"And Houston." Striker chuckled.

Houston lifted her head when she heard her name, and Reaper signaled her to lie back down.

"I'm sorry you all are dealing with the frozen slush of D.C. while I'm lying here under a beach umbrella, sipping limeade, living large."

"How's the assignment going?" Striker asked. "Is your teen giving you any hassles?"

"Nope. She's chill." Lynx's voice held a smile. "Easy days, I got a book nerd who basically wants to be left alone. I can't see her trying to slip past me to get into trouble. Nice kid. I've had worse assignments. So what's on your plates this week without me? A huddle on a Sunday night means I'm missing out on some excitement."

"Two cases," Striker said. "Strike Force was specifically requested by the clients for each assignment." Striker turned to Jack. "I'm excusing you from this first assignment. I'm not going to expose you to any fallout from conflicts of interest."

"More?" Jack, Striker's number two, pressed a shoulder into the wall and crossed his arms over his chest.

"Berry Greg signed a contract with Command this morning. When he did, he specifically asked for Strike Force to work this case." Striker turned to Reaper. "To catch you up, our team has had a brush-up with this guy. Back when there was a terrorist attack on the Bethesda prep school where Jack's wife Suz saved her students' lives by having them climb out the window, Berry Greg and his co-host Lisa Hassel speculated that Suz might be a member of the CIA."

"Putting a bullseye on her back." Jack's voice was tight. "Why would he be asking *our* team for assistance, knowing he endangered Suz?"

"My guess," Lynx said, "is that he was at work doing what he does at work. He sees himself as an entertainer—like a comedian who can say outlandish things on the stage to evoke a response. In real life, the comics don't espouse those thoughts. They use the ideas to create engagement. As P.T. Barnum says, 'There's no such thing as bad publicity.' The more emotion he can elicit, the higher the rankings. The human brain, after all, loves *schadenfreude*."

"Still, us specifically?" Jack asked.

"In his own mind," Lynx said, "he might have been impressed by both Suz's heroics and that you had set up that escape plan, Jack. I bet he put your names in a tickler file for a time that he might need help. So what's his deal, Striker? Why did he sign a contract?"

"On a transatlantic flight, he met a teen named Nia Goss."

"How young of a teen?" Lynx asked. "Did this end up in a bed?"

"Yes, to the bed." Striker pressed his knuckles onto the conference table as he hovered over the speaker. "Not illegal, though, she's nineteen. Morality, on the other hand…"

"I'm assuming he's married. Are there pictures?" Jack asked.

Striker shook his head. "Pictures and videos have not been discussed. Nia is pregnant. She tells him that it's his baby."

"He had a first-trimester paternity test?" To Reaper's great shame, when Kate told him she was pregnant, Reaper had looked into having a paternity test done.

Terrified that he'd hurt Kate when he had a PTSDemons flashback, Reaper had insisted that one of them leave their home. Kate said she'd found out she was pregnant on the morning she left Boston to go stay with her aunt in Virginia. It wasn't until she was halfway through her pregnancy that Kate finally told Reaper they were going to have a son.

To Reaper's great shame, he thought—even hoped—that maybe she'd had an affair with her friend Tim.

The test itself was a simple blood draw, that could be done after the seventh week.

But the insult of asking Kate to submit to the blood test would have been catastrophic. It might just have been the nail in their relationship coffin for him to have called Kate a cheat after all she'd put up with to get him well and to keep their marriage intact. Though, at the time, he'd been begging Kate to divorce him, to get a fresh start, to find a new guy to step into shoes Reaper could no longer fill.

The thought of Kate in another man's arms made Reaper physically ill.

Yes, he'd wanted to free Kate from the yoke of a marriage to a man who could not be what Reaper wanted for her. He was the burden, the fear, the undependable and dangerous. His head was so broken that he had little control over his emotions or behaviors.

Away from him.

Safe.

That's what Reaper wanted for Kate.

But he drew the line at blaming her for anything. For making her think for one nanosecond that he questioned her morality or integrity.

Kate was loyal to her vows—all of them. To suggest otherwise would be beyond offensive. Reaper couldn't even come up with a word that would describe such an abusive action as insisting on a paternity test.

Reaper would always—*always*—be grateful that he hadn't wounded Kate by making those accusations out loud.

The only thing Reaper could tell himself in defense of those thoughts was that his brain had been battle rattled a few dozen too many times to remain sane.

"Not yet on the paternity test," Striker said. "Nia told Greg Saturday night about her pregnancy. Greg said he'd like to go to the OBGYN with her. He was going to ask the doctor to have the paternity test done quietly."

"The quietly part is because…" Lynx asked.

"He doesn't want Nia to be offended," Reaper said. "If she's angry, who knows what she'd do. Greg is married?"

"He is." Striker nodded slowly. "And he wants to keep it that way."

"That's money and power there," Jack said. "It's not a bad star for her to hitch her wagon to. I wonder if the pregnancy was premeditated."

"Exactly his question, not that a judge stipulating child support payments would care. Though, it might be an explanation he could offer his wife." Striker focused on Deep, their team's computer guru. "Greg would like some research done and would like a plan for how to handle this. Lynx?"

"Yes?"

"I'm going to have you befriend Nia when you get home. That's Wednesday still that you're coming home?"

"Home Wednesday. I'm making friends to what end?" Lynx asked.

"Greg doesn't know anything about this young woman who is about to mother his child. He'd like to know if she abuses drugs or alcohol, if she has any debt, any associations that would add to the issue at hand."

"A baby is an innocent," Reaper said quietly.

But Striker heard. "Absolutely. It's not something we would contract to try to put pressure on a woman's choice, one way or the other. It seems that Nia has decided to continue her pregnancy—per Greg, she is thrilled."

"And he is—?" Lynx asked.

"Terrified about how this could upend his life. He's looking for information so he can make this a soft landing for everyone involved."

"A soft landing for *him*," Jack said. "I take it this is a man who wants his money and power to make his life consequence-free." It was an aside, not meant to elicit a response. It was what everyone was thinking.

"Iniquus doesn't typically take on assignments like this one," Lynx said. "We don't do infidelity. We do national defense."

"Agreed," Striker said. "Command must think there is a concern there that has to do with United States security."

"I could take a guess," Jack said. "After this guy's 'opinions' were expressed on his news show, Suz was kidnapped and nearly *killed* along with those boys. He has a lot of power to influence the public, as anyone with such a large following does. Command might have put us on this case to see what this woman wants. After all, we're fresh off the news cycle of the Russian woman working as an unregistered foreign agent. She snaked her way into high-powered cocktail parties, gathering information, spreading disinformation. Nia is American?"

"She has a social security number and has been paying her taxes," Striker said.

Lynx said, "That was my take, too, Jack. We've done so many cases where cyber and disinformation are weapons, I automatically put it in the look-see bin."

"There's nothing in my intake paperwork that flags that question," Striker responded. "But I'd say that would be a fair guess. I can have the conversation with Command."

"In the meantime, what does this assignment look like?" Blaze asked.

"A lot of research, both on the computer and tracking. While our client is waiting for the results of his paternity test, he wants a clear picture of how best to proceed. We start with finding out what we can about Nia's background and known associations, and then Lynx gets to do her thing, puzzling out Nia's motivations and personality. From there we make suggestions to Greg on how to manage the situation in a way that keeps everything calm."

"Okay. Good. I need a new BFF." Lynx laughed through the speaker. "Do you have a plan for a way to introduce us?"

"Not yet. Once we have a better picture of Nia. First, I'll have you look over the documentation and see what works. Maybe in a week or so we can slide you in place."

"Will do. Hey, my young lady is signaling that she's hungry.

I'll check in tonight after she's tucked in. As they say from the beautiful beaches of Capri, *Ciao*!"

"*Ciao*!" Striker reached out and tapped the speaker button. The green light blinked off. "Deep, you'll be performing logistics for both teams. Our team is dividing forces. Alpha is me, Gator, and Blaze. Jack leads Bravo, the primary on the Bravo mission is Reaper."

Reaper stilled. *Primary*? He was supposed to be 'trail and observe' on Strike Force.

"Jack and Randy will be giving nighttime support." Striker pointed at Randy. "Your first time back in the field on that leg. A bullet to the femoral artery is a hell of a wound. I want clear, honest feedback on how you're doing. Lives on the line, we need everyone running on all cylinders without any questions about capacity."

"Yes, sir."

Striker picked up a fob and flicked the button. A picture of a man came up on the screen. In this picture, a generically good-looking, middle-aged man in an off-the-rack suit, holding a leather briefcase, was walking down the street. "Reaper, while you're primary on this assignment, decision-making goes through Jack. Any concerns or worries, you reach out to him pronto. This is a walk-in-the-park assignment compared to what you used to do for the SEALs. But it's long hours, high concentration. I need you self-assessing."

Reaper nodded. "Understood."

"This assignment came in this morning. Charles Harlow works as an executive vice president for a private family consulting group, ClearSight. They've contracted with Iniquus in the past when they have working groups going into hot spots. Harlow will be staying in Washington D.C. for several months on an assignment that was developed to get him out of their offices. He's been accused by ten women of inappropriate sexual advances. Their problem is that Harlow brought in a good portion of the family's clientele. They're concerned that—"

"What industry?" Jack asked.

"They do futuristic business consultation out of California with a newly established Atlantic office. They look at data and find the next big thing so that they can help position their client. They want those entrepreneurs to own the lane, ready for the traffic that will follow. Sort of the Nostradamus of the business world."

"Thank you."

"The family is concerned that if they simply fire him for his behavior, Harlow will pick up his marbles and go home," Striker continued. "At the same time, they don't want a toxic workspace or to get sued by the women for not holding Harlow accountable. In Harlow's contract, there is a clause that stipulates that if he does drugs, he will be immediately terminated and a ten-year non-compete will kick in. Basically, this would prevent him from starting his own firm or even taking the clients to another group."

"That's drugs but not sexual abuse?" Jack asked.

"My understanding is that the family lost a child to a drug overdose. They want to put pressure on their staff to remain drug-free. The morality clause only stipulates that employment would be terminated. That's why the family is hoping to find him associated with drugs."

Blaze leaned in. "So they give them a drug test."

"His was clear," Striker said. "But the rumors have been swirling. It was suggested Harlow might have paid off the lab worker who administered the urine test. From what the women are saying, he's not only a user, but they're concerned that he might try to lace their drinks with date rape drugs."

"That's already happened or it's a fear?" Jack asked.

"There's no evidence that it happened," Striker said.

"Fine." Jack nodded. "They spring a drug test on him when he doesn't expect it, at a place where he can't corrupt the process. Here, for example. Just take him into our clinic, and boom we'd have our answer."

"If only it were that easy," Striker said. "The problem is that contractually, the company can only test every six months. Drug testing is done bi-annually for all of the employees. They go to an off-site testing lab of their choice."

"They know when it's coming? How does that make sense?" Blaze asked.

"It doesn't," Deep said from behind his computer.

"Harlow's test came back negative right before the dam burst and the women began sharing their experiences with their HR, when a portion of the staff was moved to Georgia." Striker turned to Jack. "That's where your team comes into play. It's game on, first thing Monday morning."

"Questions." Jack pushed off the wall and came to the conference table to sit across from Striker. "How did the company know to ask for Strike Force? Why did they reach out over the weekend? What do they expect us to do? You tagged Reaper as primary. I'm assuming it has to do with K9s." These weren't just questions to soothe curiosity. All the answers would help provide a scaffolding of understanding around this case.

"ClearSight has contracted with Iniquus before for close protection when their executives go into volatile areas. Typically, they use Panther Force, but Titus has his team in Africa right now. We're next up. As the women's claims hit their HR department Friday, the owners huddled to devise a plan and got the pieces together as quickly as possible so he would be out of the office Monday."

"That explains the Sunday morning contract," Deep said.

"Iniquus's role is to provide close protection for Harlow. They've told him that there were some credible threats against the company, and they're putting security on all the executives. That's not the truth, but they're free to tell the guy anything they want. And yes to the K9. Our client has asked that the person who is on duty while Harlow is out of his hotel room be a K9 handler."

"They want a drug-sniffing dog to tell us if he's got drugs on him?" Reaper asked. "They know that once it's ingested, a dog isn't trained for that. We'd have to catch him with the drug stash."

"Command advised them of this," Striker said. "Reaper and a K9 will provide close protection for Harlow while he's in Washington. Everywhere he goes, you will shadow him, Reaper. If asked, the K9 is trained for security and to smell explosive materials, bullets etcetera. The family doesn't mind if we scare Harlow a bit by suggesting someone could plant a bomb in the car. Not to push the pedal down too hard on that one. Just enough to let Harlow know he shouldn't be trying to subvert his security. At night, Reaper, you have the K9 clear the hotel room, so we know that no one has slipped in and left drugs for him. You're free to leave after that. Randy and Jack will take turns standing guard at night and providing you with further support during the days should you need it. Harlow is to submit his schedule to us, so you'll know when the door opens in the morning, and you can be there. This is going to be an intrusive schedule for you."

"I don't mind. But what if Harlow doesn't like the intrusion?" Reaper asked. "If he's looking for drugs, he's not going to be down with a babysitter."

"If he doesn't like the security, they would accept his resignation without question." Striker took his phone from his pocket, glanced at the screen, and put it back.

Blaze leaned in. "What was his reaction when he was told about new security protocols?"

"He didn't blink an eye, or so I was told. I think, from what the owner said on our video call, Harlow enjoyed the idea of having a security team. It aggrandized his sense of self-worth." Striker focused on Reaper. "Hopefully, this will get cleared quickly before Kate gets back from Boston. But you'll be looking at some long days until we can provide evidence to the client, or the principal goes home."

"Understood."

"If it doesn't conclude quick?" Jack asked Striker. "Reaper's on our team to observe how we function. You mentioned Randy's leg, but Reaper…we need to be aware of the stress impact of long monotonous days."

"Right. I made the assignment knowing that there should be zero issues with any physical altercations. There are no known security risks associated with Harlow."

"Unless you're a woman," Blaze interjected.

"Exactly. But I agree," Striker nodded toward Reaper, "if we get past the seven-day mark or if the days are longer than twelve hours, we may need to bring in a Cerberus team member. Since no one else on our team is K9 qualified."

"If we can at all help it, I'd like to avoid using Cerberus for the next few weeks. They're training and getting ready to host an international post-catastrophe urban search and rescue exercise. They're all hands on deck."

"Agreed," Striker said. "Now, Harlow will have a chauffeur driving an SUV, who is a local hire. The company has opted out of Iniquus providing a tactical driver as it's cost prohibitive. Since there isn't an active aggressor, it's not necessary from a security point of view. Our role is to gather intelligence on Harlow and find an instance of his using illegal drugs if that was something he were to do. To that end, we're building rapport, so he feels comfortable around us."

"Yes, sir," Reaper said. It wasn't exactly the most exciting of assignments. Reaper could imagine just a lot of sitting around and waiting. With his time in the sandbox, Reaper had learned patience. Intel was everything when it came to success. And intel was a slow game.

"There will be space for a dog crate in the back. Reaper will be sitting shotgun with the driver." Striker slid a piece of paper toward Reaper. "Harlow is taking a red-eye in tomorrow morning. Reaper, I need you to meet him at the airport at zero six-thirty. Also, I need to let Cerberus know which dog you'll be handling. They'll get the equipment packaged up. The K9 goes home with you."

"For drugs I want Max. But he's bad around Houston."

"Are you comfortable leaving Houston with Cerberus for the length of the assignment or do you need to pick another K9? With the nature of this assignment, it's best the K9 houses with you. You may get midnight calls and need to jump." Striker skated out a hand. "I hope not, but as a precaution."

Reaper gave a quick nod of understanding. "The best nose for this assignment is Max. Houston's comfortable in the Cerberus stable. They'll take good care of her."

When Reaper was in the long-term care facility, someone from Iniquus would come every day to pick up Houston take her back to the training grounds at Cerberus, work her, and bring her back to sleep with Reaper at the end of the day. It was a well-oiled machine. His brothers were stellar. They understood the situation and were there to bolster him. Yeah, Houston would be fine there. He'd have to reassess once Kate and Little Guy got home.

Kate wouldn't be down with this assignment. She was constantly worried that something might trigger a relapse.

Hopefully, Max would get a hit right away and this would never become a fight.

14

Cyn

MONDAY MORNING

JACK FROST WAS HER HERO.

This weather was perfect. Beyond perfect, it was as if Mother Nature wanted Cyn to succeed.

Parked in a hidden recess of the rural highway, shielded from view by old growth trees, Cyn's car shivered against the northern gusts. The wind was a fiend, whistling around the curves and surfaces of the rental car, clawing and searching the crevices for an entry point to get inside and suck at Cyn's heat and make her brittle.

"Your time is coming. You'll get your chance soon enough," she told the wind as she cranked the heater up to its highest setting. She was already uncomfortably warm. But every shred of heat she could stand now, the longer she'd be safe later.

She wiggled her toes in her winter hiking boots. After tugging on the silk sock liners and thick wool climbing socks, she'd laced her boots tight to give her ankles as much stability as she could.

Dressed in a silk base layer shirt and a pair of fleece-lined hiking pants, her other clothes lay beside her so she wouldn't sweat in them and make them moist, putting her at risk for hypothermia when the cold was finally allowed entry.

It might be overzealous for her to be out here so early, but Cyn had learned from her time with the CIA, and later working for The Family, that the devil really was in the details. She wanted to manage her ops from paper and pencil all the way through to victory.

Just up ahead, a few yards before a hairpin turn, Cyn had found the perfect location for this next step.

From the warmth of her cab, Cyn watched an Omega operator snake his way up the street to her marker, an old tire she'd tossed out of her trunk. He stopped his pickup truck in the middle of the road. The cab momentarily illuminated as he opened his door and jumped down.

In the stillness of zero dark hundred, he stood; a silhouette illuminated by the red glow of the rear lights.

He looked up and down the road. Waited, and looked again. Then he stepped up on a rear tire and reached over to the latch. With a tug, the tailgate dropped down and the water poured freely onto the pavement.

Cyn knew earlier that evening, the pickup truck bed had been lined with thick black rubber pond liner sheeting, then they had dropped a hose into the bowl of the truck bed and filled it full of water.

Already cold from being out in sixteen-degree weather for hours, it wouldn't take long for the water that now flooded the dip in the pavement to freeze.

The guy jumped down from the tire and climbed into the cab.

With the door still open, he drove several yards forward. Smart. No reason for him to wade ankle-deep in slush.

There, he folded the rubber back into the truck bed. With a bang of his tailgate, and a good shake to make sure it had caught, the Omega guy took one last look along the highway.

A minute later, he was down the road.

And there sat Cyn. She had time now to reflect and strategize while she waited for her Omega comms guy to ping her that Reaper was on the move.

On Saturday night, once Cyn had gotten the okay from Borka, Cyn began staging her op. The first crucial step had been to gain a steady thread of intelligence.

The Hamiltons lived in a working-class neighborhood not far from the highway entrance ramp that could take Reaper right to work on the Iniquus campus. They rented the left side of a duplex from Lexi (Lynx) Sobado. Omega said she was an Iniquus "puzzler" whatever that meant.

It sounded stupid. Like a Saturday morning cartoon villain.

But whatever.

Why Lexi and the Hamiltons lived here in this neighborhood was a little odd. They all made excellent money at Iniquus. They could afford upper middle class, even here in D.C. where real estate prices were astronomical.

It was a win for Cyn that they weren't in some high-security penthouse somewhere, or worse, living on the Iniquus campus, which was impenetrable.

Sneaking into the neighborhood in the wee hours of Sunday morning, before Reaper's plane landed, Cyn hadn't been able to access his home.

Her device detected an infrared fence wrapping the property. Expected, these were security professionals after all.

That and the dog being able to smell electronics, it meant that she'd have to be very clever about her designs.

She'd get into the house eventually. Cyn had already laid her snare. It would take time, but Kate would get back, and Cyn would get through that door. And once in, she'd have access to their lives.

Cyn would learn how best to snake her way into Iniquus Headquarters, with her spyware in hand, ready to find a port and let it seep into the nooks and crannies, undetected while she learned how to destroy the CIA.

For now, she would have to make do with external surveillance and Omega satellite overwatch.

The very first thing she did was train cameras from the telephone poles onto Reaper's house and the length of his neighborhood. She placed parabolic ears that could listen to what was said inside, and sniffers that would pull electronic communications from the air and migrate them to her. Be it a computer command that sent the wireless communication to the printer, or a cell phone call, or even the baby monitor that relayed ambient noise, her equipment would grab the vibrations from the air and send them to Cyn's computer to analyze.

Strategize.

Act.

For a moment, Cyn thought about all the things that she might overhear. All the things she would learn about Ryan James Hamilton.

He was an intriguing adversary.

A wild stallion that she planned to break.

"You know," Cyn told herself as she popped the button on her pants and pulled down the zipper, "I don't think I'd mind taking a tumble with the man." She slid her hand into her panties as her knees fell wide. She closed her eyes to focus on the sensations.

Cyn let Reaper fill her imagination. Pulling off his shirt. Her hands stroking over his shoulders, sliding down his abs. What would it be like to have Reaper between her legs, pumping into her?

The fantasy that heated her system brought her to a quick orgasm.

Heart pounding, breath hitched, she brought her fingers to her nostrils and smelled the fresh slickness of her climax.

"Yeah, I might make a good black widow. Enjoying the man before devouring him." She licked her fingers clean, then zipped herself back into her pants.

Well, that was stress relieving. She glanced at the temperature gauge again. Though toasty warm in her car, it was fifteen Fahrenheit, now.

Temperatures were dropping, *thank you Mother Nature*.

She shook off her fantasy and focused again on her immediate plans. When Cyn began this next step, she needed to be as precise as possible. The timing was everything to staying safe in this bitter cold.

"Speaking of staying safe," Cyn muttered as she reached for her purse. She pulled out her pill vial and unscrewed the top. Inside lay the same little white helper pill that she'd foisted on Nia when this whole thing started. She didn't think it would be necessary, but if her limbic system flailed, she'd miss the opportunity, and equally bad, her survival reflexes might just cause a real accident.

It would take an hour for it to fully kick in.

She had time.

She just needed to chill.

Cyn laughed at the double meaning of the word. "Or as the special ops guys like to say as they headed out, 'Stay frosty.'"

In the black of night, Cyn imagined how she wanted the next few hours to go.

She thought about her actions. Her words. Her character's qualities. A year ago, when Cyn was putting this fake life together, she wanted to call herself Cynthia Blackheart—but Cyn Blackheart was a dominatrix's name. She thought about Cyn Conway—yeah, but that would be giving away the plot in the title, wouldn't it? Eventually, she landed on Cyn Parker. That was pedestrian enough.

Time was passing very slowly.

The water on the road was freezing to black ice.

A bird decided to try out his early morning voice, it sounded to Cyn like he needed a coffee.

Cyn sure needed one. She stretched and yawned.

"Omega control. He's awake," came over her car's wireless system. "I have a light on in the upstairs bedroom in the back of the house."

"Copy," Cyn called back. "I need to know when he leaves. As you use the satellite tracking system, I want a countdown starting at the ten-minute mark."

"Yes, ma'am."

This was it. When her support said ten, it was go time.

Cyn was about to put herself on Reaper Hamilton's radar.

He might see her as a mere blip today.

But over time, he'd learn that she was a fighter plane soaring in with her heat-seeking missiles locked on him.

That phrase made her laugh, then faded into nothingness as she sat in the black of night without a single sound around her.

She jumped when she heard, "Ma'am. A figure exited the house through the back door. There was a K9 with him. He's entered his vehicle."

Cyn was immediately upright, eyes wide. With her meditative review—and probably the helper pill—she was in the mental space needed for a mission. "I need your satellite to have an X on that roof and for there to be *no* mistakes. This timing is critical."

"Yes, ma'am. I'm tracking. He's headed down Silver Lake and is turning onto the highway now."

"Keep me abreast." Cyn reached for her turtleneck, tugging it on. Then her thick wool sweater. Next came a fluffy down jacket, a hat, gloves. She looped a silk scarf around her face, tucking the end up under her hat. Cyn had seen pictures of enough people who had been in car accidents where the airbag had deployed to know that she preferred to have her microdermabrasion done by a qualified aesthetician.

"Ten minutes."

Pressing the button on her chair, Cyn moved it back as far as she could and still be able to maneuver the steering wheel and work the pedals.

Airbags deployed at speeds between a hundred and two hundred miles an hour. Cyn wasn't going to think about that. She purposefully took those thoughts and pressed them away from her.

The pill was working in her system. She felt fine. Her hands weren't trembling. She hadn't peed her panties. No sweat along her hairline. Nothing.

She was fine.

This was fine.

After this event, the op shouldn't include anything dangerous. For *her* anyway.

"Seven minutes," her support said over her wireless, encrypted with no way to trace it.

She bet Borka would be cool as a cucumber when he was in the field, no pill, no nose full of coke, no brandy that he tossed back. Nerves of steel happened when you felt nothing.

For a long time after Tom's death, Cyn felt almost paralyzing numbness. Cyn vaguely remembered dragging her butt from the bed to crawl to the bathroom to pee and drink from the faucet. She had lain there day after day, wasting away to nothing. Until one day she woke up like a volcano wakes, spewing ash and fire. She exploded from her apartment, seething molten lava, hissing poisonous fumes, just looking for someone she could strike out against.

She'd jerked open her apartment door, loaded for bear, ready to track down and kill anyone who was involved in her twin's murder.

Cyn's pain seared her insides.

Except for that little cocoon of a black void she'd survived, all she felt was pain.

And she'd do just about anything to make it stop.

When the CIA fell to its knees before her. When they begged and pleaded for her mercy, she would spit on their supplicating faces. She would grind them into the dirt with the heel of her boot.

Then maybe she'd find relief.

"Seven minutes."

"Seven. Copy." It was time for her to take this next step toward finding peace. "Is there anyone else out on the road?" she asked.

"Nada. You're alone. No one around in a ten-mile radius except for your mark."

"Copy." She put her car into drive, crunching over the hoar frost onto the country highway that was the shortest distance from Reaper's house to the airport. "I'm going to roll into position. I'll count you down once I see the tree. Moving." Slowly, Cyn brought up her speed, feeling the blacktop to see how her tires gripped the slick surface.

Since she was belted, she'd have to go faster than if she weren't. But there was no way she'd attempt this unbelted.

Peeking through the slit of space between her soft alpaca hat and the scarf, Cyn aimed for the ice patch that the Omega goon had created earlier.

Thirty-five miles per hour, the speed she needed to activate the airbag. And she definitely wanted that to happen.

She touched the silk scarf that was supposed to help protect her. She needed to be stunned and *stunning* as she set her first hook into Reaper Hamilton, war hero.

You can change your mind. Cyn's inner voice was pinging. *This is…kinda extreme don't you think?*

"Sure, if I was just looking for a date. I'm trying to bring down a nation," Cyn muttered under her breath. "This is for you, Tom."

"What's that?"

"Nada. Shut up. I need to focus."

Her headlights danced over the tire marker on the side of the road.

There was the tree that she'd decided was strong enough to take the hit without falling onto the car and killing her.

Here was her foot, steady on the pedal.

Steady.

Steady.

"Three. Two. One," she called out for the comms guy's benefit as she steered off the road with fingers crossed that the ground was cold enough to be solid. If her tires spun in mud, she'd lose the momentum she needed.

Don't flail.

Keep your hands on the steering wheel.

Steady.

It's going to be fine.

For Tom!

Boom!

15

Reaper

MONDAY MORNING

REAPER WAS in the car an hour earlier than habitual. Houston was curled up at Iniquus in the Cerberus kennel, and Max was sitting shotgun.

He was on a mission. Not exactly the kind of mission that brought glory, but a mission. Seemed like a lifetime ago that he got the call and pulled his equipment from his cage, jumped on his flight with his brothers, and headed out into the dark of night.

Track a guy to see if he happened to buy drugs?

Yeah, it was kindergarten, preschool to be honest.

Still, this was probably his last field mission of this lifetime.

Given the opportunity, did Reaper want to stay on with Strike Force? Hell yeah, he would. That was the life for him—edge of danger, adrenaline rushes, brains and body mechanics in symphonic harmony. He wanted to ride into the fray with like-minded brothers (and sister, Lynx). But that wasn't why he was hired.

Point-blank, Reaper was told he was allowed zero in the way of violence of action.

That was fine; he'd learn to be okay living vicariously.

The dogs were a good challenge. It was skilled and honest work. It served the greater purpose. Heck, he'd been training a K9 named Digger for the Asymmetric Warfare Group. While the task was to train Digger to find electronics, Reaper knew this guy was headed into the mountains somewhere. Reaper had taught Digger how to search for help in an emergency and return to his handler at night if no one was found. Persistence and focus. Digger had taken to that training. As good a dog as one would want. Command had just told Reaper that Digger saved his handler's life by employing those search and rescue skills.

Yeah, that was the kind of notch on Reaper's belt that could make him feel good about leaving the house every day at five o'clock before the family was awake. Made those bitter cold mornings worth his time and expertise.

And Kate felt better about things when she knew there would be no blast concussions rattling his brain.

My god, that woman. Talk about no man left behind. Kate was the damned goddess of tenacity and hope.

He loved her with every cell in his body.

Every breath he drew.

Every drop of his blood.

And as often happened when he just couldn't contain the emotions of being loved that fiercely, he felt the tears welling in his eyes.

With a swipe of his sleeve, Reaper cleared his blurry vision. He turned to Max. "Did you hear that?"

Yeah, he had. Max sprang up to sit at attention, staring down the road with intensity.

Though it seemed to come from a long distance away, the sound was unmistakable.

The dull thunk of a car impacting something solid.

It sounded nothing like in the movies with the screeching tires and the loud kabooms.

In Reaper's experience—and he'd had a lot of experience with this—car accidents had a muffled vibration, like calling to a friend on a snowy day where the fluffy white seemed to absorb the sounds and made the world fall into a hush.

Maybe someone swerved to miss a deer, he speculated. Reaper had seen them coming out of the woods, looking for grass to forage as the winter made food harder to find back in the trees.

Reaper's foot wanted to press down the pedal and get to the incident faster.

Slow is fast and fast is slow.

If his SUV spun out on black ice because of Reaper's haste, how would he be of any help?

While the roads had been cleared and salted, southern drivers didn't have a lot of experience driving on road conditions that were part and parcel to winters in Boston. Few southern cars had the right kinds of tires for this kind of weather. There really wasn't a need. From what Reaper was told, snowstorms down in D.C. were a day or two of inconvenience in most years, not the constant hassle they were in Massachusetts.

"We're going to take a look see." He reached out to scrub his fingers between Max's ears. "Figure out if we can lend a hand."

Max turned his ears this way and that as he tried to gather information.

This morning, Reaper had strapped him securely with the K9 seatbelt into the front passenger seat, toggling the seat all the way back so he wouldn't be hurt if the airbag deployed. Normally, Reaper put the K9s in a crate in the back where they were safer. Today, he'd just wanted the company.

Something in his gut was buzzing, and he couldn't place where the sensation was coming from.

Like he was being watched.

Paranoia was part of the PTSDemons' gig. There was a low level of terror in that creepy feeling that he was back in the crosshairs.

Reaper brought his hands back to the steering wheel as he twisted to the left then the right looking along the roadway. It had to have been black ice, he reasoned. There was no one out on the roads at zero dark thirty. And that's the way he liked it. Even though he and Kate had based out of Boston where they'd met, he hated traffic. Hated to feel boxed in. Hated to think that he wasn't in control of his speed.

Alone and in charge with maximum maneuvering opportunity was how he liked things, a holdover from his life as a SEAL when random trucks could hold deadly surprises.

Reaper slowed to a crawl.

It had to be here, somewhere.

The snow last Friday did the normal southern thing. It melted during the day and froze solid at night making everything a slippery mess. All along this stretch of road, there were skid marks off to the side, exposing the mud and grass beneath.

Sunday, fresh snow covered the old.

But the city had been on their game. For the most part, the roads were clear when he drove home last night after picking up Max at Iniquus. Reaper flicked on his fog lights, hoping to see those tracks a bit better. Another mile and he'd park and get out and track back again on foot.

Nope, he wouldn't have to; there it was.

Reaper pressed the red button on the dashboard—the emergency communications channel at work.

"Iniquus Control."

"Reaper, Strike Force."

"I have you on my navigation screen. You are fifteen minutes from your airport destination."

"I'm pulling up to a car that's off the road. I heard an impact. I'm assuming the driver is inside." He shifted the SUV into park and opened his door, putting a foot on the ground and checking out the scene. "No exit footprints. I'd go ahead and send a paramedic."

"Copy. The closest Iniquus support is twenty minutes."

"I'm not on a mission. This is a good Samaritan call. EMS should cover this fine. I'm due at the airport to meet our client."

"Copy. EMS en route. Contacting your command to deploy another Strike Force operator to the mission."

"Thank you. Reaper, out." He looked over at Max. "You stay put. I'll be back."

Leaving the car running so Max would be comfortable, Reaper rounded to the back of the vehicle and lifted the hatch.

Under the floorboard, Reaper grabbed the handle on the emergency roadside assistance kit. He took out his neon green jacket with the reflective tape and pulled it on. He was certainly visible now. Hyper visible. Not part of his comfort zone. He much preferred digital camo and secrecy.

Next came the road flares to warn other drivers. Given the road conditions, Reaper jogged farther up the street than he normally would. He wanted everyone to have plenty of warning.

Slow it down to a crawl.

With the emergency bag strap looped over his shoulder, Reaper retraced his steps, his work boots crunched through the ice, it felt like this walk was taking forever.

In the movies and TV shows, the rescue guy would sprint forward, leaping into the scene. The hero had arrived!

That was ludicrous.

And it was how things moved from "this sucks, for sure" to FUBAR.

Ambulances didn't race down the road at super-speed, it put everyone in danger. They ran lights and sirens to move the rabble out of the way. That's it.

Slow and steady wins the race.

Like everyone who dealt with life-or-death situations for a living, methodical felt like crap. Felt like the wrong thing to do. Yeah, felt craven, somehow.

Running got the heart rate up, sweat soaked the clothes, got the anxiety flowing, told the brain that this was fight or flight time; forget your training, flail!

Reaper's nervous system had taken more than its fair share of direct hits. Even though cutting-edge medical interventions and therapies got him back on track—mostly—he still found himself fighting his nervous system.

Adrenaline wasn't the ecstatic hit it had been in his youth. Like any addiction, the more adrenaline that flowed through his system, the more his tolerance went up. Reaper pushed himself to find that high. He took on the hardest and hairiest of assignments.

He wasn't unprofessional about it, just the opposite. You don't get invited to SEAL Team Six trials if you were an ego-driven adrenaline junkie.

Reaper became what is known as "an operator's operator," superhuman shit that shows up on movie screens acted out by stunt doubles, engineering, and greenscreens to make it all seem real. Hell, the day before he took the concussive blast that put him in the hospital and out of a job, his team had been tracking a submarine of terrorists transporting weapons down the Red Sea to Yemen. Reaper had jumped off their boat as it powered parallel to the sub, and he jumped.

He wasn't really thinking anything other than if he got the hatch open, the crew couldn't submerge.

He jumped.

Crazy.

And that's what addiction to a substance or a sensation can do for you.

Yeah, he'd felt the adrenaline, and it was gold running through his veins.

But after the blast concussion that turned his brain to pulp, adrenaline felt like death.

For no obvious reason, he felt like he was back on the battlefield, rifle up, approaching the enemy camp.

What did he see? Skid marks where the car slid and hit. The car itself was an igloo of snow. Had he not heard the squeal and impact, he would have missed it all together.

Had he not heard the impact, he would have assumed that car had been there all night.

Two things.

One, there were no tracks going to or from the car. That meant no one helped and no one exited. If this had happened last night and the snow had fallen to accumulate, that person would have died from hypothermia.

The person could well be dead, Reaper told himself.

The engine was running. That was thing number two. No idea how much the tank could hold, or if it had been filled prior to the accident. How long could a car idle? About thirty hours on a full tank. Okay. It could have been there since last night from a fuel point of view, but not from a tracks point of view. The tracks were fresh. The snow probably buried the car because when the car impacted the tree, it knocked the snow off the broad limbs.

There, his system was cooling.

He was chill.

Adrenaline—his former drug of choice, now the bane of his existence—waned with logic and physical action.

As he got closer, he could identify the make. Expensive damned sports car. Light, fast, and shit in inclement weather.

A rental.

Maybe the driver just didn't realize what they were driving as they hit the ice patch on the highway.

Something about that ice wanted Reaper's attention. Pulled and dragged him, "look at me!" In the past, Reaper would have followed that instinct. He would have investigated the thickness and the improbability of a length of ice that was that pristine at this point of the road. There were no natural sources of running water around. No overflowing creek beds. No reason at all for there to be ice on the road here, while the rest of the street had been chemically treated.

No reason at all.

But Reaper didn't trust his instincts anymore.

Jogging his way over to the car, Reaper just hoped the driver was still alive.

16

Reaper

Monday Morning

Reaper brushed the snow from the driver's side window. In the moonless night, he lifted his flashlight, shining it into the interior as he peered in at the corner where the side curtain left a gap.

Single passenger. Belted. Head supported by the steering wheel. A fabric puddle of a deflated airbag.

Reaper tried the door handle, locked.

He rapped on the window to see if he could rouse the woman.

Unconscious meant head injury, and Reaper knew head injuries and their ramifications all too well.

Yeah, this was hitting close to home. It had been months since his last flashback of the car crash that put him into a coma, breaking his already broken brain…

"Ma'am, I'm Reaper Hamilton from Iniquus." He raised his voice so if she was at all with it, she would know she wasn't alone. "I've got you. Just hang in there for me."

Movement. Action. Get it together. Work the problem.

Getting triggered by this accident wouldn't serve anyone, least of all the poor woman inside.

He hoped like hell she was still alive.

Reaper rounded behind the vehicle, tugging the safety tool from the side pocket of his bag. With an elbow crooked over his face, he protected his eyes as he slammed the conical point into the back passenger window, far enough away from the woman that the glass shards wouldn't rain down on her.

Reaching through the opening, he unlocked the front passenger door, but it had been collapsed inward by a branch.

He rounded to the woman's door and tried to jerk it open, but that one too was crushed.

Reaper climbed into the back seat calling, "Ma'am, I'm Reaper Hamilton. I'm a trained Navy veteran. I'm going to help you until the EMS arrives."

As the hood crumpled, the engine had pushed back into the driver's cage. The steering wheel pressed against the woman's torso, her head tipped forward. They'd need hydraulic equipment to pry her loose.

He stretched out to press the engine button to stop the motor

He checked his watch and wondered about ETA to this location.

Typically, an emergency call was ten minutes tops on a regular day. No telling on a day like today, he thought, sliding into the back seat and leaning through the gap between the front captain's chairs.

He'd have to work from here.

Sticking his fingers between his teeth, he pulled off his glove, resting it on the dash. He licked the back of his hand. The moist surface would allow him to feel even the tiniest bit of air passing through her airways.

Reaper pulled in a breath as he reached under the long strands of her blonde hair. She hadn't moved. Unconscious for this long was a *bad* sign.

The tickle of air on his skin was faint, but she was breathing.

He wasn't going to have to try to do mouth-to-mouth hanging upside down from the rear seat.

Reaper's fingers moved to her wrist where he found the pulse was strong and rhythmic. He pulled off her gloves and was glad to find she hadn't used nail polish. He pressed the nail bed until it was white then watched the capillaries refill with blood.

Circulation seemed all right.

She wasn't hypothermic—the cab was still warm. Shock was life threatening. He'd have to consider the temperatures and how quickly that could exacerbate the scene. Put her at risk.

Careful not to move her, Reaper used his flashlight to check for bleeds or disfigured limbs that might indicate a break.

"Ma'am, can you hear me?" *Where was that ambulance*? "Ma'am, move your fingers if you can hear me?" They lay limp where he'd lowered her hand to her thigh.

Until heavy equipment arrived, stabilizing the situation was the best he could do.

The northern gusts rattled the car.

With the engine off, the interior temperatures were dropping.

Reaper clawed through the roadside emergency kit and pulled out two Mylar blankets. One he draped over the woman's back and tucked in, the other he used to cover the window he'd broken out.

"Ma'am, I'm stepping away from the car for a moment. But I will *not* leave you. I'm just signaling help. Okay?"

He hoped for a "yes" or a moan or…something, but he got nada.

Reaper checked his watch to clock the "golden hour" of rescue. She was already a good twenty minutes into her ordeal.

Far enough away so the woman wouldn't hear him, he talked

to Iniquus Communications. The voice in his ear was calm and professional. "They're pulling in resources from Virginia. There was a major pile up on 395. Your wait time is sneaking up around the twenty-minute mark as a minimum. Road conditions are treacherous especially on the less driven routes."

"Copy."

"Apply what field medic aid you can to keep her alive until then."

"Wilco. Out."

Max was barking in the Iniquus SUV. Typically, these K9s were beside their handlers, running into the fray. Reaper thought briefly that Max could fit into that front seat and could add the warmth, possibly bring the woman some comfort as she—if she—came around. He tucked that away as a possibility if rescue got snarled up for longer than Comms indicated.

To his great surprise, when he climbed back into the car, the woman was sitting up and looking around, obviously disoriented.

Then she panicked.

17

Cyn

Monday Morning

When Reaper left the car to call an ambulance, Cyn blinked her eyes open. She had been conscious the whole time.

Stunned by the impact, she was grateful for all her training. She had told her brain prior to her op what was coming and how to react. She'd used imagery to train her actions and reactions. She'd told herself at impact, to keep her head down and play possum until it served her to rouse.

First, Reaper had to question if she were even alive.

As he broke the window and pressed his fingers to her pulse point, she remained still.

He would think that she'd been unconscious since she plowed into the tree. This brought up the danger levels.

He would be there as a first line of rescue; her lack of response would turn the switch to hero-mode. *Her* hero.

It was a contract. An unspoken oath. "I will do everything I can to save you." That's what heroes thought. So silly. She bet when Reaper was a four-year-old kid, he tied a towel around his neck and ran around pretending he had superpowers.

Now, Cyn just needed to play this right so she could twist him around her little finger. To that end, Cyn had practiced in the mirror last night how best to hold her face in confusion and as if pain gripped her features, attractively, like she assumed actresses did for their roles on screen.

Some of this wasn't acting. Okay, a lot of it. Now that she could assess her situation by the illumination of Reaper's light, she realized this had gone a lot worse than she had calculated.

She was trapped, crushed against her seat by the steering wheel. The driver's door was bowed outward. Cyn's hand found the door handle and she jerked on it with the full power of fight to flight.

Without planning or forethought, a scream of terror filled the tiny space to overflowing.

"Hey, hey, hey. There you are." Reaper pressed her arms down, straightjacketing her into submission. "You've come around. That's good. Hold very very still for me."

Panic wasn't so easily dismissed. She flailed against him.

"Stop!" He used the kind of authoritative voice that could make men drop their rifles.

It startled her into a gasp and a wide-eyed freeze.

"Ma'am, my name is Reaper. Emergency Services are on their way."

She blinked at him. She had wrestled herself back into control. Now was the time for her to be weak and dependent. "What… What happened?"

"It looks like your wheels hit some black ice. You've crashed into a tree. I'm going to take care of you while we're waiting for rescue to get here. I need you to be nice and still for me, Okay?"

Cyn started to turn her head to take in the scene. In front of them, a splintered windshield and the white snow mound that must have shaken loose with her impact. The side windows showed little more. Beyond the flashlight-illuminated white snow was the dark of night.

Reaper caught her chin. “Ma’am, you were unconscious when I found you. It’s best if you can sit very still and not move your head around. I don’t want you to exacerbate any whiplash or concussion.”

She pursed her lips to look like a kiss and exhaled.

Reaper had folded the passenger side seat down to the dashboard that had advanced a good foot into the interior. He was awkwardly shoved into the space. As he started to move, Cyn reached out, grasping at his coat sleeve, eyes wide with fear.

“I’m not leaving you. I swear. I’m reaching for my first aid kit.”

Cyn licked her lips and stared forward, not even turning her eyes his way. Dutiful. Obedient.

“For your comfort, I want you to know that I’m a trained medic with the Navy.”

She responded with another exhale.

“What’s your name?” His voice was warm and gruff.

He cared, Cyn thought. He was worried about her. When Cyn had started her research, she was able to find a newspaper article where Ryan James Hamilton was the victim of a drunk driver crashing into his motorcycle. It had been fairly recent, not even a year. It was spectacular enough of a scene to make it to the local news. The helmet broken into two pieces, the bystanders’ tears. The drunk handcuffed to a gurney. It all made for good television.

It also gave her the idea for this first actionable mission step.

CIA work for Cyn had been about building alliances. Shared experiences were key. While Cyn wasn’t willing to risk laying down her own bike, too much being out of her control in that scenario. She could do this much.

And it was working.

Reaper, for sure, was emotionally invested in her wellbeing, she could tell from his voice and the quality of his touch.

"Can you tell me your name, ma'am? I'm Reaper," he repeated. "What should I call you?" Reaper started down the list of questions that needed to be asked and assessed. First off, her mental orientation. Cyn knew the protocol.

"Cynthia Parker." With the steering wheel trapping her against the seat, there wasn't a lot of room to inhale. Her voice was whisper thin, barely lifting over the sound of the wind. Cyn recognized this as life-threatening. Positional Asphyxia. The lungs needed space to fully expand, or the person couldn't get enough oxygen into their blood. It was why she was taught to never cuff someone and lay them face down. Well, she shouldn't do that if she wanted to keep them alive—"Situations change. Use your best judgment," her mentors had told Cyn.

In her present situation, it would be hard for anyone to tell if she was hypoxic or if she was hypothermic. A blanket wouldn't help the oxygen issue.

As heroic as Reaper Hamilton might be, unless he had heavy equipment in his vehicle, she could well die.

She could die.

And Tom would go unavenged.

For a moment she wondered what would have happened if Reaper weren't observant, if he weren't a hero, if he hadn't decided to stop. Would Omega have figured out that Reaper drove on to the airport, and she would need rescue? She hadn't brought it up with them. They weren't her people. Omega was on The Family payroll as hired help. "Everyone calls me Cyn," she managed.

"Cyn," he repeated. "Cyn, on a scale of one to ten, what's your pain level?"

Her teeth started chattering. "I…don't know." Trapped! She'd thought that the engine block would slide under the car not in against her. That's what happened at The Farm where she learned to drive for the CIA. One night they had her drive directly into a brick wall. If she didn't crush the hood and the auto was still drivable, she'd have to do it again and again until she made the hood into an accordion. Cyn had put her foot down, closed her eyes and crushed it—in all senses of the word.

It was a different vehicle and a very different outcome.

"Do you know what day it is?"

"It's, uhm, Monday morning."

"Good. Cyn while we talk, I'm going to do a physical assessment. I'll tell you what I'm doing as I do it. Okay?"

She started to nod her head, but Reaper caught her chin again. "Words. No gestures, no head moves. You're trying to stay as still as possible. Do you know where you were going? It's awfully early to be out on these roads."

"To the park. I thought…" Her hands came up to the steering wheel, and she tried to press it away from her chest.

"I know this is uncomfortable, but I need you to be as still as possible until the paramedics show up. It should be any minute now. We're going to need some equipment to get you out of here."

Her hand shot out and grabbed at Reaper, again. A moan escaped her lips that rose up, turning into a wail.

At The Farm, they used a martial arts kihap. It usually sounded like "Ha!" as a punch was thrown at someone or on impact when a strike came against her. That sound at point of pain, released the energy and helped it to dissipate the sting of the impact. Better out than in.

Reaper waited for her to exhaust that breath. Didn't try to shush her. He didn't wait long. Cyn simply didn't have enough air to sustain any kind of tantrum.

"Cyn, don't turn to look, but the red lights are almost to us. You'll be free soon. This is a pretty quick process."

Cyn reached for his hand, interlacing her fingers with his. And he allowed it.

She held back the little curl of a victory smile.

The team that showed up was a little too efficient for Cyn's taste. She'd planned to cling to Reaper as then rescuers buzzed their little worker bee selves around them.

Boo to their efficiency!

Reaper tried to get out to apprise them of the situation and share his notebook where he'd been documenting her vitals.

Cyn gripped tighter, and he didn't fight her.

"Sir, are you hurt?"

"That's my vehicle back there with the flares. I called it in."

"Could you get out of the vehicle?"

Cyn called out, "No. No. No!" Breathless, and sputtering, and as female and damsel in distress as she could make those syllables sound.

"Are you okay in there with her?"

"Whatever is needed," Reaper said. Protector. Champion. Guardian angel. Yup, he was everything she thought he'd be. And she was going to exploit the hell out of him.

18

Reaper

Monday Morning.

Reaper stood beside his vehicle, watching the ambulance take off down the street.

The rescue workers were gathering their tire chucks and 6x6 timber that they'd used across the front of the windshield. It was a good technique; one Reaper hadn't trained.

After removing the front window, the team wrapped a chain to the steering column then around the beam, they'd been able to use the jaws of life to slowly take up the slack in the chain and lift the bent steering column. It only gave them six inches, but six inches was enough to slide Cyn out.

She'd gripped at his hand until the last possible second. She didn't let go until she was out the door.

It was a strange sensation for a complete stranger to put that much confidence in you.

It made Reaper want to be bigger, stronger.

He'd experienced little of that as a SEAL. It was pretty rare that Reaper was saving anyone. Back then, he pointed his gun and ordered folks around. Running and gunning, it wasn't like he was holding anyone's hand. What Reaper held was a leash with a ferocious war dog on the other end.

While Reaper had tried to be calm and gentle around the kids, with the women, it was best to keep his guard up.

Women could be lethal in unexpected ways.

Reaper bet the operators on Cerberus probably did a lot of hand-holding and soothing. They showed up to natural disasters and their dogs found survivors in the rubble. It was slow work to get someone out of a collapsing building. Great care had to be taken.

It was a balancing act. Sometimes slow saved lives, and sometimes careful was just too slow. Compressed chests, like Cyn had experienced, could kill.

Yeah, he'd been worried.

One thing that he didn't see in the Iniquus emergency kit was an oximeter to check her O2 saturation. The only reason he thought it might have been left out was, there was nothing he could have done to help once he knew she was low on oxygen. Except to tell people to hurry the hell up.

But then again, fast was slow.

A truism, up until a point.

Standing beside his SUV, he caught a first responder's gaze and pointed at the flares Reaper had set out when he'd arrived on scene.

"I'll take care of that." He raised a hand in a kind of half salute. "Everything you did was much appreciated."

Reaper raised a hand in response.

He wondered how this delay was going to affect his mission.

Fumbling for his phone with fingers stiff with cold, he climbed into the cab, still toasty warm from the heater.

He glanced toward Max. "Thanks for holding down the fort. You good?" He scratched behind Max's ears.

Max turned to sniff Reaper's hand then gave him thank you licks.

Reaper tapped the quick dial for Strike Force war room.

"Reaper."

"Striker. You're on speakerphone. The team is here. Everything work out?"

"Affirmative. The crash victim looks like she'll be fine. I'm sure they're going to want to check for internal bleeds, and any trauma to her head and spine. Once they got a little air into her, she seemed to perk up. How'd it go with Harlow? Who has him?"

"No one," Striker said. "He missed his flight and took one that will get in at 17:10 hours. How about you get yourself fed, cleaned up, and head over to fill out your reports."

"Wilco. Out." Reaper shoved his phone into his thigh pocket and put the vehicle in motion. With a three-point turn, he headed back to his house on Silver Lake.

"For a day that was supposed to be dull, it sure started with a bang." He gave Max a wink, then powered up the road.

Monday Afternoon, Strike Force War Room

"Did you see this?" Deep put up a picture of a woman in tactical clothing holding a cat.

"No what is that? That's not one of my languages," Reaper said.

"She's in the Ukrainian Army. They have tactical cats. I think you should take that on as a project, Reaper."

"I don't know a lot about…tactical cats. Are you pulling my leg? Is this a joke about herding cats?"

"Not at all, brother. They train the cats to find sniper's laser dots so the soldiers can find snipers."

"And it works?" Reaper's brow drew together as he took in the image of a monster-sized striped cat with fierce yellow eyes.

"This cat is honored for finding four snipers. So yeah. Do our special forces have a secret cat army that I haven't heard of?"

"Nope," Reaper said with a sniff of a laugh. "Never heard of it. I'm going to pretend that I haven't heard of it."

"Not a cat lover?" Lynx asked over the video feed.

"I'm not going to say that. Cats are cool. I'm just not up to figuring out how to train them to do anything other than perhaps domestic destruction."

The door opened and Striker walked in with Greg.

While he was recognizable from his time on air, he definitely looked different without his makeup and hairspray.

The on-screen joviality was nowhere about his posture. In fact, he looked like he was on the verge of tears.

Greg held out a hand and walked toward Jack.

The guy couldn't read body language.

Jack was lethal, his eyes hard as they slid past Greg onto Striker. "I'm heading to the barracks." He stalked out.

Following Jack's movements with a confused eye, Greg turned to Striker for an explanation.

"You nearly got his fiancée, now wife killed. Don't expect the man to put that in his rearview. My understanding is that you were warned by Command about your history with this operational task force and that you insisted on us. Let's start there. We have other forces whose members you didn't endanger. I'm happy to pass your case on to one of them."

Striker wasn't here to play.

Something sizzled in his eyes. If this were the military, that wouldn't go down well. As a private security group, Reaper guessed he'd have more latitude to be forthright.

Greg blinked and stepped back. Yeah, this guy was used to people bumbling and stumbling all over themselves to stay in his good graces. That was an easy read. He certainly wasn't the titan that Reaper had imagined.

"No. I don't want them. I…we've gotten off on the wrong footing."

"I suggest that we get this reassigned." Striker crossed his arms over his chest. "You might feel more comfortable."

"No. You. I was told to ask specifically for you by my colleagues at different news sources. You know, embeds and the like who have seen you in action."

Striker tilted his head. "Are you expecting action?"

"Not at all." He licked at his lips and seemed to search the room for something to drink, letting his gaze rest for a moment on Deep's coffee cup." He let out a nervous chuckle. "By god. This team is intimidating as hell." He looked around again, this time his gaze rested on the chairs around the conference table. No one had asked him to take a seat, and he was quivering like a chihuahua. "I was told that this is the team. I've signed the contracts. This is all rather simple." He turned and looked at the door.

Reaper could well imagine that he wanted to bolt, but at Iniquus no one was allowed freedom of movement if they weren't under contract. Guests had someone at their arm at all times, even to go to the can. And they weren't allowed within six feet of a computer.

That's why the furniture was configured the way it was, and there was a clear delineation from rug to wood floor.

Reaper imagined if Greg crossed over that line the team

would pile on like he had the football in the last moment of play and there was no way they'd lose the whole game because someone squirmed past.

"All right," Striker said, blading his hand to indicate a chair as far from Deep as one could position him. "Take a seat. Let's hear what you've got going on."

"I had a weekend with a young lady that I met on the flight from Paris. Nineteen. Legal in that sense. She told me that she's pregnant with my child. I am married and my wife...she's rather bitter about the fact that she was unable to have children of her own even though we did all of the things—hormone shots and all of that. So this would be particularly egregious if it turns out to be true."

"If..." Striker put out the lead to see where it would go.

"I went to her place and I had her do a pregnancy test in front of me. She is pregnant. No doubt about that." His words were pressed through a chest constriction that Reaper knew well. It was how he'd sounded when he told his best friend—his son's namesake—that Kate was in her second trimester. The terror of it all. For Reaper it was the fear that his injuries were harming those that he loved.

But for this guy, he was afraid for himself only. Reaper read that clearly in his eyes. He thought he could play without repercussions.

And he was wrong.

The guy was a jackass. In Reaper's book, short of violence, there was little that was more reprehensible than infidelity. To think a man of this moral character had so much sway on the nation and how they viewed the world.

"Your question then is if it's yours? Did you use a condom?"

"You know, usually it's the woman who suggests that. She didn't bring up contraception, so I assumed she was on the pill and clear of STDs—I mean she's young to have encountered them. I would assume she'd tell me."

"Did you tell her you were married?"

"No."

Striker slid a hip onto the table and stared down at Greg. "So the clear communication piece between you has never been there."

The guy swallowed, making his Adam's apple jump.

"And now? What would you like to have happen?"

"Wind back time?" His eyes settled on Deep's coffee mug again and again he licked his lips.

"Where did you see this woman to have her retake the test?" Striker asked.

"At her place. New place. She just moved. She gets money from somewhere. She was in a very nice apartment. Upscale. Doorman. That's where we were together. Now she's moved. Not far from my Washington home. It's a converted two-story garage. Again, very upscale. Lovely décor."

"So, this isn't about money." Striker pulled out a chair and sat across from Greg.

"No, she's not said a word about money. She seems to really like me. And—" He curled his lips in while he inhaled deeply. "She seems excited to be a mother."

"And you?" Striker asked. "You're the father. What would you like to see happen?"

"Honestly? I want her to have a miscarriage and disappear into the night." He shook his head, wide-eyed with disbelief. "She's seeing us as a nuclear family. Mom, Dad, baby makes three."

"You're married. She knows this now?"

"Yes."

"Has she asked you to divorce your wife?"

"No."

"All right. What role are you envisioning for my team?"

"I need to understand who she is and how best to navigate this minefield."

19

Reaper

Monday Evening, Airport

"Come on, Max." Reaper had met up with the chauffeur at his company's garage and had installed a dog crate for Max for the duration of the Harlow close protection/detect the drugs operation. The driver, Barrot, was a little pissy that his car was going to smell like a kennel.

Reaper could understand that. This is the way the man made his living. From a strategic point of view, a driver had too many ways to retaliate, too many ways to make the days that much longer and more difficult to navigate. So, Reaper had promised that after Harlow flew home, Iniquus would fully detail and doggy-detox the vehicle.

Barrot was cool with that.

Max jumped to the ground and shook his coat then sat politely on Reaper's left. "You're a damned good doggo, Max."

Max looked up and caught Reaper's gaze.

"Look, the sooner you find our scent, the sooner you get to go back and play with your buddies, okay? We going to do this?"

Max sat up a little straighter and puffed out his chest.

"That's right, good boy." Reaper straightened his security vest, checked his collar, and scratched behind his ears. "Best public manners now. Here we go."

Barrot was coming along in his suit and cap, looking very polished and professional.

They moved into the luggage area. Service dogs, like Houston, had the legal right to go anywhere that the public could go. It was against ADA law to ban them as they were considered medical equipment. You can't refuse a service animal any more than you could ban someone's wheelchair or oxygen tank.

Security animals were another story.

Iniquus had explained this to the client. Reaper could be refused entry or asked to leave at any point and for any reason, and Reaper would have to comply.

What would he do at that point? Removing Max to the SUV was a no-go, he was worth a hundred grand. And he was trained for takedowns. One of the glories of Max's life was the bite. He lived for two joys, well to Max they were probably one and the same—play drive. Sure, wrestling with a towel was okay, but a screaming fighting enemy? Bliss.

For public safety, Max could *not* be left without a handler who maintained control.

Max and Reaper would have to stand outside of the establishment, ready to rush in should there be a situation, which, of course, was a farce. Nobody wanted to hurt this guy.

One would suppose that if any drugs were used, that there would be trace amounts on the man somewhere. And that was why Reaper wanted Max, the best sniffer Reaper had ever seen in action.

Moving to the corridor where passengers would come to

gather his suitcase, Barrot held up his tablet with the name HARLOW in bright yellow against a navy blue background. With his shoulders squared and his chin lifted, Reaper thought he'd been through some training—military or police—at some point in his life. He looked like he might be nearing retirement age, and he also looked like the kind of guy who had no plans to retire. Fit. Neat. Professional.

And here came their client, dressed in the same suit and tie that was in his intake photograph.

As Harlow approached, Max stomped his foot and emitted an almost subsonic rumble.

Interesting.

Reaper had seen this in the field with his K9s when he had to speak to tribal leaders who weren't especially on the good-guy rosters. Reaper caught Max's gaze and conveyed the idea that Max's message was understood, thank you. And Max settled down to a neutral stance by Reaper's side.

"I'm Harlow. Thanks for being here. Sorry about the mix-up this morning." He clapped his hands, then rubbed his palms together. "Let's get my luggage, get me checked in, then I need some grub and a drink, or six." He sent them a wink. Pivoting in his high-shine leather loafer, Harlow headed toward the luggage carousel.

Reaper and Barrot dutifully shadowed him over.

Now that he'd met the man, Reaper knew he was going to hate every minute of this assignment.

Tuesday Morning at Home

. . .

Reaper finished typing and attached the pictures he'd taken during his turn babysitting Harlow.

Last night, after he'd handed over the security detail to Randy, Reaper had decided to grab a few hours of shut eye before he decided what to include in this report.

It had been an odd night, to say the least.

Harlow made three stops—a restaurant, a titty bar, and a blues club.

Repeatedly, Reaper had given Max a lowkey hand gesture to sniff Harlow for drugs, and each time Max said, "Nada."

What was startling to Reaper was that he saw Cyn—the woman from the accident—in two of those locations. She had her back to him both times. At first, he thought Cyn Parker had a doppelganger, but in the restaurant, she was still wearing a lime-green hospital bracelet. And, when she turned her head to look over her shoulder, she had the same abrasion on the right-hand side of her forehead. She was with a woman of about the same age. They seemed friendly but not like friends, colleagues, perhaps.

It was an odd coincidence.

Reaper was working, so he wouldn't approach. He did, however, take a picture of her left and right silhouettes just because of the oddness of her showing up in his sphere.

After dinner, Harlow moved on to a strip club, but it wasn't up to Harlow's standards. Reaper was just glad to be out of there. One thing was apparent, Harlow was a misogynistic piece of crap. Reaper had had to bite his tongue throughout his career for greater geopolitical reasons when he was tasked with high-stakes VIP's safety, and they turned out to be a dick. So he had some practice for this assignment.

Harlow asked Barrot where the "good" gentleman's clubs could be found—the ones with the "classy chicks." Then he changed his mind and asked Barrot about blues clubs.

They relocated up the street. Reaper was glad Barrot knew where these places were. None of this was part of Reaper's toolbox of knowledge. And frankly, his job wasn't to play tour director. He was here to catch the guy doing drugs, that was it.

When Harlow found his seat at *Feelin' Blue* and signaled for a scotch, Reaper and Max stood behind him in a niche out of the way of foot traffic, close enough to send the fur missile in if something went sideways.

Along the wall, facing the band, Reaper spotted Cyn and her companion again.

That made three times in a day.

A crash, a restaurant, and a blues bar.

The odd thing about it was if she was following them, she did it by getting there first. She didn't show up at the strip club. And they had changed directions at the last moment based not on what Harlow suggested but what he had chosen from Barrot's list of suggestions.

Neither Harlow nor Barrot was on his phone.

That was just plain odd.

All of it.

Yeah, Reaper would hand that data over to Iniquus and let Deep and Lynx see if they could make hide or hair of it. Reaper didn't believe in coincidences. But he couldn't fathom a reason for Cyn's proximity.

Reaper pressed send.

His next job was to check on today's weather and traffic. And just because he missed Kate, Reaper started with the Boston weather report.

After a few clicks of his mouse, Reaper pulled out his phone to quick dial his wife.

He had to wait through five rings before she answered.

"Kate." Reaper watched the radar with his cell phone pressed to his ear.

"Ryan?" Her voice was raspy, he imagined her hugging a pillow and talking with her eyes still shut.

Reaper loved to watch Kate wake up in the morning, swiping at the tangle of long brown hair as she looked around to orient herself to the new day. She'd toss off the covers, her nightdress wound around her waist from where she kicked and squirmed in the night to throw her leg between his and burrow her head into his back. Her waking was a moment of vulnerability that touched his heart. Every time.

"What time is it?"

Reaper was sorry for the vibration of fear he heard in her voice. He could imagine her hand wrapping her throat. "Early, sweetheart. Too early to call. Everything's fine here. I'm sorry but I'm about to go on duty and needed to reach you first."

"Yes. Yes. What? Why?"

"I was looking at the weather up your way."

"Weather?" Kate sounded like she was halfway between her dream and this call.

"Kate, come on. Wake up. This is important."

"Okay."

He could hear her moving around.

"I'm standing. That's the best I can do. Did you say weather?"

"A nor 'eastern is revving up. I need you out of there."

"Hang on let me…"

Reaper filled Max's kibble bowl and checked his water while Kate looked for herself at the weather system. She'd lived in Boston long enough that she knew what this meant.

"Wow. That sprang out of nowhere. You're calling me home?"

"You're at a rental. You have no food stores. No way to stay warm when you lose electricity. It's not a safe setup for you and Zack. I'd like it if you could get the first flight available and get back here."

"I could go stay with—"

"I know your friends are going to invite you to their houses, and they'd keep you safe. Normally, I'd trust that was okay, but Zack was pulling at that ear. Feverish in blackout? I don't want to take any chances on Zack. Please come home."

"Oh. Uhm. Whew. Changing plans on a dime. Okay. I'm going to get on the computer and see what there is. If I can't get a plane ticket, I'll rent a car and just start driving south."

"Plane's best. I don't like you on the roads that long alone. Especially with the baby. We've talked about this before, you're damned good at protecting yourself, but it's an entirely different equation when there's an infant in the picture."

"Yes. Yes. Whew…"

"I'm not saying this to scare you. I just need decisions to be made now—best case, second, and third. Plane. Car. Friend's house. If the plane doesn't come here, anywhere outside of the snow line is where you should go. Just fast before others wake up and see this."

"Yes. Who knew you could be such a mother hen?"

"I'm hanging up so you can get on this. Text me your plans, okay?"

"Yes. Okay. I love you! Thank you."

And she hung up before he could say the words back to her. The "I love you" was always in his heart. The "thank you" was always on his tongue. There was no way he could say either one enough.

Kate had dragged his ass out of hell.

20

Kate

TUESDAY AFTERNOON

KATE CLAMBERED FROM THE TAXI, jostling Zack as the driver ran around the car unloading her luggage and the baby seat, placing them gently on her porch.

She'd expected to be in her pajamas, laying around the house with her college girlfriends, letting them coo and fight over holding Zack. But no, she'd grabbed their things, shoved them into the bags, and with teary hugs and "I'm-so-sorries", had climbed into the taxi and headed for the airport.

Ryan was right.

But still, it was a shame.

"Are you okay getting these inside?" the driver asked.

"Yeah, they're good where they are, thank you." She handed him cash for the ride and a generous tip.

He looked down at the bills, then gave her a salute and went on his way.

"Hey, Kate."

Kate turned to see her neighbor Dave making his way up the street. Dave was the reason Kate was here in D.C. Last January, when she was extremely pregnant with no job, he'd hired her to teach CSI in a public school/police initiative.

It hadn't gone to plan.

But Kate couldn't imagine a better friend or a better place to live than on Silver Lake; the neighborhood was like one big extended family.

Kate stood on her steps waiting for him to get over to her.

"I saw you pull up. I thought you were gone all week." He nodded at her bags. "Let me help you inside."

"Big storm coming in. Ryan didn't want me to chance it with the baby."

"Nor 'eastern, I saw it on the news and wondered how you'd handle it."

Kate saw a blue envelope with her name on it stuck in her door and plucked it off, putting it between her teeth while she unlocked and pushed her way in.

After pulling off the baby's snowsuit, Kate settled Zack in his saucer. "Just there by the stairs if you don't mind, Dave," she said as she slid her finger under the envelope flap to rip it open.

"Love letter from Ryan?"

"No…no. Do you know a girl named Julie?"

"Yeah, I do. She just moved into the neighborhood. She's in the house behind yours. She's probably offering to babysit."

"Well, an exchange." Kate handed the flier with a note attached to Dave. As he looked it over, she shucked off her coat and tossed it on the chair. "Do you have time to sit?"

"Nah, I'm out the door. I'm heading into the precinct." He handed the flier back.

Kate looked at the page. A picture of a girl with serious eyes and full cheeks was at the top. Underneath was her phone number and her hours of availability for babysitting. “She was putting these fliers around? Seems dangerous.”

“Yeah, we talked to her about that. Apparently, she’s from a small town where they don’t even lock their doors.”

“I could use a good babysitter. Have you used her for your twins?”

“Not yet. She took care of Ruby and Mikey yesterday after school. Sarah said Julie did a great job. Cathy put her name and number on our fridge.” He lifted her chin toward the page. “See how she says she has references? She does. One is the principal at the local high school. The girl was an honor student but graduated May a year ago. Only high praise. The second one was from a mother who had Julie in the afternoons as a sort of mother’s helper after her twins were born. Now, that one had gossip to spill.”

“Talked your ear off, huh?” Kate came from rural Virginia. In Scarborough, she had worked darned hard to keep her life private. She hated the idea that her comings and goings were fuel to any conversation from the bored townspeople.

“Julie’s mom remarried. The new stepdad and Julie didn’t get along. She had been working to get money together to move someplace where she could go to community college. Finally, things got bad enough that Julie spent some of that money on a bus ticket out of there to go stay with her sister about a year ago.”

“Here in this neighborhood?”

“Directly behind you.”

“That house is empty.”

“Was. Isn’t now. They moved in Sunday morning. Sunday afternoon, Julie was going door to door with her fliers. I walked over to see them.”

“Welcome them to the neighborhood?”

“That and I like to know who lives in our area, get a read on them. The Baker family. Lydia and Bill Baker. Bill is a sales rep and always on the road. I didn't meet him. Lydia isn't used to the city and it's overwhelming and a little frightening she says."

"What do you think of her? Friendly?" She bent to pick up a toy that Zack had flung off the saucer tray, then lowered herself to sit cross-legged beside him. "Should I invite them for a neighborhood potluck?"

"Lydia is a decided introvert. I can't see her accepting an invitation."

"Julie must be signed up for classes already." She reread the attached note and read aloud. "Hello, Mrs. Hamilton. I'm Julie Loffe. Sarah told me that you had been a science teacher. I'm having some trouble with my class. I was hoping to trade babysitting for tutoring help."

"Proactive gal," Dave offered. "But she's an online student. She'll be following through with classes she was already taking."

"Oh, that makes a lot more sense. I bet the transition from high school and spoon-feeding to college-level classes is a paradigm shift. Babysitting or not, I'm going to offer to help her with her studies." Kate pulled her phone from her pocket. "You seem to have all the information. You'd think you were a detective or something." She sent him a wink.

"Or something. Yeah, hey, before you make that call, let me tell you why I came over."

"It wasn't to be chivalrous and help me with my bags?" She sent him a theatrically hurt look.

"Least I could do. What I was hoping for was to ask you a favor. Two favors now that you're home."

"Shoot."

"First one is for tomorrow. The gal who took over your CSI class has to testify in court. I was going to take it on, but it would be a juggling act I'd prefer not to have to perform. I just don't know anyone else vetted and qualified to take over." He pointed to the flier. "Push come to shove, you could take Zack with you.

But then you'd be doing your own juggling act. That might be worth a call to Julie."

"All right, I'll figure it out. I can take that on. And number two?"

"My twins have their scout meeting this Saturday and need to do a presentation. They just brought it up. Kids and deadlines…I was wondering if you or Ryan could go talk to the kids about Houston and service dogs."

"Saturday? Since I was planning on being in Boston, I haven't got anything on my schedule. It's a yes for me." She rubbed a hand along the line where her sweater made her neck itch. "Ryan's on this new assignment that's got him jumping hoops, so I don't know what he's going to be able to do."

"I'll be at the Scout thing, so I can take care of Zack for you."

"Okay. So, I just need someone for tomorrow. Is it really going to be Wednesday already? What time do you need me there?" She tapped in Julie's phone number. "I'll help you either way. But you're right, it would be better if Zack was with someone else. I know you vetted her, but I'm going to ask her to come over so I can help her with her science lesson. I want to meet her first before I leave Zack in her care."

"Trust but verify?"

"Something like that."

21

Cyn

Tuesday Afternoon

Cyn was uncharacteristically nervous about Borka. His tone over the phone line was…different.

Maybe she was mishearing. Maybe her nervousness had to do with how close she was to realizing the thing that had motivated her every thought and action over the last five years.

If Borka pulled the resource plug, she was back to square one.

And here he was asking if Reaper had been a good lay.

Mindboggling.

Where would he get that idea? He must be confusing her with his shelf of honey pots.

Idiot.

"It was never my intention to seduce Reaper Hamilton. How would *that* possibly work?" Cyn paused but no answer came through her phone.

Borka sat there in her video, his nostrils wriggling, but, otherwise, stoic.

She pinched at her lip. The low level of danger vibrated her bones.

"Borka, if I were Reaper's lover—first, you said yourself these men are vetted for loyalty. They aren't cheaters. If they were to take up a side relationship, it certainly wouldn't be condoned."

"True."

"And Reaper certainly wouldn't take me to work and parade me around, flaunting an affair. If Reaper were to screw around with me, then I would have zero shot at getting in there. Sex was never my goal."

"Perhaps, it is best that you explain to me what it is you are doing," Borka said in a low rumble like a rattlesnake rattle forewarning an impending strike.

"I am employing some CIA tactics to both confuse and disarm him. In the past, I've found these tactics to happily make me feel like a friend to my mark and at the same time create havoc in their personal lives and homes. Jealousy is a destructive force. A destabilized mark is distracted and vulnerable."

His face was stone over the video feed. Unreadable.

Psychopaths wore masks. They showed you what they wanted you to see—there was no truth, only manipulation. "You will share this technique." The rattlesnake hissed.

"Eventually. Right now, let's call it a theory that needs to be tested in *this* circumstance. What I am doing is weakening Reaper. My chessboard is set. I'm on a faster time frame now that his wife has returned a few days earlier. This works to our benefit."

"The pieces you will be moving around, they know their roles?"

"They are told very little. That's the way I want it. As long as Omega can provide tactical and operational support, I will get into the Strike Force war room. And I *will* dispatch the malware."

"Do it." The video line went black.

Cyn stared down at the call timer. Less than three minutes. It hadn't gone as badly as she'd anticipated. It wasn't as supportive as she had hoped.

She closed her eyes and saw Tom's face. They'd been walking home from classes at their university when Tom elbowed her. A row of booths had been set up as a mini job fair.

There at the end was a CIA booth. No one was around, pawing through the ubiquitous glass bowl of candy. The guy looked bored.

Tom grinned over to her. "I dare you to apply."

"I dare *you* to apply."

Laughing at the joke, that's exactly what they did.

It changed the trajectory of their lives—destroying both of them.

She blinked at Borka's phone number. An angel and a demon.

Cyn had her moments of self-recrimination, doubt, self-flagellation, but she couldn't let anyone in The Family know that.

Like Reaper's dog Houston sniffing out the flash drive, Borka was scent trained. He homed in on fear and anxiety—or even—distaste. He used emotions as a weapon.

Cyn's protection from the shit-for-brains who thought they ruled the world, was *always* to make them think that she was loyal to the team and that she was as ruthlessly cold-hearted as they were.

It wasn't that much of a stretch. Ruthless and cold, yes. Loyal to anyone? Only Tom's memory.

Yeah, she had some personal glee when she was able to take some goody-goody shiny object and turn their world into a hellscape.

There was a study out that said that the problem with social media and algorithms was that they elevated those who were "low-conscientiousness." Those who liked "chaos" were the ones that were spreading disinformation and riling the public, making Americans angry at each other because they believed the things that were demonstrably untrue.

The Prokhorov family had done some wonderful things to strategically create chaos in the United States. Iniquus, and specifically Strike Force, had taken down one of the family's long-running ops. That Prokhorov sent Delta Force wife was right in there, living in Fort Bragg with the other Delta Force wives, passing information about the Unit's movements.

Through her, The Family had tried to destroy Delta Force from within.

They were close.

So close.

The failure kept cirvulating in Cyn's brain. Not a day went by when she didn't feel the sting of Strike Force ruining her work.

It had been *such* a good scenario that Cyn had developed for The Family with their already running military honey pot campaign. Cyn had been enthusiastic about their progress.

And now Borka was looking for a project of equal or better destructive value.

While the CIA was Cyn's target, Strike Force was the icing on the cake, there to satisfy the sweet tooth not only for her and The Family but also the Prokhorovs' sometimes-partners the Zoric family, who were masterful at hacking and cyberwar. The Zorics would have what Cyn needed.

If Cyn could pull this off. If she could get the backdoor spyware into the Iniquus computer, The Family could make all *hell* break loose in the United States.

They could bring this nation *to its knees*.

And after the CIA killed her brother, there was nothing that Cyn wanted more.

She flung her phone on the bed and started pacing.

Did they *really* think that when they signed a check for her parents that would exonerate their behavior?

To hell with her parents for accepting the money and moving to the islands of all places. Life in the Caribbean with days of golf and cocktails. Sailing into the damned sunset. Her father in his raspberry polo shirt with pink flamingos embroidered onto navy blue shorts. Knee socks of all stupid things. He was like an English schoolboy, gleeful in his get-up.

She hadn't seen her family since Tom's death. Wanted nothing to do with them. But the Prokhorovs had kept tabs for her. Borka had shown her the pictures.

Her mother was no better than her father was. She didn't miss Tom. Didn't think about him lying there in the streets, abandoned by the murderous agent, while the rats chewed the flesh on Tom's face. While the drunk pissed on Tom's corpse and rifled his pockets. Took out his wallet and masturbated to *Cyn's* picture under the streetlamp.

Cameras caught *everything*.

Everything.

The whistleblower's video had shown up in her email. That's how Cyn learned Tom was dead. In an email.

Those images circulated in her system instead of blood.

That video was every breath she inhaled. It was the bitter scum that sat on her tongue.

They had played on the same team, Cyn and those asswipes. Trained by the same people. Equally lethal. Equally ready. But Cyn wasn't interested in taking off the head of the viper. She wanted to burn down the whole forest where it lived. Not the man, not the organization, but the government that paid to have Tom killed.

By accident.

Whoops!

And there was her mother, shopping and spa-daying, playing tennis with the girls.

Both of her parents seemed to forget that their lap of luxury was afforded by blood money paid to them for the murder of their own son.

In her mind, Cyn could hear what the CIA would say to her if she gave them the chance.

"Accident."

"So sorry!"

"Misidentification."

"Too dark to see, for sure."

"Wrong place wrong time."

Dead in the street.

Cyn wanted nothing to do with her parents since they'd accepted the bank deposit with covetous grins, left their middle-class banality, and acted like they'd rubbed the genie's lamp and been granted a wish.

Psychopaths, the both of them. Just. Like. Borka.

She reached down to grab up her ringing phone.

"Hey, it's Julie."

"I have you on caller ID." Cyn tried to take the snarl out of her voice.

"Uhm, okay. I just wanted to…you asked me to let you know if my flier worked with Mrs. Hamilton. She invited me over and helped me with my biology class."

"I told you she was a bleeding heart. Did she ask you to call her Mrs. Hamilton?"

"No, ma'am, I just… It's the way I was raised."

Cyn bet the BDSM crowd drooled over Julie's deference. Cyn could understand now why Borka had chosen *this* girl to tuck under his wing. Something was up with her. There was some other plan afoot. Cyn didn't care. She was just glad Borka was willing to loan her out. "Mmhmm. I told you to make yourself as plain as possible. Wives don't like the idea of the nanny screwing their husbands in the coat closet. You did as I said?"

"Yes, ma'am. I wore my hair in a ponytail, no makeup, baggy clothes, my glasses instead of contact lenses."

"And she didn't seem overly curious, asking too many questions? She was okay with you?"

"It went fine. She said she won't trade homework help for babysitting because she's glad to help. But she did ask me to come look after her son tomorrow at two. She'll be gone for a few hours teaching a class for Mr. Murphy." Then she whispered, "Did you know he's a detective?"

"Of course, I did. That's why we had that flier made up with your hometown references and your real-world story. Well, what portions we could use. Just an FYI, when you do something under wraps like this, you need to stick to as much truth as you can. Lies are easily forgotten."

"Uhm. Yes, ma'am. This… I don't like doing this, to be honest. And having followed through with my directives. Mr. Borka… I had hoped now that I'm pregnant I wouldn't have to do this anymore."

"Yeah, well. Just see that you keep your knocked-up status to yourself. Do a good job on this assignment, or you'll be answering to me. And, young lady, you do not want to disappoint me. It will never turn out pretty."

22

Cyn

Wednesday Afternoon

Cyn sat in her car, watching the empty street, drumming her fingers on the steering wheel and waiting.

She swiped through her cell phone to get to queue up the codes that Julie had observed yesterday during her homework help. Kate's phone was opened using a backward staircase finger swipe, same on the fridge door.

In this day and age, with the Wi-Fi alarm systems, and house cameras monitored by cell phones, the machines that listened all day just waiting for their name and a command, yup, spying now was getting to be almost childlike in its simplicity. So much data to be whisked from the air.

Data was power.

Even before Cyn got into the house, she had a smorgasbord of information.

The router codes were the most important. Last night, Cyn

had already logged in and added spyware to the computer systems. Not only could Cyn access everything on their computers—their stored passwords—well, Kate's. It didn't seem as though Reaper had anything that she could compromise. Cyn was sure that was on purpose.

That PTSD paranoia.

Well, she thought ruefully, it wasn't paranoia if the threat was real.

And here she was in the flesh, waiting in her car for the go-ahead to demonstrate that truth.

With just Julie's picture of the router number and password at the Hamilton's home, and a well-placed external camera that was able to focus on Kate's finger placements as she manually tapped her passwords into her computer, Cyn had already been able to hack much of the electronics in the house and could metaphorically just walk right in the Hamilton's lives and take a look around.

Fortunately for Cyn, Kate was porous where Reaper was not. Through Kate's computer, Cyn had accessed Kate's social media accounts with their tight privacy settings.

Their banking information showed that the Hamiltons were frugal when it wasn't at all necessary. That told Cyn that this couple couldn't be brought onto her team with a bribe.

Through the Wi-Fi, Cyn was able to connect to the Hamiltons' printer and discovered that today's lesson plan that Kate would be presenting was on "Algor, Livor, and Rigor – Clues About the Time of Death."

Cyn wrinkled her nose. She was fine creating the bodies but handling them afterward was someone else's gig.

Hacking into their television, Cyn discovered that the couple mostly watched standup comedy. She was going with the theory that it was probably a genre of entertainment they could agree on, and it was probably suggested by their therapist that they try to balance their lives with a little light-heartedness.

According to the fridge calendar, Reaper had private therapy sessions once a week; they also had couple's therapy on Saturdays. No bills went through their bank accounts, which meant it was probably Iniquus who footed the cost.

Cyn hacked into the nursery monitor and was able to pull up a visual of the baby's nursery.

It was strangely stirring to Cyn, watching Reaper's son sleeping in his crib last night.

And, of course, through the radio waves, Cyn was able to listen to everything that was within range of the monitor's speaker.

When the baby had woken up for a bottle last night, Cyn had listened to Kate singing him back to sleep. Kate had a pretty good tone and liked to sing rock and roll in a lullaby voice. Cyn thought that was kind of lazy on her part—like Kate didn't want to invest the time into learning the words of baby songs.

Before he left for the day, Reaper went into the nursery and stared down at his son, placed a hand on Zack's curls, closed his eyes, and breathed in.

If anything were to happen to that kid, Reaper would be like Cyn—relentless in his pursuit of justice. A nuclear warhead, heat-seeking a trajectory. Cyn would have to weigh that into her decision making.

Armed with last night's research, Cyn was ready to go in and place the last pieces of surveillance into place. Patting the kangaroo pockets on her coat, Cyn assured herself that all of her tools were ready to go.

In and out.

Information was key. The more she had, the better she'd be at getting her butt past the security at Iniquus and up next to a computer. Any computer connected to the supercomputer would do. She wasn't particular.

"All right." the Omega technician's voice came through her car's speaker. "I have your gal leaving through the back door. She has the baby in a stroller. They've gone out the back gate. She turned up the alley, heading toward the park. Give it five minutes to settle. I'll keep eyes on the house."

Cyn had parked her car a block over. Again, Mother Nature was her ally. It was warm enough that one could bundle a baby and take a walk. It was cold enough that a chunky scarf could be wrapped over her mouth and a beanie pulled down over her brows wouldn't bring a second glance.

Today, she'd added thick black nerd girl glasses.

She carried a grocery bag in her arms as if she were returning from the row of storefronts that included a bar called the Star-Light where that chick Lexi was supposed to perform Thursday night. The neighborhood gals were going to go watch her and drink wine. The neighborhood guys were on kid duty. So very wholesome.

The parabolic ears she'd dappled around the neighborhood meant she could have her computer search everything anyone said on that street, her computer program combed out words and phrases that Cyn had indicated were of interest to her. Anything Hamilton-related. Anything Julie-related. Anything about dogs, or missions, or scheduling vocabulary.

Cyn moved through the back gate and right up the stairs and through the door. She put her bag down, ready to grab it up and chuck it into a trash can in the alley at a moment's notice.

"Clear?" she asked into her comms.

"I've got your back. I'll let you know if anything happens within three blocks of the house."

"Good copy."

With her surgical gloves on and her hair plastered to her head under a wig, there she was, moving through the house on a primary sweep, to get the layout and to assess her options.

There on the kitchen counter lay Kate's phone. Julie's directives were to lift it from Kate's purse when Kate was bustling out the door. She was to leave it for Cyn on the counter.

So far, Julie was performing well.

It took Cyn thirty seconds to download spyware into Kate's phone that piggybacked on Kate's step count app. Now, Cyn's computer would record all Kate's phone conversations. Cyn could listen to her calls with Reaper and Kate's friends, giving Cyn a window into the impact her little campaign was going to have on her marriage.

A while back, a little over a year ago, the Prokhorov's had created a chaos attack on the United States that included a personal attack on some editor chick. They had used the woman's own phone to record her in her home being abusive to her elderly mother and posted it on social media.

Field tested, the Prokhorov's found that being able to turn on a cell phone's video and audio at will and record was a game-changing ability. Couple that with their bot farms in Eurasia, and The Family had a formidable weapon in the disinformation war.

That technology was now serving Cyn's needs.

Yes indeedy, she could turn on Kate's video or speaker at any point and just follow along with her as she moved through her day. Might as well. No reason not to.

Already five minutes into this op, Cyn wanted to be out of there by the twenty-minute mark.

Standing in front of the Hamilton's smart fridge, Cyn thought that this was probably here as part of their rental agreement and not something the family had chosen for themselves. This fridge was an odd high-tech stand out. It had a computer incorporated into the door that was supposed to help the family stay on track. As Cyn pulled up the screen, she could see that mostly it was a way to listen to music. The calendar was there—pediatrician, dentist, Lexi's music night at StarLight. Nothing about Reaper other than his counseling.

Still, a hack was a hack, an in was an in.

It was like the girls over in Eastern Europe. A sentence here, a mention there, pixels that created a bigger, more useful picture.

In Cyn's long years of doing this—since she was hired by the CIA as a college senior, and then later moving her loyalties to The Family—Cyn had learned that it was never about capturing a whole picture.

It was like being an oil painter. You put down the layers of understanding, building them up until the composition took shape, then you refined and defined and added accents of interest. Soon, enough, if one did their job well, the result would be something worth hanging on a wall, worth hanging one's reputation on.

Yes, this was a fast assignment. There was little time for her to succeed in inching her way into the inner sanctum of the Iniquus campus. But once she was there, oh the potential!

It was easy enough to add a camera that took in the whole of the kitchen to that fridge computer.

It was even easier to put a camera into the stereo system in the living room.

"Sniff that, Houston. I'd call you a shit-for-brains, but you're the reason I have this opportunity. If you survive this little adventure, I'll buy you a bone," Cyn muttered past the Phillips head screwdriver that she'd clamped between her teeth.

By the time the phone alarm signaled "time's up," Cyn was pulling the backdoor door closed and skipping down the stairs to the path to the alley. With the shopping bag in her arms, Cyn strolled out the back gate, up the alley, and onto the street to her car.

That was task number one.

She motored back to her secondary location, a place to stage her transitions. A cheap motel on the train tracks in a questionable part of the city, sitting conveniently between the Hamilton's home and Cyn's hotel where she'd actually be willing to sleep between the sheets.

Here, in the brown-paneled, dust-covered room, she pulled off her blue-collar guise and did what she could to transform into an attractive woman who would be easily noticeable.

Notice was key, Cyn thought as she put her POS sedan keys in the drawer and picked up the keys to her upscale ride that was more in keeping with her "Cyn Parker" persona.

Now, she was on to the matinee with her ticket directly in front of where Harlow would be sitting. She'd get there first, of course, to confuse the hell out of Reaper.

Then on to dinner, where her colleague would already be at the table two over from Harlow's reservation. An easy enough hack to change the reservations around at that restaurant. Cyn planned to breeze in and cheek kiss. Apologize for being late. Later tonight, she'd go for a jog around the Mall that Harlow had put on his calendar for eight. She guessed that gave him enough time to digest.

It helped that he had the room in the same 5-star hotel where Cyn was Cyn Parker, freelance consultant.

So far, everything was going *exactly* to plan.

Iniquus was going down.

23

Cyn

Wednesday Night

Cyn laid on her hotel bed with her computer balanced on her thighs. She used her mouse to scroll around the Hamiltons house, checking her connections, her view, and sound quality. If she needed to update anything, Kate asked Julie to babysit Saturday afternoon. The refrigerator calendar said, "Scout's with the Murphy's and Houston" in the morning and "couples therapy" in the afternoon.

Oh, to be a fly on that wall…oh wait, if Kate didn't turn her phone to airplane mode, Cyn certainly could be that fly. "Let's air the dirty laundry, Kate." Cyn moved the mouse to bring up her outside cameras. "I wonder if Reaper told his wife about the woman who keeps showing up on his radar screen. "So bizarre. What could it mean? Is she fate? Is the world conspiring to bring us together?" Cyn chuckled.

She'd admit it; she was having fun.

The joy of knowing her enemy would be vanquished, along with mind games and a handsome warrior? Yes, please.

Cyn toggled through the camera views from out the door and up and down the street. Some cameras were meant to capture comings and goings at the doors, others were there to watch cars and licenses. "Mmm, some of these could be better placed away from the streetlamp glare." But they weren't so bad that she was willing to take exposure risks by adjusting them. Now that the car accident was over, and the mind mushing had begun—technical term, LOL—nothing could tune the neighborhood in to the fact that they were part of Cyn's little project.

Tomorrow was going to be an interesting step forward.

Harlow handed in his schedule to Iniquus. He'd be in his room throughout the day. He planned to order room service at lunch and go out for dinner (place unspecified). That meant one of the other two operators who had shown up to watch his door—Jack and Randy—would be on duty, giving Reaper and his K9 a rest.

Kate confirmed this was the plan when she told Dave and Cathy that Reaper's close protection was covered, and he was spending the day with her and Zack. Iniquus took their required mental health seriously, it would seem.

The family was going to the Eagle's Nest for lunch, then, since the weather was going to be sunny, they thought they'd take a walk by the outdoor skating rink since one of Zack's favorite things to do was to see the high schoolers come out after school to skate around.

So now Cyn and one of her colleagues were going skating. Cyn used to be pretty good. Hopefully, it was like riding a bicycle, and after warming up a bit, her muscle memory would kick in.

And far from pretending to be ignorant of Reaper's presence—as she had done in all of their "chance encounters" when

Reaper was out with Harlow—on this particular "Cyn-sighting", she was going to make herself front and center.

Blow kisses at the wifey.

Curled up on her king-sized bed with its polyester-feeling hotel comforter, cheap shitty cover for a five-star, Cyn would lodge a complaint when she checked out.

The *when* of her check out depended entirely on how quickly Reaper fell under her control.

Cyn snagged a handful of popcorn from the bowl resting beside her as she watched the video feed from the Hamilton's living room where Reaper was picking up the baby toys and tossing them into a toy box.

From their bank accounts, Cyn knew that Reaper made really good money at Iniquus. Cyn couldn't figure out why they chose to live in a neighborhood with people who were paid by the hour and wore their names on plastic plates pinned to their corporate polo shirts.

From The Family's research over the years, Cyn knew that Iniquus offered a generous signing bonus to move the best and brightest from the elite special operations teams onto the Iniquus payroll. It was enough to put a sizeable down payment on an upscale family home in the pricey D.C. suburbs.

In the D.C. metropolitan area, a one-bedroom cottage or a trailer on a patch of land could cost upward of three hundred thousand dollars. So while Omega didn't have an exact amount of the signing bonus, it was speculated to be hundreds of thousands of dollars.

The family had probably invested it somewhere, Cyn hadn't found it and it didn't make any difference to her project, just curiosity.

Why did the Hamiltons live in *that* house?

There was something there…some weakness. All Cyn needed to do was find it and exploit it.

Granted, the duplex was nice.

Upgraded and updated.

True, it was handily placed near the highway, in close proximity to the Iniquus campus, making a commute minimal, which was no small thing when it came to drive times in the bumper-to-bumper snarl of Washington D.C. traffic.

And the duplex was owned, and sometimes lived in on the right-hand side, by Lexi Sobado.

"I'm just starting to dig into you Reaper. Just getting some insights…"

Cyn lifted another handful of popcorn and munched as she watched Reaper crawl over to the hearth and light a fire. She bet it smelled good, the burning wood and smoke.

When he stood, he pulled a cinnamon jar candle from the mantle and lit that as well.

Cozy, she thought.

He turned out the room lights by hand since there were no house-bots to scream at to set the mood.

The old-fashioned part of Cyn thought there was something romantic about Reaper's intent to stage the room and his following through with the elements himself.

A romantic gesture.

Wistfulness planted a seed. Maybe a tinge of jealousy.

"Yeah, that's not a thing I do. Jealousy, ha!" She tapped the keyboard to bring up the Iniquus photograph file that Omega had sent over. These were exterior images captured from drones and satellites. No one she knew outside of the Iniquus personnel had even been through the security check onto the main campus.

Omega told Cyn if she were able to make it past that guard station, once inside, she'd have an escort beside her at all times.

That was cool.

All Cyn had to do to compromise their system was to get close enough.

She leaned closer, licking her lips as she flipped through the photos.

From aerial images, the sprawling Iniquus riverfront property looked like a gated community on a golf course. The Family knew those who worked on the Iniquus forces all had their own apartments in the men's barracks.

Yeah, there were a few women on the forces.

Cyn had rubbed up against an ex-CIA chick named Margot in the field years ago when they were still Farm fresh. After being captured and rescued, Margot left the Agency and now did something for Panther Force.

Scanning the photos, where the women lived, or if they were required to be on rotation, living on campus, Cyn couldn't tell.

And it was neither here nor there. Again, idle curiosity.

The only thing that was important was that Cyn keep her head down if Margot were around. Time and grief had changed Cyn's appearance, but still, no point in being sloppy.

Omega said that Panther Force was in Africa, so she set that worry to the side.

The CIA usually didn't let go of their agents easily. She wondered how Margot had managed to make the career switch so seamlessly.

For Cyn's part, she had basically disappeared after Tom's death. She mildly wondered if they were still looking for her. And if they were, what would they do with her if she was found?

She imagined a dank hole in a darkly violent country. After all, Cyn's head was full of secrets.

Maybe that hole was too much trouble. Maybe just a bullet between the eyes, like Tom, and be done with her.

Flipping the computer back to the Hamilton house feed, Cyn discovered that Kate had arrived in the little bastion of warmth Reaper had created. She was sitting in the rocker, blocking much of the room's view.

Reaper brought a mug over, setting it on the table next to the glide rocker. Then interrupted her humming so he could offer her a kiss.

If Cyn had a single maternal fiber in her makeup, this scene would light it up like an incandescent filament.

But nah.

Kate bent to check if the baby's eyes were shut, then slowly stood and moved toward the stairs.

With a foot on the first tread, Kate turned and sent Reaper "that look", eliciting a wolfish grin from Reaper.

Yeah, he was going to get some.

Slowly, careful not to wake the now sleeping Zack, Kate moved up the stairs.

24

Cyn

WEDNESDAY NIGHT

REAPER PULLED the living room draperies shut. He crouched directly in front of her camera. He was so close that Cyn leaned in and kissed his image, then laughed at the absurdity of her impulse.

Sliding a CD into a slot in the stereo, soon the room was basted with the warmth of an instrumental. The music was a heartbeat of drums. It was rich and evocative. The deep raspy voice was turned down low enough to add some ambiance without being a distraction. This was old-school baby-making music.

Hm, Cyn had thought Reaper would be more of a classic rock kind of guy, metal and headbanging. Maybe that was for when he was alone in his car. Clearly, Reaper wanted to get his rocks off and was doing this to up his chances.

Little did Reaper realize that his ability to use that stereo remote to wirelessly connect to his playlist also gave Cyn the ability to hear every single word, every sigh, every moan he planned to elicit from his wife. And Cyn's micro camera, the size of a pea, would give her a front-row seat to where this was heading.

Cyn actually kind of liked this romantic set up. It was sweet without being cloying.

It had been a long time since Cyn had screwed around for fun instead of the convenience of a get.

She looked down at the popcorn bowl and tried to remember the last time she'd been on a date. And more, the last time that a man had efforted for *her* pleasure.

College.

Before the Farm.

"Come on Reaper, show me your skills." Cyn lifted a handful of popcorn to her mouth and munched at it like a squirrel, watching.

Just what was married sex all about?

Kate appeared on the screen. She was wearing one of Reaper's shirts. It hung low on her thighs.

Cyn knew that for men, that was an aphrodisiac. It was like playing King of the Hill. Planting his flag. *Mine.*

Reaper gave her a slow smile, love and desire. It wasn't hot and salty. It wasn't an "I'm going to throw you up against the wall and screw you until you're limp" look. But wow, that look was sultry.

"Good job, Kate. You know your man," Cyn told the screen.

Reaper held out his hand to her, and she accepted it. Pulling her into his embrace, she tucked in, turning the hairbrush in her hand so she wasn't stabbing Reaper with the bristles.

They rocked back and forth, swaying a bit. It was the kind of dancing Cyn had done with her high school boyfriend, Ben, at Homecoming. That night, Cyn hadn't been interested in trained dance steps or style, all she wanted was to be as close to Ben as possible. To be safe in his arms. His heartbeat in her ear. To smell the mingle of his drugstore cologne that she had loved so much and the floral laundry soap his mom used. The strength of his arms made her feel precious and cared for, protected.

Her first love.

Her last love,

+ too. Yeah, Cyn had learned that those moments should be cherished because they were as fleeting as hell.

Two days after that dance, Ben said thanks for the time together and moved on to Kelly, not a single look back. Shithead.

Cyn shoved a handful of popcorn in her mouth.

Reaper spun Kate out, and they stood there, fingers entangled, at arm's length just staring into each other's eyes. The whisper of a contented smile softened Kate's features.

"It's selfish of me, but I'm glad you came home early," Reaper said. "My bed was cold without you."

"Yup, pretty selfish." Still holding hands, she made her way to the couch. "You'll have to do something to convince me that I made the right choice."

The rumble of Reaper's laugh was Kate's assurance that he'd make sure she was well taken care of.

"Wait!" Cyn called toward her computer as she set it aside. "Don't start without me!" She scrambled off the bed and jogged into the bathroom to retrieve her vibrator, then hustled back.

Cyn thought that Reaper would drag Kate up to their bed after that exchange, and Cyn would have to shift to a different camera feed. There, he'd probably do some perfunctory kissing and rubbing. Hit a couple of positions then roll off to leave Kate lying in the wet spot.

Cyn wrinkled her nose. Yeah no, that wasn't at all what kind of lover she thought Reaper would be.

She'd bet that he made love in real life like he'd done to her in Cyn's dreams that morning.

She hustled back and climbed onto her bed.

There was no upstairs missionary positioning while Cyn was grabbing her portable boyfriend.

The image that Cyn came back to, as she tugged off her panties and threw them toward the end of the bed, was Reaper sitting behind Kate on the sofa, brushing her hair.

"Tell me two good things that happened today and a challenge," he said.

"Your son takes after you. When I got home from teaching my class, Zack was lolling in Julie's lap as she rocked him, gazing lovey-dovey at her and playing with her hair."

That made Reaper smile and nod.

Kate must have felt that because she turned briefly and sent Reaper a smile.

"Uhm. I was taking out the trash, and I saw the most beautiful ruby-red cardinal sitting on the handrail. It let me pass inches away from him as I went and came back. He was just chill. It felt like an honor that he trusted me."

Reaper leaned down and kissed her hair.

Silence continued for several minutes as he brushed.

"The challenge?" Reaper asked.

After stalling, Kate's worst burst out of her mouth. "It's weird that you keep seeing that woman that you saved." She spun around and caught his eye. Then, turned back and waited for Reaper to start brushing her hair again. "It's weird that she's *there* when you and your client arrive. It makes me feel uneasy, though, I can't say why. I guess, well, first, if someone saved my life in the dark hours of the morning in freezing temperatures, there's no way I'd be in the room with him, what five times?"

"Seven."

"Seven times, and not notice my rescuer. Yeah, I can't wrap

my mind around that. But, as you were saying, she's staying at the same hotel as your client. It could be that they're sticking close to the hotel as an epicenter and aren't interested in straying too far out. Here's another thing that you might want to take back to Striker and chat about. What if she was seeing you and ignoring you purposefully? What if she was taking surreptitious pictures of you like you're doing of her?"

"Keep going."

"Might she think that either you or your client is stalking her? Might she become so afraid and possibly go to the police and ask for a restraining order? I mean, if they take your phone into evidence, they'd find her picture at all those places."

"They would. But I don't make the decisions about where my client goes. He has control of his schedule."

"Okay." Kate took a noisy breath in. She closed her eyes for an exhale then ended with a little hum of contentment, like a kitten being stroked. "Your turn. Two good things and a concern."

Reaper leaned forward and put the brush on the coffee table. He scooped up Kate's hair and kissed the back of her neck until she giggled and shrugged her shoulders up.

"I love the sound of you happy."

"Okay, here we go," Cyn said out loud. Turning the vibrator on, she moved it from her lips, to her breasts, down to her oh-so-slick clit.

Reaper caught Kate's hand and gave a little tug, that must have been something they had done for years. Kate responded immediately by spinning around and straddling him.

"You, Mrs. Hamilton are not wearing anything under my shirt. That makes me more than happy."

She bent, cupping his face for a tender kiss.

Reaper savored that kiss like a wine connoisseur with a glass, gently swirling the ruby liquid as he held it up to the light. Letting it tease his olfactory senses, and then the sip, the swirl over his tongue.

Cyn licked at her lips. That was one *hell* of a kiss.

Reaper had beautiful lips. Full and soft-looking. Cyn wished Kate would hurry up and strip his clothes off. Cyn wanted to see him. Wanted to know if her dream Reaper and the flesh and bones Reaper were one and the same. Cyn bet he was, after all, the Iniquus uniform of tactical pants and compression shirts gave a girl a fine window into what was beneath.

Kate tipped her head. "The concern?"

"You make my dick so rock-damned-hard, it hurts every second I'm not inside you."

"I would never want that for you," Kate said as she pulled off her shirt. "Not for one. Minute. More."

25

Kate

THURSDAY AFTER LUNCH

RYAN WAS EDGY.

This was his last assignment--and the only operation since he's signed his Iniquus contract--where he was out doing his thing on his own.

Capable? Absolutely.

A good choice?

Kate didn't think so. Yes, she got the problem of manpower and certification requirements. Applying the proper expert was imperative, especially with the high-dollar lethality of the Iniquus stable of K9s.

Still, there was something worrying there. Kate could see it in Ryan's eyes.

He was back to level orange. That meant his brain was firing all the time, searching out whatever it was that this contract was concerned about.

Kate had thought when Ryan was medically discharged from the SEALs the secretive part of their lives would be done with.

Pipe dream.

Kate was just worried that now that Ryan had graduated out of the California experiment, something would happen to wipe out Ryan's progress. He'd gone from a man who laid on his bed at the assisted living facility, staring at the ceiling and incommunicative, begging her for a divorce, back to her husband.

To warm conversation and cohesiveness.

To lovemaking.

To the comfort of making family memories like there at the Eagle's Nest that had a picture window overlooking a sanctuary for injured raptors, followed by leisurely walks by the ice rink.

Today was amazing. Kate was relishing the pure normalcy of it all.

The air was fresh and crisp. The sun was bright and cheerful.

They had timed things beautifully. The students were on half-day for teacher planning periods. Wrapped up in their cheerful fleeces, they were now dashing around the ice. The girls were in clatches, casting surreptitious glances at the boys. Or, if they had some skill, were out in the middle of the rink, spinning and jumping.

The boys, too, were trying to show their prowess.

They were the plumed birds doing a mating dance by racing and calling to each other obnoxiously.

Today, the Hamiltons were walking along without a K9.

Reaper had Max at the house. Ryan said Houston and Max were bite concerns when they were together, so Houston was at Cerberus being taken care of by their kennel master.

Houston was her buddy. Kate missed her; Houston would really enjoy this walk.

Ryan stopped, turning the baby carriage away from the skaters toward the tree line.

"Hey, I told Dave that I would give a talk about Houston and service dogs at his boys' scout meeting. Do you think there's a way for me to get Houston to bring her with me? I mean, it would be much better having her there than me standing up and giving a lecture."

When Ryan didn't answer, Kate turned to catch his eye.

Ryan's face had stilled as he looked over Kate's shoulder. He reached out and squeezed her elbows. "Two seconds," he said.

She looked over her shoulder to see what he could see.

Ryan loped over the slight rise toward the ice rink. There were swirls and dashes of color as the skaters floundered and glided. An older couple holding hands moved by in meditative and synchronized swishes as they pushed the blades of their skates, left and right, oblivious to the sprawling toddlers and the raucous teens powering by.

Kate didn't see a reason for the look of…mmm—power?—of intensity in his eyes before he took off.

Until she did.

A woman in white yoga tights and a bright papaya-colored sweater.

Up on her toes with a giddy hop, she powered toward him.

Kate stood, feeling fear wash over her.

The woman's arm lifted as she waved, and she powered toward Reaper, not letting up on her speed. In her haste to get to Reaper, she was going to crash into the barrier.

Without breaking her gaze, Kate reached down and dragged a fussy Zack from his carriage. Should she go stand beside Ryan? Introduce herself? Stake a claim?

Zack pressed away from Kate's chest, and she realized that she was squeezing him too tight. His squeal didn't turn Reaper's attention around.

As the woman slammed into the barrier, Reaper's arms shot

out and wrapped her. egs thrashed to stay upright with the sudden stop, and she laughed joyfully.

Kate couldn't see the woman's face. Her hair was tucked up under a papaya beanie with a fluffy pompom on top. The only thing that Kate could clearly see was that the woman had a tight, athletic body.

Reaper held her until she steadied, but instead of letting her go, she reached out and hugged him tight, still holding onto his arms as they talked.

Kate blinked. This is *it*. This might have been *it* all along, Kate thought, only she had blinders on and had refused to see.

Back when they lived in Boston, Ryan had said they were done. One day he woke up and announced he was leaving. His PTSD symptoms, his inability to decide what was reality and what was a flashback had put her in harm's way. He had hurt her.

Not her, Kate.

He'd hurt the person in his flashback. But his hands had landed on the hallucination in front of him, and it had been Kate.

When he saw what he'd done to her, Ryan swore he'd kill himself before he'd harm her.

Ryan was a man of his word.

Kate wholly believed that his death by suicide was a possibility. Ryan wouldn't do it to release himself from the anguish of the pain—physical and emotional—that he experienced. Kate's safety, though, might have been the excuse Ryan needed to make the plan, put the gun barrel into his mouth, and pull the trigger.

Sobbing, she'd thrown some clothes into a bag, made a few desperate phone calls of arrangement, and drove by herself down south to the mountains of Scarborough, where she had grown up, to live with her aunt and uncle.

Kate didn't make that trip down alone.

She had found out the morning she left that there were two

pink lines on the pregnancy test. She kept that a secret until she was too far along to hide it anymore.

Ryan begged her for a divorce.

"You just need time to heal," Kate had countered.

Look at them wrapped in each other's arms.

Look how long and shapely she was. How nicely she fit standing next to Ryan.

Kate's hand moved down to smooth over the thickness of her postpartum waist that she had been whittling down slow inch by slow inch.

Was it possible?

Was there another reason that Reaper had wanted her gone from his life almost two years ago?

Swinging her head, Kate looked for a trash can. She thought she was going to vomit.

Moving in that direction, she put her hand on the cold steel of the rim and smelled the rotting garbage smells. But the cold and the solid under her fingers helped.

Kate had fought for her marriage tooth and nail. She thought that the pressure of the coming baby might be too much for Ryan, that's why she'd kept Zack a secret.

And she was right.

His push for divorce was a constant. He'd told her he wanted her free to find another man—someone who would be good to Kate and *her* baby. Why had that scenario popped so quickly into his mind over that phone conversation?

Was it because he had another woman in the picture? That skater woman?

Yes, something about that woman set off all of Kate's alarms.

Kate could smell the power of her BO rising from her sticky underarms. Kate's bladder screamed, "I need to pee before we go into battle!"

But no, Kate wouldn't battle infidelity.

It had never occurred to Kate before that Reaper might cheat on her. His integrity was solid. But brain damage was brain damage and finding relief, respite…men who she thought would never succumb to drug addiction did when they were finally home from the war.

It sounded wrong to her as she tried the ideas on.

But look at them…

Did Ryan want Kate out of the picture for another woman?

Now that was a paradigm shift.

Kate had told Ryan that she'd divorce him if he came and put the papers in her hand. If he gave her the pen.

Not forty-eight hours later, there he was. Papers. Pen. Conviction. "Sign them, Kate."

Kate had shredded the papers and flung them in his face.

On his way back to Boston, a drunk driver hit Ryan's motorcycle. Ryan survived.

It was a horrible life.

He lay flat on his back in excruciating pain day after day, week after week, month into unfolding month.

His doctor, Michele Carlon, knew that, while she was a world-leader in brain trauma, with what she had in her tool kit, there was nothing that would help Ryan get better. So Dr. Carlon had spent her evenings searching through ongoing studies to find a glimmer of hope.

And darned if she didn't do it. She found the thing that gave Kate back her husband.

Gave Little Guy a father.

Could it have been that while Ryan was lying unconscious in his hospital bed in Washington DC that another woman, *this woman*, was wringing her hands desperately worried about why Ryan had disappeared from Boston?

Kate ducked her head and kissed Zack's curls. Not lifting her eyes from her husband and the papaya sweater, talking at the edge of the rink. The flood of skaters glided around them like water around a protruding rock.

Baby Zack was named after their dear friend Zack.

SEAL Zack who had banded with brothers to care for Ryan. To talk him down from his rages and destruction. To navigate the VA with and for him, to make sure he ate and slept. Zack had gotten Ryan into the program that had brought Houston—hero dog Houston—into their lives. Would Zack have known if there was another woman who had made her way into Ryan's life? And if he did, would he tell Kate or protect Reaper?

Danger.

Her body told Kate that that woman was a mortal danger to her family.

It was a terrible sensation.

She tried to cast it off, to give it another name.

Maybe her hormones had her wackadoodle.

She wanted to believe that.

But Ryan hadn't turned their way. Hadn't pointed out his family—his wife and child—to the woman. He hadn't scooped his arm to call her over to introduce Kate to this papaya-clad woman with her perfectly round ass.

There was no pride in his eyes, no gentle smile as he said their names.

Kate's jaw locked as her breath hitched.

If Ryan had left behind the notion of another woman up in Boston, had finally cleaved to Kate after nine months of begging her for a divorce, was it possible that the woman followed him to D.C.?

Kate had thought that the fight for her marriage was done.

She had had almost a year of family warmth, the three of them.

Hope had bloomed into a full glorious rose.

She'd been fighting against the monster of the physical pain that had taken her husband from her.

Could she fight a choice of the heart?

Did she want to?

The papaya woman skated away.

Ryan stood and watched her until she was at the other end of the rink, then the smile fell off his face. He scowled in Kate's direction. He dropped his head, looking at his feet as he made his way over to them.

Anger boiled in her system. By the time Ryan rejoined them, she was livid.

"Kate," he said. "That was—"

She didn't want to hear it. Didn't want him to lie to her. She pressed Zack into his arms. "Ryan." She forestalled him, unable to corral her emotions. "I'm going to get us some hot chocolates." Normally, she'd say something like. "Look there's a hot cocoa stand. That would be a nice treat." And without another word, Ryan would lope off to get the drinks, to make her smile, to be her hero. It must have confused him that Kate was taking on the task herself, not even asking him if he wanted one or not. She was getting them. Two of them. She wanted some space, and she wanted the icy air on her over-hot face.

She wanted that woman, who felt like poison in Kate's veins, to go away and stay away.

But Kate knew that her next battle for Ryan had begun.

What Kate didn't know was whether or not she was up to it.

26

Reaper

Friday Morning

"Deep." The voice came softly into Reaper's earpiece.

He pressed the button hanging on a lanyard under his shirt. "Reaper."

"Cerberus is on its way to relieve you. You're needed in the war room. I have you on my screen but give me an immediate heads up on a change of destinations."

"Copy. Wilco." Reaper and Max were shadowing Harlow as he jogged up the road. His jog was Reaper's fast walk.

Luckily, Reaper knew this in advance, and he'd gone out for his morning 10k with Max before he'd reported for duty. If not, Max would be straining to move faster.

"Out of curiosity, do you see her?" Deep asked, and Reaper knew exactly who the "her" was. Even though this line was encrypted end to end, their messages could be sniffed from the atmosphere and bad actors could use AI technology to unsnarl the messages. When possible, it was good to practice to cryptic speak as well. As long as the communication was understood, it was all good.

"Affirmative, she's a half-block ahead. She and Harlow seem to like the same pace."

"When did she get there?"

"That I can't say. She came out of the park, looking like she'd been jogging for a while. We would have been right beside her, but we got stalled by a red light."

"All right. Cerberus should be with you in ten. It's Max's regular handler, and he's set to maintain and handle Max. You'll just be handing over the leash. He'll hand you the keys to the vehicle. An easy switch."

"Copy."

"Over and out."

Interesting. Iniquus Command had tried to keep this assignment in Reaper's hands to free up Cerberus for the contest. Whatever they needed from Reaper back at the war room must be heavy.

THE FACES LOOKED UP BRIEFLY JUST to identify who was pushing through the Strike Force war room's door.

Deep and Lynx were by the computer, Steve Finley and Damian Prescott from the FBI along with Striker and Blaze.

"Good. You're here," Lynx said and waved him over.

"What are you looking at?" Reaper grabbed a chair and moved it over to Deep's station.

"We've been working on the airport incident." Deep raised his chin toward the FBI, bent over something Striker was showing them. "We thought it would be good for you to be here to answer questions as to what we're looking at. It's interesting about

Harlow. Monday morning, he was supposed to take the red-eye at the crack of dawn. He came in on a later plane. Did he ever say why?"

"I'm close protection and drug-sniffing, engaging him in a conversation wouldn't be part of my role."

Deep nodded. "That conduct is correct, but I'm just wondering if he ever offered you an explanation." Deep looked every bit his Italian heritage. His accent sounded to Reaper like somewhere near New York City, maybe New Jersey.

Reaper slid his tongue along his upper teeth as he shook his head. "Nada."

"The thing that caught our attention," Lynx said, "was that he bought two tickets for that day. In two separate purchases, he bought the early morning ticket and the ticket that he flew in on."

"Which one did he buy first? The morning ticket, right?"

"Yes," Lynx said, pulling her long blonde hair around and nimbly plaited the length. "And ten minutes later he bought the latter one." She pulled a hairband from her wrist and wrapped it around the end of her braid.

"My guess is it's innocuous. He throws around money like confetti at Mardi Gras. He's not worried about that cost. What he was probably worried about was having to fly with a hangover. It was his company that set up our meet time, right?"

"That's right. Yup. That would make sense. Deep and I were trying to process a different angle. What would it serve him to tell Iniquus that he was flying in early in the morning and not tell us until after that morning plane had landed that he was coming in later?"

"He didn't call it in?" Reaper asked.

"Randy went to pick him up. We made some phone calls when he didn't deplane. He sounded like he was still asleep when he said that he'd decided to go later."

"That sounds like him." Reaper scowled. "Is that why you

brought me in?" He didn't like the idea that they pulled a Cerberus guy from his other work for this. This conversation could have been done with a ten-second phone call.

"We're working on the flash drive incident." She looked at the wall clock. "We're going to have a visitor in a short while. Prescott wanted you outside the fishbowl in case she says anything that triggers a memory for you."

Strike Force called the interrogation rooms "fishbowls' because the interviewee was the center of attention while a cast of experts watched from the freedom side of a two-way mirror.

"Let's switch seats," Lynx said, standing.

Sitting beside Deep, Reaper had a better view of the screen.

"Okay. We've been talking a lot about coincidences over the last few days."

"This is about Cyn Parker," Reaper slid forward, "and how she keeps showing up? Does this have to do with our client?"

"Not that we know of. No. Sorry, bad transition. The coincidence has to do with your finding the drive." She exhaled. "Let's start with this. Command had an interesting visitor this morning, Senator Brackmann." Lynx turned to Deep. "I think it would be faster and more thorough if you just play the video, Deep."

Deep licked his lips as he worked his mouse.

A video came up on his screen of a conference room in the command wing.

Leanne, General Elliot's personal assistant, brought in coffees, serving them from a silver tray, then set a plate of sweets between the two men. "Thank you, Leanne," the general said.

After she left the room, the general nodded. "How may I help you?"

"I made a terrible series of poor judgment calls." The senator stopped to clear his throat. "A friend of mine at the Pentagon, a buddy from back in the day when I served in the military, suggested I reach out to you. He's worried that my choices might become a security risk. I don't want to go to the FBI with this, it would ruin my career."

The general sat stoically. "You're going to have to give me a clue what we're talking about."

"A girl." He skated his hand out. "Woman. *Not* a girl. Over eighteen. Or so she says."

"Sex, then."

"Worse."

"You're wearing a wedding ring."

"Thirty years of fidelity. And then…shit." Senator Brackmann scrubbed a hand over his face and looked like he was going to burst into tears. "I don't know what happened to my brain. But this is bad."

"Okay, tell me everything you have on her and why your infidelity poses a security risk. Any photographs?"

"Hell no. I'm not a moron."

"Where did you meet?"

"First-class London to NYC."

The general continued his string of questions. "How long ago was this?"

"December, eight weeks."

"Where did you meet for sex?"

"At her hotel." The Senator's face flushed pink.

"Nice place?"

"Very nice. Not a five-star. But nice enough. Wrapped up for winter—a hat, a scarf—the way I was, no one recognized me."

"And if they did?"

"Doppelganger. I get that all the time. My face is kind of the generic everyman. At least that's what my stylist said. We used it to my advantage during the last election cycle."

"So why are you here?" Commander asked. "What do you want from Iniquus?"

"I met her at a hotel a couple days ago. She wanted me to

know that she's pregnant. I was there…I tried to convince her that she should terminate the pregnancy. She was very much opposed to the idea, crying because I wasn't as happy as she was. Anything I said just upset her more."

The general was stoic. There was no boys' club nod of understanding. Nothing negative either. "What kinds of things did you say to persuade her to go along with your agenda?"

"I offered her money." He looked out the window. "Two hundred grand to terminate."

The general nodded slowly. "Did she try to negotiate the amount?"

"No." He looked down at his lap.

"Did she threaten to tell your wife?"

"No."

The general drummed his fingers on the highly polished mahogany table. "Why are you engaging Iniquus? If we find dirt on her, that doesn't absolve you of your parental duties."

Reaper whispered, "Is it Nia? Is she trying to real in two fish with one hook?"

"No," Lynx said. "Command showed him Nia's picture, and he said the two women look nothing alike."

The senator sat very still. The only thing about him that moved was his mouth. His lips twitched this way and that, as if he were having a whole conversation that he held secret behind closed lips. Finally, he said, "This." He pushed a piece of paper forward. "She said I was to go onto the news shows and make these points." He tapped the paper with a rigid finger. "She said I'm scheduled with Berry Greg Sunday morning at eleven. That Greg's booker would be reaching out to me. How would Julep have an in at the news station?"

"Just with Berry Greg?" General Elliot asked.

"No." He sniffed. "That's just one of the places I'm to appear. Julep said there would be a list of places. I'm to go speak across

the political and ideological spectrum, so I can educate everyone about the truth."

"This information is incorrect, as you know. This is *agitprop*." The general used the term for communist agitation and propaganda.

The senator worked his hands against each other. "It's not contrary to the United States agenda. I don't know how it would hurt anything if I followed through. You know, a throwaway line, something to appease her."

"She doesn't need appeasing. Her handler is the one that needs appeasing. We don't do that. Ever."

"But why in the heck not? Everyone knows knows it's hyperbole. That's all. No harm. No foul. Right?"

"You know where that would lead. You do something for them once, and they come back with the next bigger ask. You do it once, you do it always. You'll be compromised. And in the Senate."

"But it plays here at home. News cycles these days last for the space of time between meals. At breakfast, America is mad at gas prices. At lunch, they're pissed that there are coyotes in their garbage. By dinner, all they can talk about is why celebrity X is talking smack about celebrity Y in some glitzy catfight. I say this," again he tapped the paper, "it might have about a half-hour of blowback. My words aren't that relevant in a world of information inundation."

"It gets played on American television, that gets picked up by our adversaries' television and becomes a truth in peoples' minds —but it is not, in fact, a fact. No use spinning your wheels, Senator, your tires are bogged down in the mud now. You know how this works. You got caught dipping your paw into a honey pot." General Elliot looked disgusted. "I'm going to help you. And we're going to keep this as quiet as possible. I couldn't give a rat's ass about how this affects you personally. I do very much care how it affects the country I love. And if your being compromised gets out into the public sphere in any way, shape, or form, it will weaken the solemnity and reputation of the Senate."

General Elliot pressed a button on the speaker box. "Leanne, get me Special Agent in Charge Damian Prescott. Tell him we have a situation that needs his immediate attention. See if he can cut a hole in his schedule now to come in and talk to me. Tell him it's a national security risk."

The two sat in silence.

The Senator caved his shoulders and seemed to fold down on himself.

A moment later, Leanne opened the door.

"And?"

"Sir, Special Agent in Charge Prescott is twenty minutes out. Thirty when he parks and heads up to the Commander's wing."

General Elliot nodded and Leanne moved back through the heavy door, closing it noiselessly.

The screen went black.

"Sound like anything else going on?" Deep asked.

"Yeah, Team Alpha's assignment." Reaper turned to Lynx. "Okay, I'm a little baffled. I get what's going on, but what has this got to do with the airport and me?"

27

Reaper

Friday Morning

"Let me go out on a limb and ask," Reaper said. "Does agitprop have to do with what was on that thumb drive Houston found?"

"Exactly," Deep said. "Well, not exactly. They're still working on decryption. But you're right about the finding it part."

Lynx leaned forward. "The senator met his new friend Julep on a flight from London. She upgraded her seat and spent the flight flirting with the senator eight weeks ago. So we can speculate that she realized she was pregnant about six weeks ago."

Reaper nodded. "Alpha's task is to look into the woman, Virginia Goss, who likes to be called Nia. According to the F.B.I., she's a frequent flier between Vienna, Austria and Washington D.C." Lynx pointed over at Prescott where he sat talking to Striker. "After hearing this scenario and seeing some parallels between the two stories—"

"Just the name of the news personality raises a red flag,"

Reaper said. "If both are compromised by impregnating a woman then they can be used as a tag team of disinformation. The babies —those poor children—mean that the fathers can't get themselves free from their circumstances."

Lynx looked miserable as Reaper said that. Then slapped both her hands onto her thighs as if changing gears. "With this video, Deep and I looked into Nia's ticket from Paris for the flight when she and Berry Greg met. The interesting thing about that flight was that Nia upgraded from cheapest seat to business class. And she did it at the boarding gate. Greg said she was sitting next to him on the flight. But we're pretty sure that Nia targeted him because the upgrade in seat didn't put her side by side with Greg. According to the passenger list, there was still a distance between their seats."

Reaper nodded.

"I contacted the person who was assigned the seat next to Greg, his name is Narwaz Zadari—that's neither here nor there, I just don't want the pronouns to get confusing. Zadari said that a girl wanted to sit by the window and would he please change seats for a hundred cash. Zadari said that because of the kinds of clothes she was flying in and the way she'd done her makeup and hair, he thought she was one of those Instagram people who made hand over fist with the cash. He was glad to take her money to move to an aisle seat. Besides, Zadari was afraid if he didn't comply, she'd post about it on her social media. He'd get the wrath of the immature attacking him, and who needed that?"

"No one," Deep said without slowing his fingers on the keyboard. "Not a single soul."

"Nia switched seats, and Greg comes to sit beside her. Now she has nine-ish hours to set her hooks."

"When did their physical relationship begin?" Reaper asked.

"He fingered her on the plane," Deep said without inflection. "They went through customs together. I have video of that."

"According to our client, he didn't want to go to a hotel because he was too recognizable. At baggage claim, he told Nia his driver could take her home, which she accepted. On the ride home, he convinced her to let him go to her apartment."

"So, we have the address," Reaper said.

"We have her address but when Greg was there, she said that she was moving," Lynx said. "We have that address, too. The FBI is over at the second address as we speak, inviting Nia to come have a little chat with them here. We're expecting her soon."

"Okay. And the link with the senator?" Reaper asked.

"Possibly there's a link." She glanced past Reaper to catch Deep's gaze. "Right now, we have a mess. While Alpha and Bravo are out in the field, Deep and I are trying to get some clarity about what belongs together and what belongs in a completely different box. Right now, we're trying to catch you up with our efforts so your eyes and ears, your field experience with what went down in the airport, when you found the flash drive, and our investigation can come into sync." She sniffed loudly as she filled her lungs. "Okay," she said on the exhale. "So why did General Elliot specifically call Special Agent in Charge Damian Prescott in?" She lifted her chin toward the table where the FBI special agents were conferencing with Striker.

Reaper shook his head.

"I went to the apartment and chatted with the building's security. I was told that Nia didn't live in the building. We looked back at their archived security tapes, and they said that the apartment tenant had added her to his list of approved visitors with up to three guests walking in with her. They do face scans to come through the main doors."

"Who was the tenant?"

"Some rando," she said. "John Smith. The credit card goes to a shell company. They let me work with the security guard to watch the comings and goings of John Smith. The security guy let me do this because he was curious as all get out about what was going on in that apartment. Every day, the mail carrier brought in a box of letters addressed to women's names. Military posts were in the return address area. He'd go upstairs and a few minutes later, he'd be back down with a cardboard box about the same size, all taped up for delivery with no name or address on it. The security team couldn't figure it out. And they were only trying out of boredom and curiosity."

"Okay." Reaper shifted in his seat.

"Here's something really interesting. Despite the lease date, John Smith had a mover show up Saturday night about the same time that Berry Greg got the call from Nia announcing her pregnancy. They emptied the apartment, and John Smith handed in his keys and said he was breaking his lease. Boom. Gone."

"In the middle of the night?"

"Nine o'clock was when they started. Big group of movers went up like locusts and stripped it bare by eleven. Eleven is significant because residents can't make noise after ten on weekdays and after eleven on weekends."

"What's up with the letters? They seem to me mean something to you." He pressed his feet into the ground as he leaned back in the chair.

"About a year ago there was a play to destroy Delta Force at Fort Bragg."

"What?" Reaper laughed.

"It had a good potential to work, actually. The Prokhorov family, who are associated with dark money in former USSR countries—"

"Oligarchs?" he asked.

"Mmm, same circles and money streams. But this was a Prokhorov family project. They are very into data collection, propaganda, and psyops. Bot farms and the like."

"Okay."

"Through the Delta Force debacle, we discovered that one of the ways the Prokhorovs gathered their data was through honey pot pen pals who worked on the loneliness of our deployed military. Prescott was on the ground trying to figure out the honey pot, military mail, Delta Force connections. The DIA took over the correspondence, letting those who had been caught up know about the situation. My understanding is that the DIA stood in for the military and wrote back and forth with the women in the correspondence structure. One of the women we caught, the one who was married to a Delta Force operator, gave up some information about life in the compound and what it took to stay alive and not be sold into slavery. She didn't have much understanding about how any of the system worked."

Reaper nodded.

"Prescott said the Prokhorovs got wise and stopped mailing. Prescott thinks this might show that there was more than one project going to disperse the weight, in case any one leg of the operation fell. Or that the Prokhorovs simply started a new round of correspondence. Prescott's task force is going to look into this and loop in the DIA."

"Okay, I've heard about the pen pal thing. Sort of like the World War II admonishments, 'Loose lips sink ships.' We were told to be vigilant about honey pots. You said the guy, John Smith, moved. What's happening to those letters from Nia's building now?"

"They're being forwarded to a different address. The FBI is following up. Those letters aren't directly part of our missions. I'm going to turn the page and start the next chapter. Are you ready?"

"I don't know, am I?" Reaper asked crossing his arms over his chest.

"This one has to do with the airport the morning Houston found the drive."

Reaper nodded.

"Striker?" Lynx called.

When her fiancé turned her way, he lifted his brows to ask what she needed.

"We're ready to go through the airport information."

Striker looked over at Prescott and Finley, a check-in. All three adjusted their chairs to look at the big screen that Deep was lowering. The lights dimmed.

Lynx touched Reaper's elbow. "How about we move over with the others where you can see better." After everyone was settled, a still came up of a young girl with two buns on the top of her head like cat ears.

"Ta-da. Here is Virginia Goss, otherwise known to our client as—"

"Nia," they all said together.

28

Reaper

Friday Morning

"What the…" Reaper leaned forward. His job with the SEALs was to handle the K9 and follow orders. He'd never been involved with the spycraft that got them to actionable data.

"The clarity you have on these images is remarkable," Prescott said.

"The CTV was digitally enhanced to colorize and brighten details." Lynx gave a laugh. "Up until a few hours ago, we were calling this woman 'Bunhead' because the CTV feed was so blurry. Deep's new AI program has been hard at work filling in pixels for us. Her face just became clear." Lynx walked to the front of the screen. "We landed on this woman who went into the Boston loading area, but then got on the plane across the aisle." Lynx looked over to Deep. "Why don't you play that bit while I talk. Take it to the point where she goes to sit down in the Boston loading area."

Deep queued the video to the right spot and all eyes were on Nia. Encircled by green, the highlighter moved with her, helping the viewers keep track.

"There are lots of reasons why she might have behaved as she did," Lynx said. "Across the way was crowded and noisy. Interestingly, these two seats in this one area are the *only* place that isn't covered by camera angles all along with the boarding gates."

"If they aren't covered by cameras, why would they try to hack?"

"Hack?" Reaper asked.

Prescott leaned forward to catch Reaper's eye. "We determined that on the day you found the drive, from the first flight of the day until the Boston flight took off, there was an attempt to penetrate the airport security system to disable the camera feeds."

"We're working with the idea that they wanted to disable the cameras to keep all the faces off the cameras during this time frame," Finley said. "That's the section of video feed that Deep analyzed. The computers found several people who were questionable, but we landed on this woman."

"Nia Goss flew from D.C. to North Carolina where she spent the night and got on a plane to fly back to D.C. on Sunday morning according to flight rosters," Deep said.

"How quickly after she got off the flight in D.C. on Saturday did she telephone our client?" Striker asked.

"About two hours later," Deep said.

"Deep, go back to our first marker, please." Lynx waited for a moment while Deep queued the right section of video. "Deep tracked backward to the point where Nia arrived at the airport." Lynx raised her hand to show Nia circled in green and another woman circled in yellow. "Nia walked in with this woman. Computer analysis says she's mid-fifties, five foot six, a hundred and eighty to two hundred pounds."

Reaper leaned forward. “Something about that woman. I think she might have been on my flight to Boston.”

“Her name is Mary Wise,” Lynx said. “And yes, she flew to Boston—back to that in a moment.” Lynx pointed at the pair. “As you see here, the two walk into the airport together, Mary grabs Nia’s arm and tugs her. They walk to the ladies’ room together where they are in for quite a while. Granted, with the lines issue in ladies’ rooms as a general rule, that’s neither here nor there. Neither changed their appearance or clothing while in the bathroom.”

“Maybe I should add here,” Prescott said, “we found a security notification that an off-duty U.S. Marshal saw two women interacting in the bathroom that had some red flags for her.” He stopped and nodded toward Lynx to take over.

“According to the marshal’s written description, it was Nia and Mary that caught her attention. She indicated in her report that the woman was medicating what looked like a reluctant teen. It was the kind of maneuver that she’d seen in trafficking, grooming behaviors, but there was nothing egregious enough for her to intervene. Should the teen become part of an investigation, she simply wanted to have the bathroom scene documented.”

“When the security desk got that report, they didn’t follow through?” Finley asked.

“Not at the time. It was a slow shuffle to the right hands and by then, both Nia—flying to North Carolina, and Mary Wise, flying to Boston, were gone,” Deep said.

“Nia came back to D.C. Do you know what happened to Mary?” Prescott asked.

“Mary rented a car at the airport and according to toll booth cameras,” Deep said, “she drove from Boston to Florida starting Saturday. The car was handed in at the Orlando airport.”

“Okay. Do we think that Nia’s being trafficked? Was she

following someone's directive to sleep with Greg?" Prescott asked.

Lynx pressed her lips together and looked at the still picture of a very young Nia for a long moment. "We don't know. What I can tell you from their body language is that Mary was in charge of Nia. Without any other information it's speculation," she concluded.

Prescott gave a curt nod. "Keep going."

"Deep, coming out of the bathroom, please."

Deep moved the video forward.

"There was a parting of the ways when the two women reached security. Mary Wise went through as a Pre-Check, and Nia went through the regular line. They stopped walking side by side or conversing. Now, we see Mary move off to make a purchase and is standing there, keeping an eye on Nia as she moves to that chair—out of view. She is there for what would be an appropriate amount of time to sit, look around, stick a drive in place, and then get away from it. Here, see? After a moment Nia stands, moves to look at the food kiosk. Buys nothing. Fills her water bottle. Looks at the other gate where lines are forming. She gets in the line, gets on her plane, heads out of town."

"Suspicious but not conclusive," Finley said.

Prescott caught his eye. "Agreed."

Something tickled at the back of Reaper's throat, and he coughed.

Lynx turned his way and waited while Reaper chugged back his water bottle.

"Tell me what passed through your mind, Reaper. What were you thinking when you choked?"

Reaper shook his head. "I don't know. That woman… Mary Wise."

"Have you seen her before?"

"I don't think so. If I did, this context is different enough that

I'm not recalling. Something about the way she moves. I'm trying to recall if I'm remembering something I saw that day, or if it's a different context. It may be nothing at all."

"I think from your reaction it's something. But let it marinate. If you push it'll just squirrel that memory away where you can't find it."

"Yeah probably." Reaper watched himself disappear on the video as he sat down. "Kate was there with Zack."

"Deep, if you'll move it to the next bookmark."

The team watched as Mary Wise moved to the desk and was offering a friendly smile to the staffer.

"We interviewed this attendant. She said that Mary Wise recognized Ryan Hamilton as having served with her brother and that Ryan had been badly wounded in battle. She wanted to secretly upgrade his ticket, so he was more comfortable on the flight."

"Wait, she knew my name?" Reaper asked. "My *real* name. Ryan? In the military, I've been Reaper since boot. Why would anyone write home about me? And why in the world would they use my given name and not just Reaper. We have call signs for a reason, and one of them is to protect our identities."

"Fair point," Prescott said. "My guess is that she heard Kate calling you Ryan. Or she read it on something."

Reaper closed his eyes, going over the scene, and at one point, Kate had wanted to get his attention and called him "Ryan James Hamilton." "Kate," he said. "She used my whole name."

"Mystery solved," Finley said. "Seems like Mary has some tradecraft under her belt."

"Yeah, but for whom?" Prescott asked.

"Mary paid for that upgrade, as you can see," Lynx continued to narrate the video, "with four hundred dollars in cash. Huh. Go back thirty seconds, Deep."

"What do you see, Lynx?" Finley asked.

"Without context, I'm not seeing anything, but I will point this out. There's good. Go ahead, Deep." As the video played again, Lynx walked closer toward the screen. "Look at this. Do you see that the attendant is looking in the direction that Reaper would stand? And she keeps her focus there instead of on Mary. Reaper, about this time, what would you have been doing?"

"I was on my phone talking to Striker over by the window."

"Yes, that's the direction of her focus. Now look, Mary takes a step and angles her body so that as the staff is watching Reaper, you wouldn't be able to tell. It looks like she's focused on Mary. But really, she hasn't moved her head. It's an optical illusion that Mary wittingly or unwittingly set up. After Mary went to sit down, the staffer played with her computer, then she walked over to Reaper."

"What did she say to you?" Striker asked.

"That my seat had been upgraded to first class."

"It didn't catch your attention?" Prescott asked.

"It happened all the time. It didn't ring any particular bell."

"Right," Lynx said. "He could have gotten the upgrade for any number of reasons, frequent flying back and forth to California, veteran status, cute doggo."

"And here I thought it was my rugged good looks and my flirty winks at the staff."

"Always a possibility." Lynx exhaled a laugh.

"I've always declined the upgrade because of Houston. This time, I accepted to give Kate a bit of comfort and relaxation. I took the baby back with me to my seat behind the bulkhead."

"Deep, bring up a schematic of the passenger list and seat assignments. Where was Mary Wise seated." The image changed to a still slide. "Reaper where was Kate?" Lynx asked.

Reaper looked at the image on the screen. "Back row, left-hand side aisle. We were in eye contact throughout the flight."

"Mary is right across from her. Mary Wise meant for you to

be sitting next to her," Deep said as he added Kate's name to the correct seat.

"For my clarification," Prescott said. "This is after you found the drive as you're calling it in?"

"Yes."

"Let's throw it out there just to see how it sounds out loud instead of in my head," Finley said. "Mary is Nia's handler. She came to watch how the kid did. She was keeping her eye on the pass to make sure it went smoothly. She sees Reaper. A trained eye would understand what was happening—no matter how smoothly Reaper conducted himself. She upgrades him to the seat near her so she can pull a Lynx and pickpocket you of your newfound treasure."

"Even if I had taken that seat, she wouldn't have found it on me. I put it in Houston's vest pocket."

"Ha!" Lynx laughed.

"Okay, Mary was sitting across the aisle from Kate. Did Kate chat with Mary? Do you know?"

"From my seat, I could see Kate. She was talking to the window passenger. The only time I saw Kate turn her head was when she was checking on Little Guy. He was squalling."

"Do we know anything about Mary Wise?" Prescott asked.

"I researched some of the passengers already," Deep said. "The ones sitting a row behind Reaper then forward." He tapped on the keyboard. "Here we go. Mary Wise. According to her social media profiles she had a mid-western childhood, attended university in Indiana. She's working as a branding consultant for a PR firm. Looking at their website, it looked like boutique service—very small and targeted at petroleum industries."

"I've also got the woman sitting next to Kate in that seat. She's a retired pediatrician. Easily searched. Social media is filled with family and pets."

"Okay." Reaper stood and planted his knuckles on the table-top. "I'm still stuck on that woman calling me Ryan Hamilton. She *knew* I had her thumb drive."

"She would have also seen you turning it over to the FBI when you landed in Boston. Washington D.C. is a hub, she'd have no way to know where you live," Finley said. "Is that your worry?"

"Yeah, it is. Let me be clear," Reaper looked pointedly at the FBI special agents, "if there's any chance that my family is in any kind of danger from this incident, I need to know. I *will* protect them."

"We all will Reaper." Lynx's face was as fierce as he'd ever seen. "You're not alone."

Striker's phone buzzed and he lifted it to read his screen. Looking at Prescott he said, "Nia's here in the interrogation room. Are you ready?"

29

Reaper

Friday Morning

Reaper turned toward Lynx with eyebrows raised to ask for information.

When she felt his eyes on her, she spun his way. "The FBI did a swing by Nia Goss's new apartment and invited her to have a voluntary talk with them. She said she wouldn't go to the FBI Headquarters without a lawyer. They said they'd bring her here for a chat, and she agreed."

"How old?" Reaper asked.

"Nineteen," Deep said.

Reaper popped his brows. "I guess she doesn't know enough about the law to know this is a bad move."

"Lucky us." Prescott patted him on the shoulder as he passed by. The whole group relocated to a special wing of Iniquus, cut off from the rest of the building. There was an entire corridor that was set up as a SCIF—Sensitive Compartmented Information Facility. No computers. No phones. No way to get into Iniquus proper. Locked tight. This was the place where Iniquus and their governmental partners would ask tough questions.

The atmosphere of the inquiry corridor ranged from a corporate committee room to a stark white icebox.

Nia got the icebox.

Iniquus wasn't playing footsie with this girl.

Today, Nia wasn't done up like a baby doll. Her hair was scraped back into a greasy ponytail. Her face was droopy, and she looked like she was going to hurl. Someone had put a plastic bowl on the table and some tissues.

Morning sick and interrogation would probably turn out to be a bad combination.

Prescott and Lynx walked into the room.

Dressed in fleece pajama bottoms and a t-shirt, Nia wrapped her arms around her as she shivered.

Lynx sent Nia a compassionate smile as she held out a blanket. "It's always so cold in this room," she said, "and I'm told you're expecting. I thought this might make you more comfortable." And with that, Lynx made an alliance.

She was the good cop.

Prescott, with his stone face, was going to be the antagonist. "Virginia, may I call you Viginia?"

"Everyone calls me Nia. Look, I'm pregnant, and I'm not feeling great. I haven't broken any laws. I don't want to be here. I need to go home and rest. The woman who brought me here just showed me a badge and—"

"I'm Damian Prescott. I work for the FBI. We wanted to ask a few questions."

Her eyes grew enormous as they rounded in fear. "I haven't done anything to break a law. And I don't know anyone who has."

She looked around the white room with the length of mirrors on one side.

Reaper thought she was looking right at him. He still wasn't clear why he was involved with this; he'd have to trust the process.

Lynx was an interesting addition to that room.

Everything was stark. Hard. Cold. Including Prescott.

The one reprieve was Lynx in her soft pink dress. She was like the daisy that a peace protestor would slide into the barrel of a policeman's rifle.

The protective big sister.

Nia's gaze found Lynx's, and they smiled at each other. An alliance confirmed.

"Where is this place?" Nia asked Lynx.

Lynx opened her mouth, but Prescott beat her to it. "A stopping point between here and lock up."

"After you answer Prescott's questions, we can get you somewhere more comfortable. Would some mint tea help, do you think? A friend of mine found that sniffing at a fresh lemon helped with morning sickness."

Nia shook her head, then focused back on Prescott.

"As I said, I work with the FBI. I want you to be very clear, it's a crime to lie to the FBI. We have a good idea of what kind of situation you're in. We can give you an out. You can work with us."

"No." Nia's eyelids were held wide and unblinking. "I can't."

"If you're afraid of going to jail, it's possible that we could grant you immunity for helping us get those who are exploiting you," Prescott said. He'd dimmed the hard edge. Reaper thought he was reading Nia correctly. If Nia said lawyer, they were done. If she sat there in silence, they wouldn't make progress. "If you're afraid of someone hurting you, we can give you witness protection."

"What?" Nia snapped. "And live my life as someone else? Different name, peeking in shadows. What about my baby? How would my baby visit with his father?"

"His?" Lynx said. "How far along are you?"

"I just missed my period. I took the test Saturday."

"His?" she repeated.

"I think it's a boy. And I'm not going through my pregnancy looking for people in the shadows." She stilled and seemed to realize that she's just shown a card in her hand. Nia shook her head. She looked down at the table.

Prescott gave her a moment to process. After what felt like a very long time, she whispered, "What does working with you look like? They'll know that I was caught."

"And released when we had nothing on you."

"Watched, though. They'd assume you were watching me. They'd search me to see if you had bugs on me." She talked to her lap. Her hands splayed across her abdomen.

"You'd be clean."

"They'd send me back to the compound, and they'd hold me there."

"We're aware of what you were doing for the Prokhorovs."

When Prescott said the family's name. Nia gasped and began shaking. Lynx wrapped a supportive arm around her.

"Are you referring to the compound where you write letters to the military?" Prescott asked.

Her eyes flashed up. She blanched.

Lynx moved the puke bucket a little closer to Nia as Prescott asked, "Where is your compound located?"

Nia shook her head. "Somewhere overseas. I fly into Vienna where someone meets me. I don't know how to read or speak the languages."

"You don't even know what country you were in?"

"They will know I spoke with you. And when you let me go.

They will send me away and there would be no way to pass any information on to you if that's what you want from me. I can't spy for you. If The Family thinks I'm doing anything other than a stellar job—if I were anything but loyal, I'd be sold."

Self-preservation. In the field, Reaper knew that meant that without specific conviction to a goal or ideology, that a person would align with survival. Obviously, she feared the Prokhorov's more than she feared the FBI. Unless Prescott could change that, he wouldn't get much from Nia.

"Is that what happens to the other girls?" Lynx asked. "That sounds terrifying."

Nia glommed on to the empathy that Lynx seemed to genuinely exude.

Prescott noticed. He caught Lynx's eye, and Lynx continued the questioning. "When they bring a girl to Europe, they decide who works for them and who does not, correct?

Nia nodded a tiny almost imperceptible nod.

"And only the best are brought in to work."

"They keep us if we're what they want."

"What happens if you don't make the grade?

"The girls get sold to the highest bidder. Only pretty girls are brought to the job interview, so their sale price ends up being high."

"Horrible. How do they do that, sell the women?" Lynx and Nia were now holding hands. Besties whispering secrets.

"The girls are put up for auction. The rest of us are there watching so we know what will happen to us if we don't comply. The girls are dressed in beautiful gowns, their hair and makeup are professionally done. It's like going to a high-dollar event… well, it *is* a high-dollar event. It's like being at some big Hollywood awards party. We looked gorgeous for the men. We're sitting on their laps, and they're squeezing our titties as they bid on the girls that didn't make the grade to stay at the compound.

They're every bit as pretty as we are. But for whatever reason…"

Lynx's face was a study of sadness and sympathy. Reaper knew that in Lynx's past she'd been captured and held prisoner. He was sure the emotions were genuine. She faced her own issues with PTSD. Reaper thought this was probably going to be a major trigger for her, especially while she was making herself emotionally available to this young woman.

Nia pressed her palms together and slid them between her legs, her shoulders came up to her ears.

Lynx reached out and caught the blanket that was sliding from Nia's shoulders and tucked it around her, stuffing a corner under Nia's leg to hold it in place. "There's a story there about the auctions," Lynx said.

"There are two kinds of auctions," Nia whispered. "The one for the girls who didn't make it into the program, and the ones who lived at the compound." She immediately started retching.

Lynx waited for Nia's stomach to settle. When Nia put her forehead down on the table and rocked it against the surface, Reaper recognized that move. His prisoner's systems would overheat upping the sense of claustrophobia. They'd try to cool their faces on a hard surface.

"You're having a reaction to this information that you didn't have when we began speaking about the girls who didn't make the cut. Something about the auction for the girls that were in the compound is different."

She wiggled her head side to side.

"Is it the price on the girls' head?"

Nia pulled herself up to look at Lynx.

"Is it the person who buys the girls?"

Nia's eyes stretched wide.

"Who buys the girls from the compound?"

"I don't know. It's probably a rumor." She sent a brief glance toward Prescott then focused back on Lynx.

"Okay, a rumor. What is rumored to happen to those girls?"

"They can't be allowed to go free. We know very little, but the little we know is dangerous to the people who run this show."

"Yes?"

"We're told that we're sold to sadists. That the people who would buy us were the ones who…" She was whole body shaking. "There's a phrase they like to use." The words pushed past chattering teeth. "The living will be jealous of the dead." She swallowed. "We've seen pictures of some of the girls we knew."

"And yet, here you are in America roaming free," Prescott pointed out. "But you're willing to go back to them."

"Not willing. I'm… I'm working it out. I think to survive I need to prove my worth outside of the compound. I did really good work for them. I did everything they asked, and I earned the privilege to fly home."

"Tell us about that." Lynx's voice was gentle and coaxing. "Why are you allowed home?"

"To meet in person with the soldiers that we write to. I screw them and act like we're a committed couple."

"To what end?" Prescott asked.

She turned toward him. "The soldiers are warned about the shady shit folks will try to pull on the soldiers. My showing up and pretending to be in love with them calms their nerves. They really believe what's going on between us and every time they ask me to marry them. I always accept the ring."

"What happens when they leave the military?" Prescott asked.

"They're ghosted. The mail is given a PO box forwarding address in some random city. No one ever checks it. After three months, it's closed for non-payment."

"Okay. The men feel comfortable enough with your relationship that they—" Lynx started.

"Men and women. I've done both."

"Is that one of the criteria for acceptance to the compound?" Lynx asked.

"One is yes, I slept with a man, a woman, a couple. I was asked to do role play. I didn't mind any of it. Some girls try to set limits—they won't go down on another woman or they won't suck toes or do ass play, whatever they throw at you. If you don't do what's asked of you, you don't pass."

"Then you're sold."

"Exactly—but they don't tell you that."

"What did they tell you you'd be doing?" Lynx reached out to the water bottle and poured some in a glass, then pushed it over to Nia.

"Oh, we knew we were in for prostitution. But what we were *told* was that we'd have modeling contracts and hostess contracts to entertain the wealthy elite. If you don't know what that meant you're dumb as shit. And dumb as shit will get you kicked out too. All the girls are, I'd say, really smart. Just… We all came from bad situations, I guess."

"They're sold if they don't make the cut," Prescott asked. "What gets girls from the compound sold?"

"They don't do the work, which isn't just writing notes, it's a lot of physical training and beauty ritual shit. We have to be as close to a ten as we can get." She paused and sipped some water. She placed the glass down carefully. "Maybe you get sold because you don't get any useful information. Maybe she tries to run."

"You aren't trying to run," Prescott pointed out.

"I am in my own way."

"More?" he asked.

"I'm proving myself. I'm trying to get harder assignments."

"Your placing the thumb drive was a test. That woman was observing you?"

"Exactly. Yes."

"To what end?"

"I thought…" Nia looked up at the ceiling and paused. With a lick of her lips, she spoke to the back wall. "There was a Russian woman. She came to America. She was okay on the pretty scale. Better than average. But she wasn't anywhere near as pretty as the girls at the compound. The Russian girl talked the right talk and got herself in photographs with all of these politicians, right?"

"Yes," Lynx said.

"Politicians will leave you hanging out to dry. But if you take happy pretty pictures with enough of them, it becomes a liability, right? Then you have some protection. You're safe."

"Is that true, Nia?" Lynx asked. "I mean, that woman went to jail for eighteen months for failing to register as a foreign agent, right?"

"How long would it have been if she didn't have those photos?" Nia asked.

"Good point." Lynx nodded. "But you also know that some people prefer that anyone who has dangerous information disappear, did that ever concern you?"

"Yeah. But I figured if I were in America and the news outlets were talking about me and putting my photo up… I'm good at manipulating men. I figured I'd work my way up as high as I could, find me a sugar daddy. He'd protect me. I'd have security and all that. Billionaires don't care."

"You planned your pregnancy to protect yourself?" Prescott asked.

Nia blinked at him.

"Do you think it will work? The Family could always call you back to Europe. Then what would you do?"

"I … I…" She shook her head.

"This is why it's so important that you speak truthfully today, that you're helpful. You can either become a cooperator or, I'm guessing down the road, you might be hiring your own lawyer to fight your own failure to report as a foreign agent charges. Conspiracy to defraud the United States. Oh, I can think of a laundry list of things that might turn your life into a hellscape."

Nia blinked.

Prescott pulled a manilla folder over in front of him. He pulled out a single 8X10. It was a picture of Cyn. "Do you know her?"

Reaper looked over to Striker with a scowl that asked for information. "Are you kidding me? Cyn might be a Russian asset?"

"Fishing. Cyn Parker showing up when and how she did, we're trying to figure out what's going on there. It makes absolutely no sense to any of us. The how. The why. Or if it's even a thing."

"No." Nia rolled her lips in and shook her head. "I don't know her."

While Prescott put the photo away and picked another one, Reaper focused on Striker, "They're not going to push?"

"No. Fishing, like I said. And Lynx there, she's a human lie detector. If that wasn't genuine a genuine 'no,' Lynx would be on it like blowflies on a body."

"Nice visual."

Striker chuckled as he focused back on the interrogation room.

Prescott had moved and Reaper couldn't see the picture that was laying in front of Nia.

"That girl, we call her Julep. Like a mint julep, some kind of alcohol drink they have in the South. That's where she's from. She—she's a very smart girl. She came home to meet with a soldier but caught this guy's eye. An important man in the government. And she got pregnant with his baby. I overheard it being talked about between our handlers at the compound. They were packing up her things to ship home. She gets to live in

America now so they can put pressure on the father. It gave me the idea that I could do this, too. Home isn't perfectly safe, but it's *safer*. It's much more comfortable money-wise. I have a pretty nice apartment. And all I have to do is screw Berry when he wants. It's a lot less work."

Prescott turned the photo over and stuck it into his file. "Julep, do you know where she is?"

"No." Nia shook her head. "No idea."

Prescott picked a third image and slid it forward where Reaper could see Mary Wise standing by the kiosk with a bar of chocolate in her hand. "What about her? Do you know this woman?"

"Yes and no. I don't know her name. She picked me up when I was flying to North Carolina. I was with her for about two hours. I don't know anything about her. She wouldn't talk to me unless she was scolding me or telling me what to do."

AFTER ANOTHER HOUR OF QUESTIONS, Nia went to the bathroom behind a pocket door on the side of the room.

A worker showed up at the SCIF with a lunch tray.

Lynx and Damian excused themselves and left her to eat and be alone with her thoughts. They walked out of the interrogation room, and into the viewing room. There on a buffet, there was food already laid out and available for them. The team made plates and went to sit down.

Prescott broke the silence. "We have a politician, and we have a national commentator. The politician says X, the commentator drives the message. Followers take this to be the truth. Disinformation is the new geopolitical warfare, apparently fueled in part by infidelity and baby-making. It seems we might have a modus operandi."

Lynx frowned at her plate. "The only innocents in this

scenario are the future babies. A baby deserves a mother and a father who want them and will love them. The baby deserves a family. I wonder if Nia even realizes the implications of this situation." She took a bite of her apple. After she swallowed, she said, "Someone with a very decided worldview now has two formidable weapons. And two future babies are the priming charge."

30

Cyn

FRIDAY NIGHT.

BORKA PRESSED a piece of paper forward, and Nia scooped it off the desk. "What's this?"

She seemed unusually nervous tonight, Cyn thought. But what did Cyn know? She had confused morning sickness with nerves in the airport. Maybe this is how breeders act when they're first knocked up.

"You will call Berry Greg and ask him to come to visit you. When he does, you will hand him this paper. He is doing an interview with Senator Brackmann on Sunday morning. Here are the questions and talking points that will be covered."

Nia folded the paper without reading it. "What if he doesn't come when I call?"

"Then suggest that you will show up at his work. He wouldn't want that now, would he?"

She folded the paper in half, and half again, then again. She folded it until it could disappear in her palm, then she made a fist around the wad. "I'll do my best."

"See that you do." Borka's voice was soft, he kept the threat level pretty low.

Cyn wasn't feeling that generous. She chuckled.

Turning on Cyn, Nia shouted, "What already?"

"Oh, I was just thinking about my last trip to St. Croix. I had a lovely day taking a catamaran out to Buck Island."

Nia blinked at her. She did that a lot.

"Buck Island is a national monument with lovely corals. I was snorkeling there and saw a lobster in the wild. Tropical fish. A wonderful day." She canted her head. "The interesting thing I learned about Buck Island is that there is a tree—the manchineel tree—also, called the 'death apple' tree. This tree is pure poison—the bark, the sap, the fruit, all of it is just toxic as hell."

Nia blinked. *Stupid, insipid girl.*

"The fruit looks delicious, especially back in the days of Columbus when the shipmates all had scurvy, and they were desperate for fruit and vitamin C. But, if you were to take a bite, your mouth and throat would blister and swell. Swallow the bite and you'd die." Cyn smiled. "They say the death from the manchineel fruit is like if you were exposed to nerve gas, *torturous* and slow. The indigenous people in the area knew better than to eat the fruit. And they used it for their own needs. They would paint the juice on the tips of their spears when confronting their enemies. Or, if they captured prisoners, they might tie them to that tree. As the sap or even the raindrops drip, it burned the skin of the prisoner, forming horrific blisters. Even the vapor, just sitting under the tree breathing in can kill you. Yes, the manchineel tree looks like a lifesaver, but in reality, it is death."

Nia blanched. "Why? Why would you be thinking about that?" She audibly swallowed. A frown tugged down the corners of her mouth.

"Oh, you know," Cyn shrugged, "it's so cold and unpleasant in the city right now. I think I need a frilly drink on a beach somewhere. St. Croix is lovely."

"Go home, Nia," Borka said. "Call Berry Greg and invite him over. I want you to have sex and while still in bed hand him the paper and tell him about his assignment. At that point in your conversation, make sure Greg knows that the entire apartment is like a porn studio filled with cameras and microphones. I want that sex to be as compromising as possible."

"My apartment is bugged?" Her face flamed red, then dropped to sheet white.

Interesting.

"They are taking care of that now." Borka flicked his hand at her, and Nia left.

When the door snicked shut, Borka turned to Cyn with a look of amusement. "You are a master of psychological warfare aren't you?"

"Me?" Cyn let her hand drift to her chest as she sent him her most innocent expression.

"Why did you tell Nia the apple story?"

Cyn shrugged. "I felt catty, it was fun to play with a little mouse."

Borka laughed. "So." He slapped his hands onto the desk. "We have some new power moves, and they're coming together." He drummed his fingers on the surface. "I have mentioned your efforts with Iniquus to Medved' Zoric to ask him about the spyware and malware to introduce to the Iniquus systems. I have not mentioned it, however, to The Family. I would like to present it as a *fete accompli*." He narrowed his eyes. "But you wish to strategize with me. Tell me, what is the newest?"

"Reaper is very open with his wife and has told her about each instance where our paths have crossed. It means she's got her women's antennae in the air waving around. Jealousy and worry.

Reaper will be exhausted from long hours of paying close attention in the field, and he will go home to strain and subtle digs. I want to move the babysitter et al out of their house immediately. I've used them for what was needed. Now, their presence becomes a potential liability."

"You don't think that their moving in and out of the neighborhood in a single week would be a red flag?"

"I'm afraid that Kate is a smart cookie. She's home all day worrying this knot. She will unravel it if our players are available. Having observed the girl, she seems to want to be in that neighborhood. She seems to enjoy the inclusion and normalcy there. Too young and too weak, I think to be a significant asset for The Family beyond her ability to brood and babysit. My professional assessment is that Julep, well, Julie Loffe, would ask for help getting out from under The Family's thumb if she at all saw a route."

"This is not true. Her sister works at the compound. If Julep —" he flicked his hand in the air, "fails to comply, we sell her sister at an auction. Julep will be tight-lipped. However, if she is no longer serving a purpose, there is no reason to have her exposed. I will remove them in the morning. We need to do it in such a way that this won't cause issues with the Hamiltons. Raise questions."

Cyn thought about it for a minute. "Julep is babysitting for the Hamiltons tomorrow while they go to couples therapy."

Borka lifted his nostrils in derision.

"Perhaps, we could have a domestic dispute in the house Saturday night. Julep could call 9-1-1. The 'husband' could be arrested. You have embeds on the police force who can handle this, don't you? Put some guy in the marked car and move him out?"

"Of course."

"So the police seem to arrest the husband, and the two women move out while he's in jail."

Borka picked up his phone. "Saturday night?"

"Yes."

"Consider it done. Go home. Strategize. Kate's being home cuts the length of your time frame. You must act."

31

Reaper

Saturday Morning

"Hey, man, glad to see you here." Standing on the 1970s brown and orange industrial carpeting in the church's assembly hall, Dave stuck out a hand for a shake.

"Happy it worked out." This morning Reaper's alarm clock sounded followed immediately by a text message from Randy. Harlow had drunk himself into oblivion last night. Jack had listened to him singing drunkenly into the wee hours. He was sure that Harlow was going to be sleeping it off and would be dealing with his hangover at least until Reaper was scheduled for his counseling session. Randy would cover the door.

Mental and physical health were of prime importance to Iniquus Command. They made sure that everyone had a chat with the shrink at least once a month. Reaper got a double whammy of intervention, even though he wasn't—well, hadn't been up until this assignment—out in the field, he was to have counseling weekly. More, Kate had signed papers that for Reaper's first year on the job, she'd accompany him to couples therapy each week.

Their session this afternoon was contracted and not even Harlow took precedence.

This morning, one of his brothers at Cerberus brought Houston over as planned for Kate. Since Max was in the house and Houston was territorial and hyper-protective of Kate and Zack, they'd decided to just load Houston into Reaper's SUV and head on to the church where the scouting group met. For the rest of this assignment, Max would get crated at Lynx's next door, and Reaper could keep watch over the "baby" monitor.

Pushing Zack's buggy back and forth to keep him happy, Dave and Reaper watched from the back of the room as the kids sat in a semi-circle around Kate and Houston.

Reaper was happy to answer questions, but he wasn't big on talking in front of groups. Kate was the teacher. *Look at her, she has those kids in a learning trance.*

"Now, this is Houston. She is still very young. She was training to be my husband's personal PTSD dog. When Mr. Hamilton had a flashback—a bad memory from his time fighting the war, Houston would bring him a ball. Mr. Hamilton would stop what he was doing and go outside to play ball with her. It was a good distraction. It really helped. Now that my husband is doing much better, Houston is being transitioned from being a service dog into a pet. Those roles are very different. The way we interact with working dogs and pets is very different. Mainly right now, we're looking for a doggy job for Houston. We think she might do a good job as a tutor dog to help students with their math."

"What?" the kids chimed and chuckled. "Math?"

"Oh yes, Houston *loves* to do math."

The kids laughed.

Kate looked down at Houston and said, "Math?"

Houston immediately jumped up and circled in front of Kate, his tail scraping against the carpet as she wagged her pleasure. Houston knew she got cheese for this trick.

"Good job. Okay, Houston, what is two plus one?"

Houston barked three times.

Kate looked at the kids. "Too easy?"

"Yes!"

"Okay, let's try this one." She focused back on Houston. "Houston, what is twenty-five minus twenty-three?"

Houston barked twice.

The kids gasped and looked around to see if the others shared in their astonishment.

"Houston, are you ready for a really hard one?" Kate asked. "What is thirty-two divided by eight?"

The kids were slapping their hands onto their heads and coming up on their knees to see if Houston could really do such a hard problem.

Houston barked four times.

With each correct answer, Kate had pulled off a thumbnail-sized piece of cheese. "That's right!" Kate said. "Good job, Houston!" She turned to the students. "Let's give Houston a cheer."

Dave chuckled beside him. "She got Fletcher doing his math homework with that trick. If Houston can do it, he can do it too."

"He knows it's fake, right?"

"Yeah, Kate promised if Fletcher got a good grade on his last math test, she'd teach him how it's done. The kid got a hundred for the first time in his life. Kate said she'd show him today. Look at him, squirming all over the place, can't sit still he's so excited."

"Now," Kate said. "That was a pretty good trick. But it's a trick." She gave Houston the hand signal that asked her to lie down and rest. After Houston complied, Kate continued. "Houston is as smart as they come, but she doesn't actually do math. Let me tell you how we taught Houston this trick, and you can go home and teach your dogs, if you have one, how to do math."

A boy reached out his fingers along the floor, reaching for Houston.

"Whenever a dog is wearing a service dog vest," Kate told him. "We never distract the dog from their job."

The kid immediately pulled his hand back and clutched it to his chest.

Kat smiled and gave him a nod of approval. Focusing on the group she said, "When Houston barked on her own, I would make this hand signal." She made a yapping mouth with her fingers. "I'd say, 'good bark'. And then I'd give her a treat. One treat, a small piece of cheese about the size of my thumbnail. That's a good amount. Soon Houston associated the word 'bark' with making the sound. At that point, I stopped using the word and simply made the hand signal. Little by little I pulled my hand closer to my eyebrow." She demonstrated making the barking signal up by her eye. "Then I would lift my eyebrow when I was making the hand gesture and drop my eyebrows when I stopped. Can you all raise your eyebrows? Good. Now drop them. Perfect. After I got there, and this is weeks of every day practice. Very slow. Very gentle. I started just pointing to my raised eyebrow. Houston barked when I lifted my brows and stopped barking when I lowered my brows, that's when she earned her treat. This went on for another few weeks. Do you see the time and patience it takes to train a dog?"

"And lots of cheese," a boy yelled out.

"Yes, and lots of tiny pieces of cheese," Kate agreed. "Then I started talking and saying random numbers while she was barking. The number of times she barks has nothing to do with the numbers that I'm saying. It has everything to do with how long I hold my eyebrows up. If I said no numbers at all, Houston would bark as long as I've given her the command 'Math' and then lifted my eyebrows." She stopped to sniff. "Why do you think it's important that Houston learned to only bark with raised eyebrows when the command 'math' was used?" Kate asked.

"Because otherwise," Fletcher said, seriously, "when Mr. Hamilton was talking and he was surprised or his face changed up, Houston would keep barking at him."

Kate pointed at Fletcher. "Exactly. And because service dogs are out in public, it's important that they are very well behaved. That means they don't make any noises unless they are commanded to do so by their handler."

"That is so cool!"

"Isn't it?" Kate grinned. "Now, here's a question for you. What to do if a dog with a service dog vest came to you without anyone holding their leash?"

"Don't touch!" They shouted.

"Right, don't touch, some service dogs have been trained to go get help if their person is having a problem. Like someone who has seizures might need a helper to come. If you see a dog with a service vest you could ask the dog if it needs help? Simple words like 'show me' or 'help?' or 'find it.' One of those might turn the dog around and lead you to the person. Once there, if you don't know what to do to help the person, you can use your phone to call for help."

"What's the phone number for emergency help?" the scout leader asked.

"9-1-1," the kids chanted mechanically.

"Perfect, yes." Kate smiled.

A hand went up and waggled in the air. "Can a dog find drugs on you?"

"If that's their training then yes," Kate said then pointed at the next hand that shot up.

"My aunt got a dog that used to work at the airport. It was a beagle."

"That's a nice job for a dog," Kate said.

"My aunt lives in the city, and she had a lot of trouble walking the dog."

"Why is that?" Kate asked.

"She said the dog would be walking along and people would walk by and the dog would lie down. That's the signal for drugs. She says now that it's legal to have marijuana in the city and everyone smells like that. Their whole walk, her dog takes a few steps and lays down."

The kids laughed at the image.

"What did she do about it?" the girl beside him asked.

"She just says, 'leave it', and the dog stands up and walks again."

"Cool," the girl said.

Watching Kate teach was a source of pride for Reaper.

Kate in a classroom was a fish in water. Natural.

He thought about that woman Mary Wise and that she knew Reaper's legal name. All of it. Kate had said "Ryan James Hamilton."

Just the *potential* that his family would land in someone's crosshairs because of him made the beast that lived in his chest roar.

This was a very different adrenaline rush than he had back in his days as a SEAL.

Then, Reaper's adrenaline rush came from the types of assignments he'd volunteered to take on. Kate was in the picture, but he never took her into consideration when he made those kinds of choices. He'd always assumed that if something happened to him, he'd just cut her loose to move on to a healthier relationship. After all, very few SEALs maintain their marriages. It seemed inevitable that Kate would give up on him, on *them,* and move on to greener pastures. He'd just enjoy their relationship until she said that's enough.

Cynical? Maybe. Reaper framed it as pragmatic. He loved her and wanted what was best for her. As wonderful as Kate was, someday she'd open her eyes and see that she got a raw deal and move on.

He was who he was. He owned that.

Reaper was other-side-of-the-tracks. He was from poor and hungry. From cold and filth. Ignored and rejected by a family that wanted to drink beer and vegetate in front of the television, he was an angry youth that enjoyed the release of a brutal fight. Reaper's straight-A report card—earned with zero effort—meant Reaper got plenty of attention from the kind of guys that wanted their intellectual inferiority to be supplanted by physical authority over him. Fights of one kind or another were part of Reaper's every day.

He trained for it.

While the other boys were still snoring in bed, Reaper got up early every morning, pounding out five miles at five a.m., every morning. Like a prizefighter. Rain, sleet…didn't matter, five miles. A stop at the park for plyometrics to get his fast-twitch muscles firing. Pullups on the monkey bars, pushups until his wrists ached, Reaper pushed and pushed until a single punch could put someone in the hospital.

Reaper recognized the wolf inside him. The one that wanted blood for blood's sake. The one that felt pride when an ambulance was called, and all the eyewitnesses scattered.

One day though, his image was caught on a cell phone camera.

A video of a punch straight to the nose when Reaper caught a guy on top of a screaming girl.

The video didn't show her. It just showed Reaper dragging the guy onto his feet and Reaper's fist flattening the guy's face. Blood spurting.

At Reaper's trial, the girl showed up at the arraignment and said, "Ryan is a hero. It would have been bad if he hadn't been there to protect me. He shouldn't go to jail for being a decent human being."

The judge also recognized that wolf inside Reaper. "Son," he said as he lifted the school transcripts Reaper had brought to show he wasn't a gangbanger. "That punch might well have been an act of heroism like this little lady says, but I can see you're on a deadly path." He put the pages down. "That punch isn't new to you." He laced his hands and looked over to the flags that stood in the corner of the courtroom. "I'm going to give you my very best advice." He turned to look Reaper in the eye. "You need to train your violence. It feels good, I know. I was there about your age. Anger has to come out. And even if you wouldn't admit it to me, you can admit it to yourself: You're looking for your next punching bag. When you look up at this bench, you see an old balding man, and you might discount my words. But I was you. I. Was. You. And the way that I kept the fight in me from being a destructive force was to put those impulses to good use. I joined the Marines. I served my country with honor. I used my GI money to go to college, law school, and eventually made it to this bench. If I hadn't, I would have ended up in prison. My life would be completely different. I'm suggesting you leave here and go talk to a recruiter from each of the branches and see what they have to say about you. See if that might be an answer to that beast that wants to get out."

"Yes, sir." Something about that judge, the look in his eye. Reaper believed him. Realized how close it had come to his getting a felony record, a life of under the counter jobs because who hires a felon? The wrong judge… Reaper's life would have been so different.

He wouldn't have joined the Navy.

Wouldn't have qualified for SEALs.

Wouldn't have considered being good enough for a woman like Kate.

She was...*everything* to him.

And he loved her enough, that while he'd ask her to marry him—he selfishly wanted a slice of joy in his life—he always knew he could only have her in his life but for so long.

Someday, she'd wake up and be over him.

He'd hate every damned minute of his life after, but he'd always planned to graciously let her go.

He wanted her to be happy.

After the blast concussion, he'd begged her for a divorce.

After she got pregnant, he'd insisted on it.

Kate was cement. He couldn't budge her. Couldn't make her see reason—that he was a broken man with nothing to offer anyone. Zero.

And in the end, it was Kate who found the doctor for him who was as tenacious as she was. Dr. Carlon had gotten him into different FDA trials, and damned if they weren't able to fix him.

And now, for the first time, Reaper saw the potential that Kate was right, that they had a forever future together.

Saw that he could keep the vow he hadn't believed in when he'd said it, "Until death do us part."

Had he endangered all of that?

32

Kate

Saturday Afternoon

"Just watching you walk into the room, Kate, I sense some tension." Their psychiatrist waited while Reaper and Kate took a seat on the sofa. Avril was an Iniquus approved mental health provider who maintained clearance credentials to work with people associated with the government, especially the CIA, DIA, FBI…those who need to process through their emotions centered around things that they did and things they failed to do on the job.

For example, they might need to talk to someone about how a botched assignment ended up killing an innocent child. While the agency might clear them of any misconduct, that didn't mean that the operator could emotionally separate from the outcome.

In the old days, these men and women were basically told to stick it in a mental file cabinet and keep on keeping on. It wasn't a great game plan. Those people often broke. Some suicided, some lost their humanity, their empathy, became violent trying to get control of the voices in their head telling them that they'd done monstrous things for their country and therefore they were monsters.

The problem with the monstrous self-talk was that the brain was malleable.

Through the stories that Ryan told her, Kate had realized that being out in the field, undercover, could break a person. Make them antithetical to what they had once been. It could turn the kindest of people into devils.

The plasticity of the brain was amazing. Just look how far Reaper had come in his journey back from brain trauma and PTSD.

But he was also a human being.

And humans needed help, from time to time, an outsider who could be an interventionist. And that took someone like Avril.

In the Hamiltons' case, they were here as part of Reaper's Iniquus contract. Reaper had his own team bringing him along the spectrum of physical and mental health. But Iniquus was wise enough to know that operators could get lost in the weeds of their job. They faced evil on a day-to-day basis. So those who worked in the field had to attend monthly assessments, and take regular R & R.

The Hamiltons, on the other hand, had been through familial trauma and Iniquus needed to make sure that their home life was solid. Iniquus was all about family.

Reaper sat in the middle of his cushion, on the brown leather love seat, pulling his leg over his knee to the classic 4-shape that Lynx said men often used as a body signal of the barricade, "I'll only let you so far in. I'll only expose so much."

As usual, though, Reaper's leg barricaded Avril and opened toward Kate. He wasn't keeping Kate out. It was almost as if he were closing the circle. "It's us against them, sweetheart."

Typically, Kate accentuated the intimacy of that circle by

crossing her leg in the opposite direction, their dangling feet coming close to touching. Sometimes, her hand would rest on his knee.

After Lynx had pointed it out to Kate and explained the significance, that seating configuration had been encouraging while they worked through the depth of emotional pain they'd experienced as a couple. From the time Reaper was knocked unconscious by the blast concussion in the Middle East, and was subsequently released from his military contract, up until the birth of their son, Zack, there was a lot of hurt there, Kate would readily admit it.

Today was very different.

Kate pulled a leg up under her hip, forming her own physical barrier between the two. She leaned her elbow onto the couch's armrest, thus moving her as far as she could physically move away from Reaper.

"What's on your mind, Kate?" Avril asked.

Kate glanced briefly at Reaper then pinched her lips with a little shake of her head.

"We missed a session because you were up in Boston. How did that trip go?"

"Good."

"And when you came home…"

"I went back to my daily routine."

"All right." Avril turned her attention to Ryan. "How's your assignment going?"

"I'll be glad when it's done."

She clicked her pen, ready to write. "Why?"

"It's close protection, as I told you."

"Right."

"I don't love that I'm working these long hours. It takes me away from the family."

"Iniquus is usually family-first," Avril said.

"Typically, they'd use an operator without a family for this. But it's short-term. It has to be a K9 handler."

"Ryan volunteered," Kate threw in.

Avril let her gaze settle on Kate for a moment.

"I *accepted* the assignment," Ryan clarified, turning to face his wife. "I didn't volunteer. You weren't supposed to be home for most of this." He turned his focus to Avril. "I'm finishing up my time with Strike Force. I'll be with Cerberus when this wraps up. I won't have to worry too much about long hours after this."

"But you accepted this assignment because..."

"I'm supposed to know what the operators need in terms of K9 training. This is an opportunity to see that firsthand." His gaze shifted to Kate who was looking straight forward and scowling. "It's more than I thought it would be," he finished.

"In terms of time?"

"Yes. They hired Strike Force specifically. hey wanted a K9 team with him when the client is out of the hotel. He's out of the hotel a lot."

"How do the dogs do on those long days?" Avril asked

"Max's been chill. It's not a demanding stint. Just long."

"On the topic of those long days then, how is this impacting you, Kate?"

Kate shrugged.

"Kate?" Ryan asked.

Kate skated her hands down her thighs. Self-soothing. Wet palms. She should say this out loud. She should confront her inner demons. "The time away is fine. It's fear, to be honest."

"That I'll screw up my head again?" Ryan asked. "I'm standing around watching a guy talk on the phone and eat. It's boring work."

Kate shook her head.

"This is obviously a difficult subject for you. Can you give your fear a name?" Avril asked.

Kate swallowed. This was either going to break her marriage or she was going to come off as petty and silly. If she let it fester, she'd keep banging around the kitchen and snarling at her Ryan. Either way, it was going to be a problem. Might as well be honest. Brave. Might as well face this head on. "Cyn."

"Sin…so this is a religious issue?" Avril asked.

"No." Reaper's voice was gruff. "There's a woman named Cyn, short for Cynthia. She was in a car accident while Kate was in Boston. I was first on scene."

"And now she's *always* on the scene," Kate said through clenched teeth.

"I'm listening." Avril let the pen rest on her pad of paper.

"It was Thursday, we went for a walk by the skating rink," Ryan started.

"Zack loves to watch the skaters." Kate focused on Avril's bright yellow legal pad where Avril wrote in shorthand so most people wouldn't be able to read her notations.

"Cyn was skating there with a friend," Ryan said. "She came over to give me a hug and say thank you."

"She only saw you the day of the accident, or were you in contact, to check in on her?" Avril asked.

"I saw her at the accident. She was trapped but didn't seem to have any major injuries. I just put it in my rearview. She recognized me and skated over."

"Mmph." Kate crossed her arms tightly over her chest.

"That was a problematic show of gratitude, Kate?"

"She is *always* showing up. Everywhere. There isn't a day that goes by that Ryan doesn't see her multiple times in multiple locations."

"And I tell you every single time. I don't want to hide anything from you, Kate. I can't help that our paths cross the way they do."

"I think I need more context." Avril turned her gaze on Reaper.

"Show her the pictures, Ryan." Kate glowered.

Ryan paused at the fierce lines that turned Kate's soft features to stone.

The therapist sat still, observing this interaction.

Kate tugged her attention away from Ryan and focused on Avril. "I opened Ryan's phone to take a picture of Zack. He was standing up and looking determined. I thought he might want to take a first step, so I grabbed a phone."

In her peripheral vision, Kate saw Ryan's face flush pink.

"Zack didn't take a step. He fell to the floor and crawled to his toy. But I took a picture, then realized it was Ryan's work phone. Our phones are the same model, and I have access with the code I use to open my own phone. Iniquus allows my accessing certain parts of the phone in case of an emergency. Though, Ryan's vigilant about keeping anything personal separate from his work."

"Yes, that's quite common among my clients who are in similar jobs. It's to protect their loved ones."

"I get that." Kate closed her eyes and kept them closed. "Realizing that I had made a mistake and taken photos of Zack on Ryan's work phone, I went to delete them. And there they were, Cyn pictures."

"Not nudes," Ryan said right away. "Work photos."

"I'm not sure I'm following along at this point. Can you orient me?"

"When did you do that, Kate?" Ryan asked.

"Yesterday."

"And you didn't ask me? You didn't bring it up? What, did you think that you'd just hold your cards close to the vest and then spring this on me? A gotchya moment in front of the one person you could bring this up in front of? What's the purpose of the delay, Kate?"

"Hey. Hey. Hey," Avril stopped him. "I hear your words. I understand from your tone that you're upset. I would like to have some context, so I can help you navigate this very important conversation."

Ryan put both feet on the ground, then leaned forward, resting his forearms on his thighs. "I go for a jog, Cyn's there. Already sweaty, coming in from a different path. I'm the one who shows up in a space Cyn was already using."

"She was a row ahead of Ryan and his client at the theater. She was at the table next to the clients at the restaurant. She was browsing the art gallery, and there she was contemplating a canvas. She was having a drink at the bar. She is *everywhere* Ryan is."

"But not just when you're with your client, right?" Avril asked.

"Recently, I'm either with my client or with my family. Otherwise, I'm driving. I'm not in public on my own."

"Do you think she's shadowing your client?"

"If she's a spy she is terrible at her job. It's almost like…" Ryan turned his head and looked out the window.

"I'd like you to finish that thought."

Ryan turned to Avril. "It's almost like she wants me to see her. Wants… I don't know what the want would be." He leaned forward. "There is no get with me. I'm dedicated to my wife and child. I'm finishing up my time with Strike Force, then I'll be hanging out with dogs all day. I'm a simple man. There's no—there's nothing that would make sense."

"Kate, do you have a theory?"

She pursed her lips, she exhaled vitriol "She's after my husband."

Ryan threw his head back and laughed.

Kate sat like a stone.

"Stalking?" Avril asked.

"Possibly? Maybe. When I was looking through the photos, I was remembering back to a psych class I took in undergrad about proximity studies. Granted, it was a very long time ago." She rubbed her hands over her cheeks, leaving them there over her eyes. "But that would be crazy train. I mean, could that work?"

Ryan leaned forward. His brows knit.

Avril tapped her pen on her pad. "A theory was put forth a theory around 1950 that postulated that proximity to someone—be that physical, like what you're describing in how Cyn shows up where you do, or whether it's psychological, like when you were thrust into the savior role at the car accident—increases a person's attraction. Is that what you're referring to, Kate?"

"Yes."

Ryan shook his head. "I don't find her attractive. She's a burr under my saddle."

"It's literally a numbers game. You see someone who is say medium attractiveness to your tastes. To use a hideous idea, let's consider him a five on the attractiveness scale. I'm not just talking about physical appearance. This includes personality too. As in, 'he was a five, but he was so gentle and kind, his smile so genuine that soon I saw him as an eight or nine, and I decided to accept his invitation to dinner.'"

"I'm following." Ryan sent a quick glance toward Kate then settled his gaze on Avril.

"Now you see them all the time when you go get your mail out of the mailbox. Over time, that person becomes more attractive to you."

"That works or it's a 1950s theory?"

"Yes, it works. Research has proven that proximity does increase friendships and even lifelong partnerships."

"*Marriages*," Kate said.

"Yes, in the last decade another researcher added to that body of work. First, increased exposure isn't all good for a relationship.

If Ryan had an opinion of Cyn then that preexisting opinion would solidify."

"You had a good opinion of her didn't you, Ryan?" Kate's voice was accusatory. "She was a damsel in distress. You were the knight in shining armor. You love that, riding to the rescue is 99% of your DNA."

"I—" Ryan shook his head. "I saw a person who might well freeze to death. Are you suggesting I should have called it in to 9-1-1 and just driven on by?"

"You couldn't," Kate said through gritted teeth. "It would be like asking a fish to climb a tree."

"Are you angry that he stopped and rendered aid, Kate?"

"No!" she yelled as she crossed her arms tightly over her chest.

Avril observed her for a long moment. "This is affecting you deeply. I've never seen you exhibit these emotions before—please, don't censor yourself because I said that. I'm validating that this is an emotional subject."

Kate tapped an angry foot on the floor. "Keep going with Schneider. I want to know what he concluded."

"Okay…so if someone didn't have a preexisting emotion around someone, the more they saw them the more positive feelings they develop."

"Ha!"

"I *don't* have positive feelings about her, Kate. I just don't. I took the pictures—and had you asked me I would have explained—"

"Stop with that tone. I'm not going to be placated."

"Fine, be pissed then. I took the pictures to take back to my team. I'm on close protection duty, and I was worried that she was tracking my client through me."

"And?"

"And we can't find any evidence that's the case. We also haven't found any evidence it's *not* the case."

"You save the woman when she wrapped herself around a tree, and what? And it was really some movie cliché where the universe keeps tossing her into your path all of a sudden?"

"Ryan." Avril leaned forward. "I don't know anything about your client, and I'm not on the team to figure that all out. But I do want you to hear about what Schneider et al discovered in their research. It may have some bearing on how your team wants to proceed." She paused and when no one offered a complaint, she continued. "When someone sees the same person over and over, they feel like they might have similarities that either do or do not exist."

Kate leaned forward. "We shop at the same store, we eat at the same restaurants, we jog in the same park, we have a lot in common."

"That's right. And that's reassuring to people. Makes them feel comfortable, even feel warmly toward someone."

Kate thrust back against the cushion. "They might even develop an attraction."

"Woah, Kate. Hell no. I don't know how many times you're gonna need to hear it, so I'll just keep hammering until I drive it home. I am *not* attracted to that woman."

Kate twisted away from Ryan.

"I love *you*, Kate. I *love* you." When she didn't turn back toward him, Ryan addressed Avril, "This doesn't seem to be attached to my client. It is freaky, admittedly. I brought it to my commander. We did a deep dive on her. There's really very little to know. Nothing that we can turn over of interest. We tracked her for a few days. It's cost-prohibitive on this particular case to keep her in our scope. She just seems to be going on with her day. But her day and my day and my client's day seem to overlap."

"Ryan tells you every time he sees Cyn?" Avril asked.

"Yes." The s hissed out between clenched teeth.

"Do you think he's having an affair?"

Kate sat on that for a moment. An answer didn't immediately form. Did she think that Ryan was having an affair—even if it were an emotional affair with this woman? If he were he wouldn't have brought it to his team to investigate. Iniquus was a family first organization. They would find breaking an oath to a wife to be intolerable. If you could break faith within that relationship, you could break faith in *any* relationship. Loyalty and honor were paramount. Iniquus would not abide a cheat. And certainly, wouldn't protect the wrong doer.

"Do you think she's stalking Ryan?"

"I don't know. Maybe? But like Ryan said. She's at the restaurant finishing her meal when they go in and are seated. If she's stalking, she'd have to be high-tech about it. And she'd have to be determined. It doesn't make sense to me. But my inner danger warning system is on high alert."

"Kate, I'm thinking of your own recent past. You were targeted. You and your unborn baby were in life-threatening circumstances from three different killers." Avril tipped her head. "You understand that even one incident can be life-altering. Most people have never had a similar experience, even once, let alone three times. Has it occurred to you that you too might be suffering from PTSD?"

"She has nightmares," Ryan said. "They seem to have gotten worse since she's been home from Boston."

"Kate?" Avril lifted her brow—an invitation for Kate to share.

Kate shrugged. "How would one know?"

Ryan reached over and captured her hand in his. It felt warm and the pressure was reassuring. Was he gaslighting her? Was he pretending about their relationship so he could have his cake and eat it, too? The image that came up with that thought made her blush hard. Poor choice of idioms.

"How would one know…?" Avril and her darned open-ended phrases.

"PTSD or women's intuition?"

"They can indeed feel like the same thing. Mainly because they have the same physical response. Fight or flight. Aversion to pain. Adrenaline and cortisol. All of it. This is especially true when you're right in the middle of a series of events."

Kate was looking at the potted plant, disengaged.

"Okay."

"They're right. But I haven't seen anything, my team hasn't come up with anything. And the guy is just unpleasant to be around."

"He's unpleasant, and you aren't able to give the client what they need. As I remember it, you're hoping to find drugs on the man."

"Right."

"Kate, I sense a bit of aggression in your eyes as Reaper says that. Does this case impact you as an individual or you as a couple?"

Kate looked toward the window.

"I take that as a yes. Is it the situation that's difficult or putting your feelings into words?"

Kate opened her mouth and exhaled.

"If you could give this situation one word, what would it be?"

"Infidelity," Kate said, then opened her eyes wide as if she were surprised as hell that it had popped out.

"Whose infidelity?" Avril asked.

Kate gave a tight shake to her head.

"Mine?" Ryan swiveled to full body face her. He was either an excellent actor or he was genuinely shocked and hurt for her to say that.

Kate didn't turn toward him. She did lift the arm that was

closest to him and rubbed the back of her neck—this was both a pain in her neck and she was putting up another limb barrier.

"Kate?" Avril prompted.

"Okay let me ask you this, Ryan," Avril said slowly. "Have you had any physical contact with Cyn? Anything that could be construed or misconstrued as intimate?"

"Yes, during her accident, when she was semi-conscious, panicked at being trapped. I held her hand while we waited. The responders let me be the person who stayed with her under the canvas blanket since I had developed a rapport. Then she was loaded in the ambulance, and I moved on with my day."

"You didn't mention the accident to me in our one on one when Kate was traveling."

"No. It didn't register as important to bring up."

"Did you bring it up with Kate?"

"Yes. I told her. I tell her everything I can about my day."

"Our time is up for today," Avril said with a glance at the wall clock. "Let's talk about this again next week. Kate, final words?"

"I am willing to fight like a demon for my marriage if it's against any of my vows. Poverty? Fine. Sickness. I'm there. But infidelity?" She turned and looked Ryan directly in the eye. "You can pack your damn bags and hit the road. There is no coming back from that kind of cruelty. Done. Do you hear me? *Done*."

33

Cyn

Saturday Afternoon

"What did she say, this Kate woman? 'Done?'" Borka threw his head back and laughed. "And his response?"

"Was stunned. Reaper had no idea what to say to her. I think I've touched a marriage nerve."

"This is probably true. Now, as you requested, I tell you that the 'Baker's' extraction from the neighborhood will happen tonight. However, Julep was moved to her new apartment as soon as the Hamiltons got home from their session. The senator wishes to come visit and check on her tonight. He will probably be asking her to let him put off delivering the message on tomorrow's Sunday news show. I have placed a protector in her home, a strong arm to stand in the shadows, so the senator has a better picture for what his future will look like."

"She'll have to look much different than she did as a babysitter. She looked like an unmade bed."

"She is newly pregnant. Sick and tired." Borka shrugged.

"What an aphrodisiac for the senator. But I guess now that she's knocked up, it doesn't matter how she looks anymore."

"Not at all." He held out a hand to indicate the chair in front of him. "I wish to speak with you about your plans."

"Yes. Everything is going very well."

Borka tipped his head back and forth. "Kate is a smart girl, as you said. Yes, she is weighing the possibility of infidelity. Science teacher, yes?"

"Yes."

"Then she will want facts. Proof."

"I have a plan to push her buttons with proof."

"How is this?"

"I have lots of photos from Reaper's time with Harlow. I'm using an Omega digital artist to put Reaper and me into intimate moments together." She stopped to smile. "Bed. Shower. Couch. Kitchen."

"To what end?"

"She is a stabilizing force. If I cut her from his life, along with the baby, he'll be vulnerable. I think of his brain like making mashed potatoes. Every time I press the masher into the pot, the more the contents become purée."

"This is an odd analogy from you. Domestic. This is not your style."

Cyn exhaled a laugh.

"So what do you do with these photographs you're developing? She will confront him. She will pick them apart. I'm assuming the artist is putting Reaper's head on another body. Naked body."

"Yes."

"She knows her husband's body."

"Granted." Cyn gave a nod. "Low lights. Me as the main character, the focal point. His face visible. And, get this,

Omega has an app that I've already applied to Kate's phone."

"When was this?"

"When Julep was babysitting."

"What does this app do?"

"It allows me to send a message or an attachment from any phone number in her contacts list. She'll recognize the name and open the text. Here's the genius part. I can put a timer on the attachment. As soon as Kate swipes, the attachment opens as if it's a picture in the feed. I give her a moment to look at it, then the whole message disappears. So she swipes, there's a picture of hubby and me embracing in the park, or screwing in the shower. She's shocked and stares down, trying to get her heart-broken mind to take in the image, and then it disappears as if it was never there."

"There are many good applications for such a program."

"I agree."

"It is nowhere in the phone records?"

"I'm told no. It comes through the app not through the carrier." Cyn put her hands in the air. "I have no idea how that works. Nor do I care. Soon enough, early next week, they should be ready. When Reaper is out on his assignment guarding Harlow, Kate will start receiving her special messages."

"This is a difficult assignment that you've taken on in a time parameter that I find unworkable. When you explained the plan to me, I warned you about fast." When Cyn slid forward in her seat, Borka held up a hand. "I agree with you that you are working within time parameters that are outside of your control. I have seen from your reports and agree that Reaper's particular medical diagnosis gave us the potential in that we haven't found before. The right key, the right lock." He lifted his brows. "The wrong amount of time."

"Kate holds the key. He's devoted to her in a way that I

haven't seen by men I've known. I remove her, his brain is toast."

"I agree with this, too. However, she mentioned the science you are applying. This is a good ploy when you have time. You pushed too hard and showed your hand. As with any ploy, once you see the secret move, the brain goes right to the movement every time from that point on."

"Yes, sir. Now is the time to pivot."

"And do you have a next step?"

"Yes, I will weaponize Harlow."

"To what end?"

"I thought that I could do this clean and quiet. I'm afraid that my pivot will be loud and bloody."

"With Harlow? This is fine. He is disposable. And will you leave the wife and the baby in play?"

"I'll think it through."

"Carefully. If the man is pushed too far, he may break in a way that is a lock instead of a key."

"Soldiers are used to death. They process it differently. And work is typically the place where they can retreat and feel a little bit normal."

"Yes, well. You will be very careful if you decide Kate is getting in the way it looks like an accident. Clean."

"Yes, sir. That I can do. I've already laid the groundwork. It's just a matter of pressing a button when the time comes."

THERE WAS something about Borka's behavior that wasn't sitting right with Cyn.

Yes, Julep had seen the senator and made a desperate and well-timed move to gain control over him as a gift to The Family.

Yes, Julep had been offered as a piece to play a role in Cyn's game, and Cyn should probably feel grateful.

Yes, Julep had set a precedent that Nia had followed, when she too found a dupe and got knocked up with her own baby as a control mechanism.

And yes, a bird in hand was better than two in the bush. Or in this case, two pregnancies in hand were better than anything that was happening in Cyn's bush. Cyn chuckled at how that phrase had turned out to mean something quite different than she'd intended. There wasn't, and hadn't in a long time, been anything happening in Cyn's "bush." There was, however, something very important going on with Cyn's chaos efforts.

Where these girls were putting long-term pressures in place that would serve The Family, Cyn was more about the violence of action, rather than subtlety. This wasn't The Family's normal route, though. A few years ago, they too had been pushed for tight time operation. There was a major vote coming up in the Senate and Borka needed to apply pressure to make it fail. That, or Russian oil would suffer. The Family believed they could hand this win to the Russian government and improve and strengthen the alliance.

Borka had his people attack a school to gain control over a senator, now retired. Borka failed. And look at that catastrophe with Delta Force when Strike Force helped take out his cell of goons, all because Borka didn't listen to Cyn's good counsel on how to manage the problem.

He was such a proud man; Borka probably believed that if he couldn't thwart Strike Force, no one could.

No, that didn't feel right, especially since Iniquus was only collateral damage. This job was about destroying the CIA.

What was it about Borka that made her feel like she was dangling over a precipice?

Why would he not be cheering her on?

Cyn scoffed as she walked through the frigid night to her car.

Borka's birds in hand theory was weak tea.

34

Cyn

SATURDAY NIGHT

REAPER, just why in the hell was he taking up so much thinking space?

If it was about her mission, getting through the Iniquus doors, that would be fine.

But this wasn't.

She'd gone at it hard in the gym. When lifting the heavy-weights wasn't doing it for her, Cyn had jumped on a treadmill and taken off like a bat out of hell. She cranked the dial so high, her feet flying. An hour. Ten miles. That earned her a round of applause from a handful of old-geezer types who were following doctors' orders, trying to get their heart rates up to get their blood pressure down, along with those pesky cholesterol numbers.

She'd swiped at her face, mottled red from exertion, as she lifted her other hand in recognition of the attention. She wanted out of there before one of them sidled up and asked her for a drink.

Reaper. It was eating her up inside.

It was like…it was like termites all up in her house. Nope, you can't see them from the outside. Everything looked fine. Pretty. In good shape.

She pressed her butt against the wall of the elevator as it climbed to the twentieth floor and her room. All she could think about was peeling away her sweat-soaked clothes. Getting in some water.

Once she got there, Cyn treated herself like she had come down with a fever and needed to be gentled back to health, she sobbed as she let the water run.

She was robbed of her future when they killed her twin.

There was no life for her beyond retribution.

Before Tom was left dead in the street for the rats to gnaw at his corpse, Cyn had anticipated a time when she'd be a wife, like Kate. A mother to someone like Zack. A house. A dog. Stress over the water bill and anger at the neighbor kids for trampling her flowers.

A husband who was big and brawny, smart and capable, who would hold her in bed at night.

The damned CIA covering for Uncle Sam meant Tom's corpse lay in the streets for the dogs to piss on.

Cyn could never clear herself of the images.

Gasping in a deep breath, Cyn plunged her head under the water and screamed as long and as loud as she could. Bursting through the surface, she panted more oxygen into her system then submerged again. And again. Screaming. Then, Cyn leaned her torso over the lip of the bath, sobbing and dry heaving until she was spent.

She lay there in a stupor, letting the water turn cold, then pulled the drain plug, and stepped out.

The light from the little entryway shined into the bathroom.

Cyn stared at her naked body in the mirror.

Yeah, she was eaten up inside. She rubbed a hand over her belly, lifted her breasts, watched her damp hair fall across her cheeks. She looked like a hag.

Alone in a hotel room, cold and impersonal.

Not wanting to stare at her own walls. She'd been living out of hotels for a while now.

She didn't want her own stupid furniture. Her family albums and the pictures on the wall.

She stilled and listened to Tom's ghost moaning with the wind that bent the trees in tonight's storm.

Blinking at her image in the mirror, Cyn reminded herself that not everyone lived with a haunted soul.

She gasped and groaned as she pulled on a pair of sleep shorts and t-shirt.

Kate got the white picket life with Reaper and Zack while Cyn had nothing and no one.

Of course, Cyn had found that alone was easier, usually. No one to ask her *What's wrong?*

"I'm eaten up with grief. I can feel the poison of it in my veins. I can smell it when I sweat, like a decaying body lying out in the summer's heat, attracting flies and disgust."

Nope, not everyone was terrified to go to bed at night where the nightmares were woven into the fibers of their sheets.

Combing the tangles from her hair, Cyn wound the wet strands into a braid that she held together with an elastic band. She wondered what technique they'd used to fix Reaper's brain. He'd seen some shit for sure.

At one point in her life, when she was the do-gooder trying to protect the homeland, Cyn had lived in a single-wide trailer in a base camp in Afghanistan. She'd done the intel work, forged the relationships, banged some heads, got what was needed. Her work was life or death.

It was fate wasn't it that she was aiming her intentions at Reaper Hamilton?

At one point, she, Cynthia Demitrova, was also called Reaper, pointing her bony finger and sending the enemy to hell. She'd always liked that image of herself. When she arrived at the base, she'd simply decided to introduce herself that way. "Hi, I'm Reaper Demitrovoa." No one blinked at the nickname.

Back in the day, based on Cyn's intelligence, those Deltas, the SEALs, the Rangers, they'd drag on their battle rattle and run out into the night. *She* was the angel of death. Special ops were *her* tools of destruction. If she did a good job, it was the enemy who moved on to the next world. If her intel was bad, it was American boots that took the brunt.

She always tried her best.

Always.

Then the video showed up in her inbox.

Now, she'd be in pain forever, while her fellow spooks moved on.

All the special forces folks that left the military to sign their lucrative contracts with Iniquus, they moved on.

How did they do it?

Maybe once Reaper was hers, he'd tell her the secret to life after death. Maybe he could help her get her brain fixed, too.

Cyn blinked at the wall. Did she just think "once Reaper was hers?"

She slid her laptop over and pulled up her connections to the Hamilton house. She wondered if they were sitting around the kitchen table after Reaper's long day dealing with his family. Were they having a beer and playing a hand of cards to unwind? Was Reaper listening to wifey complain about shitty diapers and not enough sleep? The banality of the laundry piles and what do you want for dinners this week? The "I'm making a shopping list what do you want me to add?" triviality?

"Let's see how you two are doing after your little counselor's office confrontation. Bedlam in the bungalow?" Yeah, it was a shotgun-styled house, but Cyn liked the alliteration.

A quick scroll through the different camera feeds, and Cyn came upon Kate chopping vegetables. Baby in the highchair. No sign of Reaper.

Cyn checked the outdoor feeds and found Reaper's Iniquus vehicle out front. The one he was driving that day, anyway.

Cyn had not attached any kind of tracking device on Reaper's vehicles—it would surely expose her hand.

From Omega intelligence on Iniquus, Cyn had discovered the force operators handed in their car every day and picked up a different one from the pool. Cyn assumed the work bees in the Iniquus garage would run a search on the car for any tracking apparatus, get it cleaned, make sure everything was top-notch under the hood in case the operator was zipping through traffic trying to save the day.

Turning her feed to the backyard camera, she found Reaper taking out the trash. *How domestic*. Tracking him back through the kitchen door, he was already at the sink washing his hands when Cyn switched to the kitchen camera.

With Reaper directly behind her, Kate stuck out her butt and rubbed it against Reaper's. Cyn read that as mollifying. An olive branch.

Cyn needed discord from Kate. What the heck was this woman doing? "Have some damned respect for yourself, Kate. You think your husband is screwing around on you and you're placating him?" Cyn grumbled toward her computer. "Tell him to pack a bag and get the hell out!"

Reaper dried his hands then turned to wrap his arms around

Kate as she continued to chop. He bent and kissed her hair. "That smells good."

"Casserole. Simple." She stilled her knife while she leaned back into Reaper's arms and closed her eyes.

"Hey," he dropped a kiss onto her hair, "today was emotional."

"Mmm."

"I'm feeling unsettled. After Little Guy goes to bed, I think we should talk this through. Maybe we can come to a shared understanding."

Kate said nothing, just opened her eyes and reached forward to start chopping again.

How very adult of them. The amount of time they'd spent in therapy was showing. This was all phrased in those stupid psychological phrasing with "I" statements.

Here's an "I" statement. 'I want you to go to hell, Kate, you wimpy little shit.' And luckily, I have the skills and equipment to make it happen.

Cyn continued to watch until Kate slid the casserole into the oven and put a salad in the fridge. "Thirty minutes," she told Reaper as he set the table.

"Thank you."

She plucked Zack from his highchair, then Kate moved into his arms. "I love you." There was the slightest, teeniest, tiniest question in her inflection. But it was there.

Cyn smiled. Her flash photos would grow that question mark in Kate's mind, Cyn felt sure.

"This is a bump in the road." Reaper brushed a strand of hair from Kate's face. "We'll figure it out."

Kate came up on her toes to receive his kiss. She wrapped her arms around him and got a second one. Then another. With the baby held to the side on her hip, Reaper deepened the kiss.

Yeah, Cyn thought, that was going to turn into sex later.

Kate took a baby bottle from the microwave and shook it.

Cyn had to flip through her cameras as she followed the couple up the stairs.

In the hall, outside of Zack's nursery, Kate stopped. "After I get Little Guy down, I'm going to take a shower," she said. "I need to clean this day away, these feelings."

Reaper pressed his shoulder into the wall. "And me? Are you trying to clean me away too?"

"I'm not going to let that woman do that to us. But, if you'd like," and she swayed her hips, "you can come shower with me."

"Yeah, I like." He grinned as Kate pushed through the door.

Mr. and Mrs. Clean, huh?

Cyn looked over to her vibrator, washed and charging on her side table. She thought the maids had probably been disgusted, but meh, what did Cyn care about the help's comfort?

Cyn toggled her camera to the master bath.

Some folks felt that putting surveillance in bedrooms and bathrooms was against the rules. For some odd reason, they thought that their marks should have privacy while they took a crap or got dressed in their rooms. Puritans. Cyn thought those were the two rooms that most revealed a person. They *thought* they were all alone and could do what they wanted outside of societal niceties. Vulnerabilities were exposed by the products in their medicine cabinet and in their personal care drawers. What was this person trying to compensate for with their creams and salves? If a guy was going to spill hundreds of dollars on a product to keep his hair in his head, that was information. So was a bottle of little blue dick plumping pills.

It wasn't unusual for combat veterans to experience some level of sexual dysfunction.

Interesting that after his injuries, Reaper didn't have some on hand. And from their sexual gymnastics on the couch the other day, he definitely didn't need them.

But had they been there when Cyn did her intelligence sweep, that would have been another little bit of information to exploit.

It seemed the Hamiltons used sex to confirm their bond. What if Cyn had replaced Reaper's hard-on pills with a placebo? Cyn chuckled. "Look, Kate, even with the little helpers, I can't get it up for you." Ego slap for sure. Yeah, too bad his cock was rock solid.

"Well, Mr. Domestic, I need a drink." Cyn pushed her laptop to the side. "Intermission!" she called.

35

Cyn

Saturday Night

Cyn moved to her overnight bag and dragged out the bottle of vodka. She considered walking to the end of the hall and the vending machines for a soda and a bucket of ice.

Meh. Too far. Too much trouble to get dressed.

She took a swig from the bottle and came up coughing.

Yeah, she wanted to drown the voices in her head, but she wasn't going to do it like a back alley drunk.

Not bothering with a bra or panties, Cyn yanked a sweatshirt over her head. Tucking her key card in her pocket. She found a roll of quarters that she kept in her luggage for just this reason. Wrapping her hand around them, she slid into her shower shoes and walked out the door.

Her thighs were still quivering from her sprint. The hall looked long and…empty. It was all barren and cold. It was industrial and indifferent. Cyn slogged her way toward the snack room, past rooms with low level conversations, and humming televisions.

The whir and the ka-chunk-chunk of the ice machine jangled her nerves—she hated that sound. She'd been in a hotel in Turkey with that clatter and bang going on all night the night she'd gotten the news about Tom.

Ghosts.

Cyn's nostrils expanded and quivered. She felt the devil in her head yelling "Coward!" at her.

As she moved past the last room, the door snicked open.

A monster of a man stood there with a crisp dollar bill pinched between his fingers. "Hey there."

She glanced over her shoulder at the guy. She carefully opened the top of her quarters roll and pulled out the six coins she'd need for her soda. Then she folded the paper down tight. She gripped that in her right hand as she reached out and pressed A12. The soda tumbled to the slot below.

"I said, hey there."

"I heard you." Angling her butt away from him, she bent and pressed the flap to retrieve her can.

"That's not friendly."

She stood slowly. Her blood boiling. A sneer on her lips she squared off with him. "We aren't friends."

The universe was good to her.

There were a few things that could assuage the monster that hissed inside of her.

Sometimes sex could do it.

Sometimes exercise.

Violence *always* worked.

The more damage she could inflict, the better she felt.

Cyn knew this guy's type.

She'd slapped his ego in the face, and he'd want payback, and all she could think was that a punch in the jaw might just feel good. It would give her a legitimate reason to feel pain.

Of course, she'd never let someone actually punch her.

Her last sentence pressed the guy's throttle.

The man puffed up. "Someone needs to teach you some manners."

"And just who's gonna do that?" She pushed. "You?" She threw her head back and laughed. It was a wicked dangerous laugh that should have made this guy fear the Reaper that she was. Apparently, he didn't have a lot of self-preservation instincts, didn't see that she was wearing a black cloak and carried a scythe in her hand.

The man roared forward, his shoulder down at her waist, he grabbed her behind the knees and folded her over his shoulder.

Cyn bet that he expected her to fight, to kick and scream. Punch him in the back.

Nah, she wasn't going to waste her energy.

He was actually helping her out.

She waited for him to take her back to his room.

After he kicked the door shut, he flung her onto the bed.

No crying. No begging. No cowering. The guy looked at her confused as she just lay there, quarters in one hand, her soda in the other.

Yeah, real confused.

"You've done this before, attacked a woman," Cyn said conversationally.

He undid his belt.

"You were looking for someone to grab. You heard me in the hallway and thought, 'dinner time!'"

"Shut up." He popped his button.

Cyn rolled over and propped her head up on her bent arm. "How many?"

"Shut up!" The zipper came down.

"How many women have you dragged into your hotel rooms to rape? What do you do with them afterward?"

"I said shut up!" He raised his hand to hit her. Cyn rolled out of his way and was back on her feet. "Strike one." She laughed. "But you don't play baseball. Football, right? I don't know any football phrases. Sorry, but it's a stupid sport." She lifted a finger from her soda and tapped her temple. "Too much brain damage. Weakens the gray matter."

He swung again. Missed again.

Cyn was unaffected by the hate she read in the man's eyes. If only he knew about her pact with the devil. Her soul had been sold so long ago. She didn't fear death except that it would stop her from her goals. Destruction. Pain. Yeah, pain should be a shared experience. The devil would keep her alive to do his work. "I bet you already cased the hallway. I bet there are no cameras. You wouldn't have been that brazen if there were cameras. Thing is, if there are no cameras to protect little old me from the big bad wolf." She fluttered her eyelashes at him. "Then there are also no cameras to save the big bad wolf from me."

His snarl turned into laughter. He closed his damned eyes and tipped his head back. She wanted to throat punch him, to dig her fingers in until her knuckles bent around his trachea as she crushed it. But that kind of death was a hard one to mask as accidental. She didn't need the cops moving up and down the hallway, knocking on doors, asking their questions.

Just how was she going to do it?

Different scenarios flashed through her mind. Once Cyn had set up a mark to make it look like he'd died of auto-erotic asphyxiation. A plastic bag over his head, a dick in his hand. She bet his family had trouble explaining how their son kicked the bucket. Oh, the shame of it all.

Cyn put her coins on the bed and moved to stand near the table.

She considered the terrace but rejected throwing him over the banister. There was an apartment house across the street from this side of the hotel and surely someone would be looking out.

Mores the pity.

The goon had watched her positioning with amusement. “Nowhere to run,” idiot cooed at her then lifted his hands like a cartoon evildoer wiggling his fingers.

Cyn put her hands behind her back to shake the soda can. She rolled her eyes at him as she pushed the chair between them with her foot.

“Shaking like a leaf. That’s right. Be afraid.”

In that moment, he must have realized the issue. What to do with the chair blocking her?

Pick it up and throw it on the bed? Nah.

Pick it up and put it on the table?

Pick it up and swing it behind him?

So so stupid. No matter his decision, he was either going to have to come at her from over the bed, put himself off balance with a kick, or he was going to have to pick up a cumbersome weight in his hands.

Either way…

“Let’s go.” Cyn’s voice was painted with boredom. “I’ve got a project I’m working on, and you’re distracting me from getting it done.”

He lifted a foot and put it down. Dumb oaf.

“Time’s ticking.” Cyn thought the soda was primed. “Do you need help? I’ll tell you what, why don’t you just pick up the chair and turn it sideways, then you can put one foot on the seat and step over and get me.”

He was so confused by her behavior that he looked back at the door like he might want to flee.

“No. No. None of that. You made your bed. Time to sleep in it,” Cyn said.

Brains were funny things. They stuttered when they were needed most. Cyn had thrown him off his game, interrupted the modus operandi. She confused the shit out of him. So he did what often happens to confused stuttering brains, he did the last thing that he heard.

The man actually picked up the chair and was turning it.

The idiot was making this too simple, taking away all her fun.

As soon as his foot hit the seat, Cyn popped the top of her soda and let the liquid shoot full blast right into his eyes with one hand. Her other hand dropped to his shoelace, sliding her fingers under the knot and grabbing the bow in a solid fist.

The natural inclination is to back away from acidic bubbles on the eyeballs.

Blinded, he tried to do just that. The scene got that much more confusing when Cyn jerked the laces, and his body went in two different directions.

Down he went—trapped by his size between the bed and the lowboy.

In that split second, Cyn went over the bed, dragged out the bottom drawer, lifted his head by the hair, and with her full jumping bodyweight, banged his temple into the corner.

The thud was stomach churning.

Now his eyes were a fixed stare as blood trickled from the impact.

Cyn sighed as she picked up the soda can and wiped her prints. She positioned the can near him.

Yup some cop was going to have to tell this ogre's mom that he died because his pop exploded, and he hit his head.

One less prick in the world.

Cyn got her roll of quarters and went back to the ice room where she bought another soda.

As she rounded back into the hall, a group of soccer kids came off the elevator hooting and cheering. She joined in with their group as they made their way up the carpeted hallway, and let herself back into her room, not even winded.

As Cyn poured herself a congratulatory drink, having just performed her societal duty as a vigilante, she remembered that she had wanted the drink for when the Hamiltons were screwing around in the shower.

She took a satisfying sip of her cocktail then tapped her computer back on.

Fighting always made Cyn horny.

Violence, she had found, was a superb aphrodisiac.

With Reaper's hands rubbing soap over Kate's body, Cyn reached for her vibrator.

That's right, big boy, show me your moves.

36

Cyn

SUNDAY MORNING

DRESSED IN A CONTOUR-CLINGING, teal, woolen wrap dress and brown boots, Cyn looked up at the sky. “Thank you, Mother Nature. Once again, you’re my ally.”

The snow mounded in patches in the shadowed spaces. But the air was unseasonably warm. The cloudless sky was a resplendent blue, and the scent of spring drifted with the light breeze.

Along the sidewalk, spring bulbs had pushed green ears out of the ground as if listening for the command, “It’s time! Come out and play!”

Cyn stood at the stoplight waiting for the little white walking man to flash into place, telling her she could cross.

She had chosen this particular church on purpose.

This was Strike Force territory, and her being here would put Reaper on high alert.

There, across from the park, was Grace Del Toro’s art gallery,

The Bartholomew Winslow Gallery. Grace was the Strike Force operations guy Deep Del Toro's wife.

Grace had walked out onto that portico when a sniper aimed between her eyes. Sadly, they weren't quick enough on the trigger. Deep tackled her. And the rest, as they say, was history. Very quickly after, according to the file Omega kept on the guy, Deep and Grace were married.

Deep and Grace were the reason that the Zoric family ended up imprisoned for trafficking East-European teens. The Zorics and the Prokhorovs had very similar game plans, but for the Prokhorov family it was the inverse, they took the American girls to Eurasia. There, nobody gave a damn about the young women's wellbeing. The Prokhorov plan was easier. But everybody needed to work their own game plan. Do the thing that got them closer to their own goals.

Cyn's game plan was for the Zorics to want their retribution enough that they'd happily give her the spyware that she needed for her own mission to succeed.

Stepping off the curb, she thought, See? Deep was just another example that the hero saving the delicate flower and then riding off into the sunset was a thing.

It was going to be *her* thing, Cyn had decided. Her prize for her impending success. Her and her little mush for brains would become a D.C. power couple for sure.

She'd now waited through two cycles of the light, and she'd need to move, or her odd behavior would catch other's attention. Harlow was supposed to be here. She traversed the street grinding her back teeth. Where was he?

Cyn stepped onto the sidewalk and turned when she heard, "Excuse me?" She lifted a bladed hand to protect her eyes from the sun.

Ah, he was coming from a different direction than the one

she'd advised. Harlow jogged toward her in his Sunday go to meeting suit.

"You know," when he reached her, he took a pause to dip his head and send her a smile, "I see you everywhere I go. If I didn't have security with me, I might even think you were stalking me."

Cyn looked toward Reaper then back to the man. She put her hand to her throat and took a step back.

"This feels like fate," Harlow said. He really did have a nice smile with just a touch of the devil in it. "Honestly, I'm not surprised at all that I ran into you today." He pointed back at the church. "I guess that's one more thing we have in common. A shared faith."

Cyn focused on Reaper and asked with her eyes whether she should mention that they knew each other.

Reaper was busy being hyper-soldiery, scanning the environs.

Harlow reached into his jacket, and Cyn brought her fists to her chest and squeezed her elbows tight against her ribs.

Yeah, that pulled Reaper's attention around right quick.

"So much so that I brought you something." From his inside pocket, he withdrew the small, wrapped package she'd orchestrated to be quietly delivered to him by his Omega chauffer. Between the three of them—Harlow, the chauffer, and her—Strike Force had no idea how Cyn was getting to each location first. Enemies hiding in plain sight. Cyn suppressed the bubble of glee that this was all coming together so beautifully.

Harlow didn't have bad acting skills, she thought as he handed the parcel out to her.

Cyn looked at the package dubiously. "For me?" She let her gaze drift over to Reaper asking, *should I?*

Reaper focused down on Max and gave a hand signal. Max's posture changed and his nose worked the air. When he looked at Reaper for his next command. Reaper scrubbed behind his ears.

With a small nod and a lick of her lips, Cyn accepted the

package and ripped off the paper. It was a book about Desdemona Piccard. Cyn's gaze flashed up. "I love her work. But how did you know?"

"I told you. I see you all the time." He chuckled. "You were admiring one of her works at the museum the other day."

"I was. You were there?" She extended the wrappings to Harlow's outstretched hand.

He balled it to toss basketball-style into the nearby trash bin.

"Unbelievable." She paused as their gazes caught. "You were paying attention. I'm not sure how I feel about that. It's…very disconcerting." Her voice trailed off as she feathered through the pages.

"Maybe you would be so kind as to accept an invitation to lunch? Have you ever been to the Bartholomew Winslow Gallery?"

"No." Cyn looked up. "I'm not familiar."

"They have a new piece by Piccard." He tapped the book. "I'd love to show it to you. We're right here, after all." He pointed to the gallery. You can't see it from here." He turned and pointed in the opposite direction. "There's a little café. They have a winter garden where they set out food for wild birds and other animals. It's always full of life, or so I read in the reviews. It seems a wonderful place to eat, especially on a beautiful day like today."

She looked back at Reaper.

"Do you two know each other?" Harlow asked, spinning to send a look toward Reaper to see if he might be competition. *Well played.*

"I think lunch would be nice, thank you," Cyn replied.

Harlow pivoted to stand beside her and offered Cyn his arm.

"It has been such a strange week," Cyn said. As they fell in step, she refrained from looking at Reaper. She was now aligning with Harlow.

Jealous, Reaper? She smiled to herself.

As they walked onto the park path, Reaper positioned himself just behind Harlow's right shoulder. Max paced along as a tight group. Of course, Reaper was supposed to be close enough to "personally protect," and he was trained to ignore the principal's conversations, but Cyn had to focus on every word out of her mouth.

His job, after all, was to report back. So he'd be listening, even if this seemed to be an impromptu date.

"I should properly introduce myself. I'm Charles Harlow. I'm in D.C. working on a project for ClearSight."

"I'm Cynthia Parker. ClearSight out of San Fransisco?"

"No, the new office, Atlanta. You've heard of us?"

"I've actually done some gig work for them. This is making me feel weird." Her mouth dropped and her gaze shot up and down the tree line, then over to Reaper with a question in her eye.

When he was passively stoic, Cyn focused back on Harlow. "Why do you have security?"

"ClearSight had some threats come in. They're taking them seriously and giving all of the executives close protection. No one would think to look for me in D.C. Personally, I think this is overkill. Ha! Probably the wrong choice of words."

"But why would anyone threaten you?" She stopped and stepped a little closer to Harlow as if she might need his protection.

"There was some illegality that was covered up by advisors. And we—you've stopped. Have you changed your mind about lunch?" He tipped his head.

Cyn started up the street, once again tucking her hand into the crook of Harlow's elbow.

A moment later, Harlow stepped forward and pulled open the door, holding it wide for Cyn. "Here we are."

Cyn sent him a smile as she passed him.

Harlow performed all of the niceties. "Two for lunch and if

you had an adjacent table for my security, I'd appreciate it." He turned to Cyn. "We're early for the brunch rush. Good timing, I think. After we eat, shall we cross the street to the Bartholomew Winslow Gallery and see the Piccard's painting?"

"I'd like that. Thank you."

He pulled her chair. He asked her what she'd enjoy and placed the order. He was convivial as a "date", well-practiced in his metro-styled manners. Suave without being oily.

And oddly, yes, very strangely, Cyn felt like she was being disloyal to Reaper.

As if she were cheating on him in front of his eyes.

Cyn had to work to keep herself from sending him furtive looks.

Harlow was a handsome man. Salt and pepper hair. Bright blue eyes, that might be contact lenses, Cyn couldn't tell. Impeccably dressed from Windsor knotted tie to Italian leather shoes. And he smelled good, too. The kind of cologne that might entice Cyn to curl into his arms, lay her head on his chest, and inhale deeply as she rested.

Under other circumstances, Cyn might have just given herself a little stress relief with a tumble to see what he was like.

But honestly, that would be fleeting, and she couldn't imagine that he could satisfy her desires. Reaper was more to Cyn's taste. She liked that he wasn't as polished and primped for polite society. He wouldn't be able to talk artists and vintage wines. He wouldn't have exotic locations in common with her like Harlow might.

She liked rough, angry sex. Sex with passion, pain, and ultimately satisfaction.

That wasn't the sex Reaper had with Kate. He was attentive and slow with Kate.

It was sweet and salty at the same time. Definitely not missionary and wet spots.

Yeah, rough and hard, both in body and spirit was what revved Cyn's motors.

But if her goal here was to ensnare Reaper. Harlow's line of conversation was too sophisticated, too removed from Reaper's sphere.

Reaper wasn't the kind of guy who lusted after an up-town girl, wanting punch above his weight with women. Just look at Kate. You couldn't get much more suburban housewifey than she was.

"Since you've seen me around enough that you brought me this book. I'm sure you figured out that we're staying at the same hotel." She stretched a hand out. "I saw you getting off the elevator. Maybe you were visiting someone?"

"I'm on the tenth floor."

"Did you hear about what happened on my floor, the twentieth?"

She could feel Reaper's antennae buzz to life.

"A guy died last night. I talked to the maid who found him this morning. He fell and hit his head on a drawer. That's why I was in church this morning."

"You knew him?" Harlow asked.

"No, I just. Ha! I was feeling superstitious. I thought I'd better go get some prayers in for safety's sake."

It was a split-second decision when Cyn put her hand on Harlow's. "Instead of the gallery, why don't you show me your room, and we can compare décor?"

Harlow held a finger in the air. "Check please." He wiped his mouth and put the napkin beside his plate.

Cyn tried to see Reaper's reaction as she tipped her head down to take a sip of water. Jealousy?

Would that emotion be what she needed to untangle Reaper from the tight knot of his marriage vows and to start thinking about indulging in a little…experimentation?

She was having a hard time gauging his thoughts.

A hero…

She'd started this mission by having Reaper save her…

That's who he was, a knight in tarnished armor.

That's what she had to do, Cyn decided. While Harlow signed the bill, Cyn fantasized about Harlow doing something horrible to her, preferably while she was naked…no, in her sexiest lingerie. A real movie moment where she was fighting…no, *flighting!* Running through the bitter night to stay alive while Reaper fought to save her.

Then she'd fall into his arms in gratitude.

And that's where she wanted to be—professionally—for the sake of gaining entry to Iniquus, and personally.

He *loved* Kate. Would do *anything* to protect their marriage and relationship.

Cyn just needed an opportunity to screw Reaper's brains out, and then she'd control him. He didn't need to care for her.

In recent circumstances, this had proven true.

Julep and Nia had shown the power of the snatch if one were willing to use that power as a weapon.

Cyn was more than willing.

37

Reaper

Sunday Evening

Reaper rounded in to the Iniquus War Room. "This case is just getting more bizarre."

Max waited for Reaper to sit, then slid behind his shins to tuck himself out of the way.

Reaper reached down to reward him with a quick rub between the ears. "Good boy."

Striker looked up from the computer screen. "Harlow?"

"And Cyn Parker."

"*And*?" Lynx asked.

"Exactly. I wasn't the only one to notice that she is often in my path. Cyn seems to come within my sphere, as I've outlined in my reports."

"We cleared her. Happenstance," Deep said.

"Is it though?" Reaper had been so focused on what he wanted to share with Lynx, that he hadn't been aware that Deep was in the room. Cold washed over him. That had never happened to him since his first day in Navy boot. He was losing his edge.

"What happened with Harlow?" Striker pushed a hip into the table and crossed his arms over his chest.

"They had a date today."

Lynx sent him a scowl. "Cynthia Parker had a date with Harlow?"

"I was pretty uncomfortable letting her go into his hotel room with him."

"It advanced to the hotel?" Deep asked.

"What about that made you uncomfortable?" Lynx asked at the same time.

Reaper decided to answer Lynx. "Harlow gets pissed at the drop of a hat. I've documented his misogyny, his racist, xenophobic bigotry in my reports."

"Jack and Randy have had the same reports," Striker said. "We've speculated that these are more reasons that ClearSight wants to give him the heave-ho. But the company needs something like drug use to have an easy out that won't end in litigation or high payout costs," Blaze said. "Nada on the drugs?"

"Absolute zilch," Reaper said.

"It seemed so easy—an alert from the dog. A quick blood test. Boom, out on his keister," Deep added.

Reaper frowned. "My take, if he liked drugs, he'd have looked for a hit before now. This is a road with a dead end."

"The date?" Lynx asked.

"He's mercurial. He got dressed in his suit and suggested a walk while custodial cleaned up his room. And, as usual, Cyn was out and about."

"Mercurial? Why? What happened before hand? What needed cleaning up?" Lynx asked.

"After I relieved Jack, I was outside the door waiting for Harlow to go out for lunch. From the sound of things, Harlow had an early conference call this morning. After he hung up, his normal tantrum turned violent. He was in there throwing things around and yelling. He's unpleasant on a minute-to-minute basis. This morning was a significant notch higher in his inappropriate behaviors. But very quickly, Harlow turned from the Tasmanian devil into a suit-wearing choir boy."

"Huh. I wonder what that was about," Lynx canted her head.

"He needs a hit?" Deep speculated.

"Maybe. I don't know. He seemed to be able to switch it off."

"Where'd he go dressed in his suit?" Lynx asked.

"He had his chauffer drive to some park up the road. We were walking the perimeter. He bumps my arm and points, there's Cyn coming out of church. She walked down the steps and was heading up the road when Harlow takes out after her. And get this, Deep, he thought he might see Cyn, so he got her a present, an art book with a painter she likes. Piccard."

"Grace has a new Piccard at her gallery."

"I know, Harlow invited Cyn to go see it."

"Did they?" Deep's brow furrowed. "I want dangerous behavior nowhere near Grace."

"I would have protected her and her gallery if he were to suddenly go off. Harlow was night and day when her was with Cyn, though. Seems he can pull off the gentleman act when needed. Tells me that Harlow knows that he's crossing boundaries. They went back to his room after lunch and skipped the gallery."

"What did you do when Harlow was going off this morning?" Striker asked.

"I let him vent. Following orders. We're there to protect his bodily safety from others and try to gather probable cause for a drug test."

"Nothing there?" Blaze asked. "You're sure Max would find it?"

"No hits. I'm a hundred percent on Max. He's got the best nose on our team for this. But as I explained at intake with the client, Max isn't going to pick up something in the guy's blood. And if Max were to sniff something that Harlow ingested, there are medications that are legitimate that could be smelled and then show up in the blood. If it's on his hands or clothes, any of the opiates, for example, that doesn't mean the guy is a user. Though, it sure would explain a lot of his behaviors."

"What's happening with him now?"

"When Cyn left his room, he said he was going to take a nap and read. Probably order dinner from room service. Randy has him covered."

"I'm glad you came into the office on your own," Lynx said. "I was going to see if you couldn't swing by. I wanted to go over something with you, and it has to do with Cyn." She walked over with a file in her hand. Sitting beside Reaper, she opened it up and handed Reaper a photograph. "Is this where you were at the ice rink when Cyn came over to thank you?"

Sliding the photo over to him, he turned it to see a picture of the park from someone on the ice in the rink. "Twelve o'clock from where I was standing, facing her was the concession stand. Right behind us there was a bench and a trash can." Neither were visible in this photo.

She pulled another one over, same spot, different angle.

"No," he said, "we were here." He put his finger on the photograph.

"You're sure."

Reaper closed his eyes and played it out in his mind's eye. It was part of his SEAL training. When the team came in from a mission, they held a hot wash. Each man walked through their movements and decisions. He'd say something like, "I came in through the door on the north side of the building, I cleared the rooms to the right, as I moved down the hall, I spotted two tangos with rifles and dispatched them." Knowing where he was and what he was doing was a habit that never left him, even when the PTSDemons were ravaging his thoughts. "Yeah, I'm sure."

Lynx pursed her lips. "Isn't that interesting."

"How so?"

"I went out and skated that rink." She stuck a pointer finger into his chest. "You should thank me. I suck at skating, and I took out the knee on my favorite pair of jeans."

He canted his head.

"These are some of the photos I took of that area. This," she pointed to the first picture that she'd asked him about, "is the single spot on that side of the rink that can be seen from on the ice."

"I'm not following."

"If you weren't standing in this exact spot," she tapped the photo again, "Cyn could not have seen you to recognize you from the ice."

Reaper shook his head.

"She would have to have known you were coming or have been aiming," she pulled out the other photo where Reaper had identified his spot, "for this area that was open by the branches. It had to have been timed." Lynx's job with Iniquus was "puzzler." It was a title developed just for her. She had the admiration of all of Iniquus, though, she was super young. Maybe mid-twenties. Her ability to figure things out from odd angles was legendary.

"I don't mean to be dense here, but I'm not privy to your thoughts up until now. I feel like I entered this conversation halfway through. Can you orient me?"

Lynx pulled a topo map of the park over. "From your report, you and Kate came down this path with the baby carriage."

"Yes."

"You were walking by this spot when she skated over to you."

"Yes."

"The skaters in the rink were skating clockwise."

"She should have skated on by me if she were skating clockwise. The people who do tricks go out to the middle. Maybe she was there, recognized me, and came over."

"Until you were in this spot," Lynx put her finger down, "she couldn't have seen you from the rink. I bet she lifted her hand and waved, maybe called out to you?"

"She did."

"From pretty far away?"

"Far enough that I couldn't make out her face."

"But she made out yours, walking parallel, talking to Kate. Either back of the head or side of the face to her."

"Shit." Reaper laced his fingers and planted his hands on top of his head.

"Yup."

"That means someone was watching my family and called it in to her." Reaper was completely back on his heals.

How could that be?

Why would that be?

"It's a theory. I've been going over it and over it, and I don't know how she's doing this. We've laid traps and tried all of the tricks to figure it out… I'm not figuring it out. And to be honest, it's kicking my ego in the teeth."

"I've got one for you," Reaper said.

"What's that, a theory?" Lynx gathered the photos up and put them back in the manila folder.

"More like a question. Kate doesn't wear much makeup." Reaper pinched at his nose. He nodded at the screen. "I'm going to move your mind away from Cyn Parker and ask about Mary Wise. Don't laugh, okay?"

"Never."

"I've been long hours in the hallway. I've been rerunning the security videos in my head. Do you have a copy of it?"

"Deep?" Lynx turned and said over her shoulder.

"Pulling it up," Deep said. He pulled a pen from behind his ear and pointed it toward the wall. A screen came down. The lights went out. "When do you want this to start."

"From the time Kate and I move into the area. But when you play it, is there a way to get the focus on the woman Mary Wise?"

Deep adjusted.

"Okay, pause there for a second. Okay, slow motion. I hate this angle but look at how she leans over and picks up that piece of paper on the floor. Then look how she stands."

"Ouch," Lynx said as Mary Wise stood and knocked her stomach into the corner of the staff station. "Wait. Play that again, Deep." Lynx walked toward the screen and put her hand on her forehead. "Holy moly! One more time Deep, slower this time." Lynx's finger came up and pointed. "Nothing. Her stomach hit into that sharp edge, and she had no response whatsoever. She didn't recoil. She didn't wince."

"She didn't feel it." Deep tinkered with the keys and pulled up a close-up of her face.

"Possible. Probable." Lynx turned toward Reaper. "A minute ago, you told me Kate doesn't wear much makeup—that's not new to me. You're wondering if this woman is in a disguise?"

"You do that when you go out for the Strike Force don't you?"

"Absolutely. My mentor drummed that into me like I was the timpani section in an orchestra." She grinned. "So, disguise. There are some very easy things that one can do—that I do. I could, for example, put in some temporary hair coloring, the kind that I can wash out in a few shampoos. Contact lenses to change my eye color. Women have it easier with using makeup, so using contouring can change the shape of the face." Lynx stared in silence at the still frame.

"Let's just suppose for a moment that this woman is in

disguise. We started with the fact that the sharp corner of the desk didn't seem to register in any way," Reaper said.

"That could be a fake belly," Deep offered. "I had a friend once who had a fake baby bump made out of silicon. No one in the spy field looks twice at a pregnant woman, they're not allowed to operate in the field."

"That's interesting, Deep." Lynx sent a smile over her shoulder to him. "I think I'm going to see what I can do about getting one for me." She turned back to Reaper. "I'll have to look for any telltale signs from other angles. But with the heavy winter clothing, I'm not expecting to see anything. The hair, though. That's interesting. Heavy bangs hide the forehead and brows. Those are the parts of the face that human's eyes go to first in identifying someone. Obscure those, it's much harder for someone to make an identification." She stepped up to the screen and pointed where she wanted the men to focus their attention. "No part to her hair, so no scalp and hair follicles showing. I'm not saying a hundred percent this woman is wearing a wig. I'm putting it on the possibilities list."

"Hey, we have some new AI software," Deep threw in. "This might be a good application for it."

"What does it do?" Reaper asked.

"I'm fairly new working with it. But what I can do so far is take various photographs and the software can peel things away. So we start with her head, and I can change her eye color, her hair, add pounds, take away pounds… I can take off makeup and reapply it. It looks at things like the knuckle and bone prominence in the hands to try to decide fat percentages. It helps us to see what the person looks like without bulky clothing."

"I think that was advertised in the back of my comic books when I was a kid," Lynx said. "Are these X-Ray glasses?"

"I always wished they were real," Deep snorted. "I had such plans for them."

"I don't even want to know." Lynx put her hand up. "Can you work on this for us, Deep?"

"I can. Is this life or death or do we have some time?"

"Not time-critical," Reaper said. "I'd say time-sensitive, brother. I am confused right now. It's not like the SEALs here is it? It used to be we got a target package and headed out the door, do our duty, and get home. This? It feels like I'm in a carnival funhouse with those distortion mirrors."

Lynx sent him a worried look. "Are you sleeping?"

"Not much to be honest." Reaper scratched his shoulder. "The hours are long. When I work close protection, I'm at level orange. I'm not complaining. I'm not in a hot zone, clenching my stomach muscles against incoming rounds. But I take my assignment seriously."

"We're trying to find drugs," Striker said.

"While I provide him with security."

"That's not in the contract," Deep pointed out.

"Granted. But the guy *thinks* he's being covered by security. I told him that. If he believes it to be true, I think I have a moral if not legal obligation to see that that's correct.

"This isn't okay. We need to pull dogs in from Cerberus's training." Lynx's voice held her worry. "You need help cutting some of these hours off your schedule."

"Please don't do that, Lynx. I want to pull my share. And those guys have been working darned hard to get those skills honed. I don't want them standing behind Harlow as he cracks his Alaskan crab legs and reads memes all day. It's basic work—"

"Except for the ever-present appearances of Cyn Parker."

"I'm starting to think she's a ghost, and she's decided to haunt me."

"Could be robots," Deep suggested. "Straight off the factory floor. I've always been a little concerned about that since my high school English teacher had us read *Stepford Wives*."

REAPER PARKED in front of his house and unloaded Max from the hatch. He stopped to scan the neighborhood before he made his way into Lynx's house to feed him and play for a bit before Max moved to his kennel to sleep.

Making sure Max's "baby" monitor was functioning on his phone and that Lynx's door was secured, Reaper walked across the porch to his own door, bending in the foyer to love on Houston. Before he could call out that he was home, Reaper heard Kate's "drinking wine" voice. "Cyn—sounds like a stripper name. Everyone give a warm welcome to our next dancer, Cyn Full!"

"Wow, that's…not like you, Kate." Reaper recognized Grace De Toro's southern accent.

"No? I'm not very generous when it comes to this woman. There's something going on—something very wrong."

"What does Reaper say?" That was Faith, Blaze's fiancée.

Kate lowered her tone to try to sound like Reaper. "We have a buzz in our antennae, sure. We're working the situation."

Kate's impression of him made Reaper grin.

"What does that mean, exactly?" Grace asked.

"It means, they're checking her out," Faith said. "Doing what they do."

"But I. Don't. Know. What. They. Do," Kate complained. "I'm not in the loop. Everything is 'classified' and 'need-to-know'. It's actually worse than when Ryan was with the SEALs. He deployed. He came home. I got the home part of his life. This? It's different. And I don't like it."

"What does the team say?" Grace asked gently.

"That at the end of the month he'll be working the dogs, and he'll be able to tell me all about their shit and slobber."

"Ha!" That must have been Faith.

"Really?" Grace asked.

"Look, I get it," Faith said. "All of the wives and girlfriends get it. It's a very strange way to live. It makes us stare into shadows and wonder if someone might have wired a bomb into our cars. I can't tell you how many times I've sat there, my hand shaking, forcing myself to press the start button."

"You, too?" Grace asked.

"All the time," Faith said. "At least, Kate, you know that the threat will be gone at the end of the month."

"God, I hope so," his wife said.

Reaper re-opened the door and shut it loudly, then called, "Kate, sweetheart, I'm home."

With a buzzy lisp Kate called, "Ryan James Hamilton, don't you dare wake that baby!"

38

Cyn

Sunday Night

Cyn sat in her car outside of Borka's building.

His office lights were the only ones on in the whole building.

This was it. This was the culmination of their decade-long relationship. Once she did this, took down Iniquus and the CIA and whatever fallout that came with it, she was going to disappear.

She had her new life all set up. And it was lovely, beautiful, and calm.

Cyn's mind flashed back to the Turkish apartment in the iffy part of Istanbul where Borka had introduced himself to her.

Introduced, ha!

He wrenched a bottle of vodka from her hand. She'd fought him off. Not for self-preservation's sake. Quite the opposite. Cyn had drunk herself into what she hoped would be an alcohol-induced coma, followed by asphyxia via her own vomit.

That seemed a fitting way to go, alone and unknown.

Years of cutting ties and building fake relationships, who would miss her?

Who would give two shits?

She'd thought, "Bye world!" as she tipped the bottle back and let the clear liquid blaze down her throat.

But *they* were watching her. Waiting for rock bottom.

Borka had picked the lock and gently shut the door behind him. No, she didn't see any of that, she was passed out. But she could imagine the scene clearly.

He said that he'd stuck his finger down her throat and made her vomit until it was only dry heaves. Then he gathered her into his arms and carried her to the bathroom. Still fully clothed, he climbed into the tub. The iced cold shower hit her in the face.

It shocked the hell out of her—the water. And being alive.

She was so angry that she was still alive, that she'd have to live another day pressed flat by the pain of having her brother, her twin, ripped out of her life, that she became a fire-breathing dragon, trying to scream and claw her way free.

Borka held her tight against his chest, letting her feet dangle mere inches from the bottom of the bath. Her arms were now pinned to her sides. Even her spit was ineffectual, as he simply ducked his head under the water jet.

After a while—a long while—Cyn lost any motivation to fight.

Her skin was purple with cold and pebbled with gooseflesh.

Her teeth chattered so hard that she bit her tongue, and the copper tang of blood filled her mouth.

Borka suspended her in one bear arm as he adjusted the water. Then, both fully clothed, he lay down in the tub as it filled with hot water.

All she could do with her clanging head and churning stomach was rest her cheek on his chest as he petted her hair. "Shush.

Shush. Shush, my child. You have been through too much. I am here because your drinking yourself into oblivion serves your cruel masters. What you really want is to Make. Them. Pay."

He was right.

How would her self-destruction be of any consequence to the murdering bastards?

What she really wanted was revenge.

She still wanted that.

She got out of her car and walked with long clacking strides toward the security guard. Recognizing her, he gave her a deferential bow and held the door wide for her to pass through.

Up the elevator to the top floor, she walked through the empty reception room and tapped lightly on the door before cracking it and poking her face through.

When Borka looked her way, she smiled and went in. "Have you got it?"

Borka lifted his brows and dropped them.

"The Zorics came through?" She rounded the chair and sat on the very edge. Excitement effervesced along her hairline.

"I have what I need from them."

Cyn laced her fingers and gripped her hands together as she leaned in. "Did they explain it to you?"

His chin dropped slowly to his chest, rose halfway and bobbled.

"Wow. Bad, huh?"

He pulled out a drive and put it on the desk between them. He tapped his index finger on the table.

"Interesting." She licked at her lips, desperate to reach out and grab it up. "You're hesitating. I've never seen that before."

His eyes were silver and cold like a shark's as he stared at her. "I don't think you understand what is here."

She lifted her chin to indicate the drive. "What is it?"

"Death. Destruction. War."

"For America."

"America is woven into the structure of the entire world."

He linked his fingers as he scrunched down in his seat and rested his hands on his chest. "The Zoric family thinks that if they were to gain access to the Iniuquus supercomputer, it would be a wonderful opportunity."

"And you don't?"

"My life is pleasant. I enjoy myself."

"Mmmm."

His eyes focused on the drive. "It doesn't seem to make you hesitate. To think. This has the potential to destroy a nation. Your nation." He paused for a response.

"Potentially?"

"Nothing is ever a hundred percent. *Nothing*."

"I want the CIA."

"I know."

"Ask them for something else," Cyn said, reaching out and gripping the edge of the desk with white knuckles.

"And how would we trust what they give us?"

"We can't." As she slid back in her seat, she pricked a finger through her hair and scrubbed at her scalp. "My brother—"

"You could see how the mistake was made at his death. It was a *mistake*. You understand this, yes?"

She looked at the tips of her brown shoes. There was a little bit of mud that had worked its way into the stitching while she was in the park with Harlow on their way to brunch.

"What you hate was the desecration of Tom's body."

"Take his name out of your mouth," she growled.

"It was staged, that desecration. It was meant by American enemies to make its way into the intelligence circles and to rob their morale. I stopped this by destroying the films. They do not know it happened, the CIA."

Cyn looked up.

"It would have manifested a greater pain in your heart if you knew others witnessed what you saw in those films. But I saved a copy. I knew you would want to see them. And so, I made sure that that happened."

Cyn set her jaw.

"These actions… What do they say in America? I put skin in the game. Because I saw potential in you. And I was right. But your hatred is becoming lunacy."

"I am so close!" She clasped her hands together and pressed them into her thighs. "So close! Tomorrow, I plan to be at Iniquus. Tomorrow Harlow is meeting me at a rental home for a date. It will get out of hand. Reaper will take me to Iniquus to get cleaned up and make a report. Omega told me that's how they handle things. I can slide it in undetected. Like a micro dick into a prostitute, they will feel nothing."

"At Iniquus? You still think that's possible?"

"You don't?" Cyn scooted closer to the desk.

"I think that it is admirable what you have done to injure the CIA over these years. If you continue with that… The Family would be grateful. But this?"

"What did the Zorics give you?" She reached out to pick up the drive.

Borka's fist slammed into the desktop, making everything jump, including Cyn.

When she looked down, the drive had flipped. It was the cartridge from a 90s child's game.

She stared at it, stunned. "You brought me in here to laugh at me?"

"Your behavior is laughable. The Zorics say they are busy with their own strategies, and they do not wish to help with this project lest you destroy their intentions."

"So, I've been working my tail off, getting everything in

place, and you are too craven to walk through the door I'm opening?"

"Language." He pressed the pads of his fingertips together. "I am your mentor. I understand your disappointment, that does not mean that I would allow you to speak to me in this manner."

Cyn ducked her head, the effervescence of excitement turned to a sizzle of fear. "My apologies."

"I will caution you, again, you are a *wound collector*. Every perceived slight, every painful experience, you tuck it away. This is one of the qualities that we see in serial killers and mass shooters. It is a good one to have in some respects when monitored and guided by a strong hand." He paused and waited for her to meet his gaze. "I read in the paper, by the way, that a man died of a freak accident involving a can of soda on your floor of the hotel."

Cyn snorted as she laughed.

"Wound collectors use their inner rage to allow them to do heinous things. And The Family appreciates that in you. But you are like a pig in the mud, wallowing in your vengeance. The problem is that wound collectors are always looking for the next grievance like a magpie looks for the next shiny object to bring to its nest. Be careful that this psychological trait is used to reach your goals, and that they not be ill applied. You do not want to be a detriment to The Family."

"No, sir. I do not."

"We have long agreed on your ultimate objective. And you have done much to cause the CIA problems. We nearly took down the Delta Force last year. That was another way that you were able to inflict pain on your government. The information that you offered us, the names and locations of your colleagues in the CIA, they have served the Family well. And for that reason, and that reason alone, I will allow this one outburst from you."

"Sir."

"I believed that we had an interesting adventure ahead of us.

And circumstances dictated our time frame. Better to put you into place and have the scheme unfolding while we discovered if this was possible. As it turns out, the Zorics had very much the same idea. Not with Iniquus, no one has been able to thwart their security. However, with the FBI and the CIA, our families have people within their walls. This scheme has already been attempted. And thwarted."

"If they've already got the malware, if it's been tried, maybe it would work on the Iniquus system. I know from a colleague who interfaced with Strike Force on a mission, that they have a supercomputer that is connected to government computer systems. Consider this, what if spreading malware was not the intent? What if we just got a look around their data?"

"Iniquus would see the breach. They could warn everyone."

"And lose their trust."

"To what end? All this would do is bring scrutiny. We dislike eyes on us."

"The information though…"

"Cyn, define your objective on this mission."

"It is—as we've discussed, as you've promised me that we would—to take down the CIA."

"And how are we going to do this with your current scheme?"

Cyn could feel the emotions piling up behind her eyes. And oddly, all she wanted to do in this moment was to find Reaper and let him hold and comfort her.

The room was silent for a long time.

Cyn wrestled with her new revelation. She loved him. She wanted him for hers, always.

"Cynthia," he barked to pull her back into the conversation. And when she focused on him again, he lowered his voice. "If you simply leave this mission there will be many questions. I don't want them to be asked. I want you to start to unwind what is going on for you. Remove your players from the playing board one by one in a natural way. Something that brings no attention."

"Slither away."

"If that is the quietest route." He snorted then pulled a tissue from his pocket to wipe at his nose. "I have another assignment for you starting next Monday. I need you at your best. So close this down, and go to a spa to rest yourself. We will continue to make the CIA miserable. And we will do it by diverting their resources, their money, time, and energy away from things that would bring them success." He tossed the tissue into the trash. "And I will make sure it is your hand that brings many of those strikes."

A weight sat on Cyn's chest. She could not believe this interview. She had been there. *Ready*. She had one more act and surely Reaper would have gathered her and Harlow and taken them to Iniquus for safety's sake. One. More.

Everything had gone to pl—everything had been working out.

Borka lifted his hand to make a shooing motion of dismissal.

Cyn knew not to say a single word after he waved her away. She stood and offered a deferential bow of her head. "Thank you, sir."

She headed out into the night to grapple with two new truisms.

One, Cyn wasn't going to destroy the CIA and avenge Tom. *Yet,* she reminded herself. She wasn't going to destroy the CIA and avenge Tom on *this* mission. The future lay ahead of her. She needed a new route to get to them was all.

Two. And almost equally as disturbing of a revelation, Cyn didn't want to go away to the spa all alone when this mission was over. What she wanted was Reaper Hamilton for her very own.

Crap.

39

Reaper

Monday Morning, Crack of Dawn

Berry Greg looked like shit.

Under his expensively tailored long wool coat, he was wearing a pair of gym shorts and a T-shirt with what might be a soup stain dripping down the front. Unshaven, rumpled hair, grey bags under his eyes.

Reaper slid into the room and over to the coffee pot, wondering what had been discovered that he was being pulled into Headquarters at this hour.

Not that he minded, Reaper couldn't honestly say that his time watching that garbage of a human being Harlow was anything but painfully long. This would break up the day for him.

Bringing the mug to his lips, Reaper focused on the typed page that was projected onto one of the war room drop-down screens.

There were bullet points that read as pro-Russia takes on a variety of subjects.

Striker said under his breath, "We talked about this with the senator yesterday. The senator had his marching orders already. But Greg didn't accept Nia's invitation to go over to her apartment Sarurday night. So, Nia went to Greg's work this morning. The network security took Nia to a waiting room until Greg got off the air. He found her there, waiting for him."

Reaper glanced over at Berry Greg, his face almost purple with emotion.

"I need the can," Greg said and moved to the bathroom at the back of the war room.

"Nia handed him this." Striker pointed at the screen. "Since Greg didn't have the list of topics at the time their interview aired, the senator didn't have to say any of the things on the list Julep had handed him. Unfortunately, that only means a short reprieve. Along with this list," Striker hitched a thumb over his shoulder, "both men got phone calls from the expectant mothers early this morning, letting the men know that they were expected to follow through on air this morning."

"If he wasn't sure before," Deep said, "now he knows his balls are in a vice."

"Exactly." Striker settled his hips against Deep's station.

Prescott wandered over to join them at the conference table.

"When are they going on air with this?" Reaper asked him.

"This morning at zero seven hours. The drive-to-work hour over the radio programming."

"The best way I see to handle this," Reaper said into his coffee cup to keep his words from Greg's ears should he be listening at the door, "is to call their wives, tell them that they were targeted, then go on air and explain the whole thing to the viewers. Let the chips fall where they may."

"That would take balls," Striker said, "and as Deep said, both of these men feel like theirs are in a vice."

"Sucks to be them." Reaper took a sip of the aggressively strong coffee. "Is someone going to clean him up before he hits the airwaves?"

"Not our job," Prescott said. "After Nia's last revelations, at least we know what we're up against. The Prokhorov family is formidable, well-placed, well-funded, and a consistent, sharp pain in my ass."

"Glad you chose the adjective sharp over penetrating," Deep said from behind his computer.

Reaper chuckled into his mug as Greg moved back into the room.

Striker's phone buzzed. He pulled it out and read his screen. "And that's that." He rounded toward Greg. "Iniquus is terminating your contract. We're handing this situation over to the FBI."

Greg looked startled, then tears welled in his eyes. "Terminating." He splayed his hands on the conference table. "Look. I know that Strike Force is mad at me. Especially Jack McCullen. And understandably so. Back when the school was attacked, I was on-air, and they told us to fill time. Thirty seconds. Thirty seconds is a long time when you're on-air to riff. Do you see what I'm saying? We just needed to fill some time to get to the commercial break. I was speculating. Imagining. It wasn't meant to cause any harm." He put his hand to his chest. "I didn't mean to create problems for Miss Malloy, well, Mrs. McCullen now. I learned later that my words were taken for reality. I'm an entertainer not a journalist. I opine. That's it."

The men in the room stared stonily at him.

"Look, I decided to hire Iniquus to help me with my issues. Y'all aren't cheap. That's for sure. Man, this has been expensive, and I haven't even gotten to the part where I pay child support. I mean, worth it, yeah. When I came in with the letter, no one was surprised, your team already had this figured out. But at the time I got Nia's first call, I thought who could help me. I thought win-win. I could make up for my words causing Mrs. McCullen harm by throwing some business toward Strike Force. I know an apology is inadequate but I'm…yeah. I'm embarrassed by all of this."

Striker looked at Damian. "Do you need a private room?"

"I'd be grateful." Prescott turned to Greg. "Let's go have a chat about how this is going to play out."

Blaze opened the door. "If you'll follow me."

"Can you believe that joker?" Deep asked once the door shut behind them.

Reaper took another sip from his mug. "Did you make this swill? What were you trying to do, experiment with rocket fuel?"

Lynx walked in and smiled at Reaper. "Good, you're here. How long are you here?"

"Harlow was three sheets to the wind last night. Jack's babysitting. So Max and I are just waiting to get tagged. I do know that he has a dinner date with Cyn. I'm planning on a long day." He set his mug down and posted his knuckles on the table. "Did you figure out anything about Mary Wise?"

"Yep," Deep said. "It's why we called you in. we wanted you to see it for yourself."

"Granted, it's a computer mockup and another issue might be that it was Deep that did the work with the AI."

"Why would Deep's participation be an issue?" Reaper asked.

Deep, put up the image on the screen.

Reaper was stunned to see Cyn Parker's face staring down at him.

"Grain of salt, Reaper," Lynx said. "The problem with Deep doing this is that he's been working with both Alpha and Bravo teams and has been looking at the faces. It most certainly had to have corrupted his objectivity."

"I 100% agree with that," Deep said. "I don't give this image a high-reliability rate because of my exposure to Cynthia Parker's images. I sent it over to Nutsbe. He's really good with this kind of thing."

"I thought Panther Force was in Africa," Reaper said.

"Twiddling their thumbs." Deep tapped the keys and brought up side and three-quarters views. "Nutsbe's over there running their command center. He said he was glad for a distraction. He's on this."

Reaper posted his hands on his hips as he stared at the side by side of the woman in the airport and what could be the woman he'd met at her car accident.

Mary Wise sure did look an awful lot like Cyn Parker.

40

Cyn

Monday Morning

"I've spoken to Charles Harlow," Borka's voice came over the line. "He said that he's scheduled to take you to a house this evening?"

"A little rental on the river." Cyn sat in the POS car associated with her rundown motel where she changed her guises. For the moment, she was in a Mary Wise outfit. "We'll be making a lot of noise, and we'll need the privacy."

"I see."

"If we're to leave by tomorrow," Cyn measured her words carefully, "I thought you would appreciate it if I left a little pain and destruction in my wake."

"To what end?"

"Payback to Strike Force for helping to ruin our wonderful strategy to damage the Delta Force. I'm quite angry that they trounced on my plan just when it was paying dividends. You can tell the Zorics that even if they were unable to help me, I'm still willing to dent the Strike Force armor. It's a gift from me to them to show I harbor no ill feelings. Maybe I can sweeten their attitude toward the Prokhorovs enough that when we ask for assistance, they're willing to offer it. After all, Strike Force was part of putting their family members in jail."

"Careful not to expose yourself or The Family. You will not target an Iniquus operator. The Family has zero interest in going to war with Iniquus without a clear strategy to win. And with that understood, you have my blessing to proceed." Borka's words were without any energy or even much interest. "I caution you, however. Cyn, you *cannot* hurt the dogs."

"Why the hell not?"

"Because this is America. Americans are crazy when it comes to dogs. They treat them as their children. Often better than their children."

"Excellent, imagine how much that will hurt."

"Out of self-preservation and concern for The Family's ability to stay under the radar, leave the dog alone. Both Max and the other one."

"Houston." Cyn pressed the flat of her palm against her forehead, soothed by the coolness of her touch. "I'm not going to let a dog hurt *me*."

"You're not getting my point. If you do anything to Strike Force, Iniquus is coming after you, *us*. They will capture you, there is no doubt. They're just to good at what they do to miss. Once you are held in custody, if it is mentioned in the press that you killed or injured a dog—not just a dog, but a service dog for a Navy SEAL, not just a service dog for a Navy SEAL but a hero dog who has accommodation from the DCPD for saving a pregnant woman's life—they will crucify you. There will not be a juror in this land who will let you go free. No judge who will listen to your story of woe and how the CIA is ultimately to blame for your behavior. You will go to a maximum prison, and you will stay there for as long as laws will permit. Then you will be met at the exit gates by the CIA, and they will drop you into a black site never to be heard from again. This all would be a shame."

Cyn paced. "You're assuming they'll catch me. I don't think they can."

"Don't be a fool. Of course, they'll catch you. This isn't a bureaucracy cocooned in red tape. This isn't a desperately overwhelmed police force. This is *Iniquus*. And if you don't know how they move mountains for their people, simply do an Internet search on India Alexis Sobado—this is that Lynx woman--and Omega."

"I will."

"If you harm the dog, your image will go viral. Every dog-loving American will be beating the bushes and dragging you to a station by your toenails. There are many things that the American public is too bored and sad to pay attention to, harming a dog is not one of them."

"Fine. I leave the dog alone."

"Prudent of you."

"Thank you. I'll talk with you later."

After their connection ended, Cyn pressed the phone between her hands and rested it on her chin.

Cyn had been at this game for a long time, Borka thought he ran her.

Cyn, in reality, used him. In this instance, she wanted the best spyware and malware to do the job. And she knew it was the Zorics who could deliver that to her. And the way to get the Zorics to cooperate had been through Borka.

He failed her.

Cyn turned to Plan B. She didn't get as far as she did without being prepared. She put the car in drive, heading for the mall where an up-and-coming black hat hacker was going to meet her and hand over his version. He'd done some work for her in the past that had been very satisfying in getting her goals met. He didn't have any ethics issues with not knowing what his work was used for, he simply a teen who liked the money and the women that he could impress with cash.

"Starting down the degenerate path so early these days." Granted, it wasn't going to be the same level of hack that she'd expected and wanted from the Zorics, but at least she'd gain access to the Iniquus supercomputer.

And from there, she'd see what she could do to make her enemies pay.

Cyn didn't give a rat's ass about the welfare of the damned dogs.

41

Kate

Monday Evening

Standing outside their house on the sidewalk, Ryan grabbed Kate into his arms and hugged her with a vengeance. "Kate Hamilton, you are a miracle of a woman. Thank you."

Kate laughed. "You're welcome, I guess. Where did that come from?"

"Love burst. It happens with alarming regularity. You just happened to be standing by my side while that one exploded in my chest."

"Exploded in your chest? Mmm, no. That's not at all a good description. Choose some other analogy and never say that to me again." She tipped her head back farther to catch his gaze. "Are you done for the day?"

"Sorry, no. The client wants to go to dinner. I'm on duty."

"Again?" Kate sent him a pout. Her phone rang and her

muscles jumped. "Ha. Nerves. It's Faith." Kate swiped her screen. "Hey there." She held up a finger to keep Ryan in place.

"Kate, hey. I hope I didn't catch you at a bad time, I have a favor to ask."

"Shoot."

Ryan leaned in. "Dangerous word choice, I don't want you to say that again." He punctuated his sentence with a wink and a smile.

"I was riding with a friend of mine and her horse spooked and threw her. I'm following the ambulance to the hospital and I'm not sure how long I'm going to be. I'm worried about my dogs. They haven't been out all day, and they need to eat."

"I can go get them and bring them to my house."

"I'm so used to calling Iniquus and having them send an ISO—but for once Jack is home. He's on close protection duty. I can't ask him."

"I can do it. No worries."

"When you get there, just ring the bell, and I'll open the door remotely. Blaze hates that I have that app, but at times like these it makes everything so much easier."

"Reaper's the same. No smart functions in our house. Well, the fridge, but you can't hack that to get into the house."

"I'm pulling into the parking garage now. Thank you!"

"No worries. Glad to help."

"Help with what?" Reaper asked as he trailed her into the house.

"I'm getting her dogs to take care of them while she deals with a friends' emergency. I figured that since Lynx is letting you kennel Max at her place, that's not a worry. I'll just put Faith's dogs in the backyard and let Houston play with her friends."

Ryan followed her into the house and up the stairs where Zack was playing quietly in his crib.

"Is that woman Cyn still showing up?" Kate asked

Reaper's voice was tight. "She started dating my client."

"What? Is that weird?" Kate dragged a tiny sock onto Zack's foot.

"Doesn't matter if it's weird or not. Listen. If you ever see that woman anywhere, I want you to leave immediately. I want you to stay as far away from her as possible. I can't say more. But you have to promise me."

Kate stood poised with the other sock in her hand. "Promise." Her brows drew together.

"And call the Strike Force war room immediately, or Iniquus Control if you're in your car."

"Ryan." Kate froze, fear painted over her. "Is she a danger to Zack?"

"I don't know what she is other than a great big red waving flag."

Kate pulled the other sock on and reached for the moccasins that Ryan held out to her. "I don't like this—I don't like how this makes me feel—I don't like how it makes me feel about you. About us. I want you to request someone else take over the assignment." She walked to the closet to get Zack's snowsuit. "I'm asking you to hand back this case and to start immediately with Cerberus."

"I promise to talk to Striker about it tomorrow. Okay? But I need to go in tonight. The client was in his room all day, which let me off the hook. Jack and Randy need a break."

"Okay." She came up on her toes to offer a kiss. "Well, I hope tonight is boring." She zipped a squirming Zack into his suit then scooped him up, heading toward the door.

"I expect it to be. Look, it's dark already."

"Your powers of observation, Ryan, are extraordinary. Maybe you should have chosen a scientific profession."

"I don't like you driving alone at night, especially coming home to a dark house."

Kate laughed as she handed off the baby to pull on her hat. "With four dogs in the car. Listen, I've been alone at night for most of our marriage."

He followed her to the door. "Take Houston with you. That will make me feel better."

"Fine. I'll take Houston with me. Five dogs in the car, then." She turned and called out, "Houston! Go bye bye!"

There was an immediate scramble over the wood floor in their bedroom.

"Kate, can you do me a favor?"

"What's that?" She turned to the stairs. "There you are, good girl." She peeked over at Ryan. "Can you attach her leash, please?"

Ryan moved to the hook and grabbed the lead. "I want you to stay the night with Faith."

Kate froze. "Why?" she whispered.

"This thing with Cyn Parker is obviously an issue. I want to work with Strike Force to solve it. It's throwing me off. I'm not sure what's going on here. More than meets the eye. I need you safe. And I need Zack safe. Just for tonight, then I'll let Striker know that I'm done."

"Okay." Kate's system lit up. She had a few brushes with death this last year. So had Reaper. For some reason, in her mind, she'd thought they'd met their quota of crap, and they were done, ready to live, love, laugh. Ready for their happily ever after. "I'm sure Faith will think it's fine." She pressed Zack back into Ryan's arms. "I'll just throw a few things in the bag for Zack and me."

Her skin burned and buzzed as she climbed the stairs.

Something was telling her to grab Ryan too, jump in the car and drive like the bat out of hell.

Kate remembered her conversation with Avril; how could one tell the difference?

Was this PTSD or was it women's intuition?

42

Cyn

Monday Evening

"Faith's house?" Cyn pulled up the map on her computer. Looking at the time, Kate would be snarled into traffic. It was normally a nice country drive to get from Kate's inner-city home to Faith's. Cyn had already mapped the routes to all the Strike Force and Strike Force adjacent (fiancées, girlfriends) homes. She'd put them through a program that told Cyn how long the drive time was based on the day of the week and the hour to account for city traffic. It also offered options to cut that time by taking the roundabout ways even if they were longer distances on a map.

Accessing Kate's car computer, Cyn saw that the program automatically changed Kate's route to the shorter one timewise. Ah, but that route was so much easier for Cyn to stage for her next steps. Rural. Dark. Poorly traversed. *Perfect.*

Faith's calling for help played right into Cyn's plans and made everything so much easier.

Cyn called into Omega Overwatch and Surveillance and told him to tag Kate's car and follow it. "Also, I need you to follow a truck for me. He'll be moving in a few minutes. He's parked on the side of the road. Ready for the GPS coordinates?"

"Go for Omega surveillance."

Moving right along. Easy day.

Cyn made another call to a new trucker friend introduced to her by the Omega chauffer who had been driving Harlow around. The truck driver was low scruples and had been more than okay with a little windfall moolah in exchange for a small favor.

Twisting a suppressor onto her pistol, she set it in the recess on her car console. With her car in drive, pressing her foot on the gas, by her computer's readout, she should be in place twenty minutes before Kate hit Cyn's X.

She wanted as much time as she could get.

Driving aggressively through the city, applying the behind the wheel driving techniques honed at The Farm, Cyn buzzed past her fellow drivers.

With this next move, Kate, Zack, and even Houston became her pawns.

The next move would be Reaper's choice.

One, Reaper could try to protect Cyn and take her to Iniquus for her safety. Cyn would insert the spyware into their computer. Reaper's family would be gone, and he could choose to fly off with Cyn to see how they did together as a couple, a new family.

Two, Reaper could try to protect Cyn and take her to Iniquus for her safety and Cyn would insert the spyware into their computer. Reaper could choose his family, but too bad so sad, they were no longer alive. He could live out the rest of his miserable life in mourning and self-accusation.

Three, Reaper could refuse to take her to Iniquus, at which

point Reaper's family would become her ace up the sleeve. Reaper *would* take her to Iniquus, and much like the thwarted tiger kidnapping that had made the Zorics so mad at Strike Force, Reaper could try to comply, but his family would die once they were no longer useful.

Four, Reaper could put a gun in his mouth because he was a mush-for-brains, and he'd realize he'd brought death and destruction into his home. Then, the family would die, and Cyn would have to weigh any available options at the time.

Yeah. Four. Those were the most likely outcomes.

The thing that Cyn never considered was Kate might slip through her fingers, because Cyn was better at her job than any of these bozos.

OH, so many years ago now, when Cyn was at The Farm training, she sat beside her instructor, driving him to the get a snack and chat about how she thought her training was going.

As they rounded a bend, her lights caught on a string of sawhorses in the road. A figure dressed in black, a gator covering his lower face held up a hand to stop.

Cyn looked over at her instructor who leaned forward squinting.

Not planned?

The man's arm came up and in Cyn's headlights, she very clearly saw the gun in his hand.

The rule Cyn learned through that exercise was that there is only one way to survive that situation.

At the time, out of sheer panic, Cyn had pressed her feet down as she pressed her body back into the seat, away from the steering wheel.

One of those feet was already on the gas pedal.

Her startled tires slid and shrieked until they mastered a grip on the road, then she barreled forward, her car's exterior peppered with paint balls.

She was the only person who had reacted that way.

And the only person to have passed that test.

Kudos to her limbic survival powers.

Back in the lecture hall they were told:

If you back up, you die.

If you try to go around, you die.

If you stop, and negotiate you die.

The only way you have a chance to not die was to drive forward, even if that meant driving over people.

Our brains are horrified with that idea, even under such dangerous (seeming) circumstances.

After the instructor explained this to them, her class was told to lie down, close their eyes and practice running people down to get free.

For that reason, Cyn wasn't afraid at all as she stood in the middle of the road, Omega in her ear, taking in the progression of Kate's car, a pistol in her hand.

If Kate did anything but stop and try to negotiate, Cyn would pop her off.

Dead.

With any luck, Zack and the dog would be okay. Borka was probably right about not hurting the dog. And baby Zack was a good enough pawn.

In Cyn's other hand she held her phone all queued up.

One of the people that the CIA had brought in to lecture them was a DARPA scientist who was working with the dangers of the newest vehicles. They were very computer component dependent. And they were hackable. DARPA had successfully hacked into cars and taken over their braking systems, their steering systems, their phone systems and other controls. The scientist had said that he was particularly concerned with the new automatic driving cars. Those systems were ripe for hacking.

The easiest hack, the scientist said as he taught them just how to use this new tool in the spook black bag of tricks, was to hack into the car's accident-avoidance system.

This system was designed to preserve life and limb by taking over the car's braking system and stopping on a dime should the driver be distracted and miss something out in front.

Whatever Kate thought when she saw Cyn in the road didn't much matter.

Cyn would merely tap her screen and Kate's car would come to a screeching halt.

As an added layer of protection, as soon as Omega let her know Kate was rounding the bend, Cyn would cut on the jammer.

Any phone call that Kate might be having would drop. There would be no startled gasps that the person on the other end would pick up on, no emergency buttons to press.

Nothing.

Isolation.

Houston was there in the car. And according to the newspaper, last year when Kate was attacked in her house, Houston bit the guy so badly he lost his arm.

If Houston wasn't in her crate in the back of the vehicle as she normally was, then Cyn had a fast-acting vet dart in the delivery pistol in her utility belt.

That and a stun gun in case either woman or beast needed persuasion about good behavior.

The pistol, though, should give Cyn the visual leverage needed to make Kate do whatever Cyn wanted.

43

Kate

Monday Night

Kate couldn't breathe.

Her heart was too big. It was the Big Ben, the Liberty Bell of gonging clanging hearts.

It was hard to hear past the sound.

"Kate, pay attention." Cyn snapped her fingers. "I told you to roll down the window."

When Cyn had stepped out into the middle of the road, Kate had decided to simply swerve around her. She'd reached out and pressed the red emergency button that was an immediate link to Iniquus Control and help.

For the first time ever, no voice came over her radio speaker.

As Kate pressed her foot onto the gas pedal, her SUV stopped so hard, she was thrown forward, her seatbelt snapping at her chest and holding her firmly in place. She slammed back against her seat, the air pressed from her lungs and now not filling again.

Cyn had a gun trained on Zack.

Of course, Kate would comply.

"Unlock the doors, Kate."

Her hand trembled as she pressed various buttons, the windows swirling up and down until she hit the right one. The locks popped open.

Cyn climbed in to sit next to Zack. "Kate," she said as she pulled the door shut and released the brakes on the car, "I bet you've learned a thing or two from your husband and his buddies over time. Since I have a gun at your baby's head. You won't do anything other than what I tell you to do. Say, 'yes, ma'am.'"

"Yes, ma'am."

"You can start driving forward, I'll direct you. Slow and steady. There you go."

Kate was gelatin in an earthquake, a quivering shaking mess with no control.

"I'm not showing good trigger control back here, Kate. My finger isn't aligned with the trigger guard. In fact, it's wrapping and pressing just a bit on the trigger. A bump, and I might make a mistake."

Kate lifted her gaze to her rearview mirror and saw that the barrel was pressed against Zack's head.

Houston was going ballistic.

"Shut up the dog or the first bullet's for her. I don't need the racket."

"Houston. Silence. Leave it," Kate called desperately back.

Houston gave a series of whines and paw stomps then lay down.

"Good. Now, here we go. Forward, nice and slow. Nice and quiet. It's up the street about five miles."

What happened next made Kate's brain stutter. She was so confused. This was nothing she'd ever seen or heard of.

Along the road was a tractor-trailer, ramps lead to a yawning back opening.

Cyn had exited the car and told Kate to drive in.

Why?

That was the question that cycled through Kate's brain.

Scenarios spun forward, reasons, explanations, but none of them mattered. The only thing that mattered was keeping her son alive in this moment. She'd worry about the next moments when they presented themselves.

Cyn had ordered her to drive into the truck. It wasn't easy. Her car's width and the truck's interior were about the same. At least she knew that Cyn couldn't get back into the car with her.

As Kate drove into the black maw of the trailer, without conscious thought, Kate's fingers found the switch to open her sunroof. The cold night air helped her brain regain some clarity.

Pitch black, Kate was all ears.

She heard the door's shut.

Heard the locks fall into place.

She waited for the rumble of the truck engine and the swaying movement as she was driven away.

But that didn't happen.

Long minutes went by.

Was this a trap?

Was Cyn waiting to throw the doors open to…she had no idea what Cyn would want with her. But Kate was done waiting. She needed to figure this out and find a way to escape.

Her phone and the comms switch went nowhere.

Cyn must have set up a jammer. Jack's fiancée Suz had experienced that when she was trying to save her class during the terror attack at her school.

Kate crawled out the sunroof and slid down the back of her car, clinging to the luggage rack as long as she could, so she could land on the metal floor with as little noise as possible.

Kate put her ear to the side and listened.

"Like I said, I've parked here before." It was a man's voice. "Never had me no hassle about it. You're good to go."

"I have somewhere I need to be. I can give you a lift as far as the grocery store. Is that okay?"

"You aren't going to leave that lady in there very long, though, right? I mean, I saw she had a baby and a dog."

"Not long. Let's go get in my car. I'm running late."

And then Kate heard it. The *Pop-Pop-Pop* of a suppressed triple tap.

Kate peed down her leg, emptying her bladder.

Cyn had killed the man. Kate was sure of it. Just chatting, then dead.

Kate waited for the sound of Cyn's car to disappear down the road.

Freezing cold, Kate would have to change quickly into the extra pair of pants she'd brought to stay with Faith.

Not knowing how long Cyn would be gone, Kate needed to get them out *now*.

First things first.

Kate clambered back up and over the roof, down through the hatch to turn off the engine. That meant no heat, but there wasn't enough ventilation in the truck to stop a buildup of carbon dioxide.

She flicked on her interior lights and peered around at her son, sleeping through all this, wrapped up in his snowsuit despite Houston's earlier ferocity.

Kate slid off her shoes and quickly pulled off her wet socks, pants, and panties. She used a diaper wipe and drool cloth from Zack's bag to get herself clean and dry so she was functional. While her mind scanned over what she knew about trucks—nothing—and the equipment that Iniquus required her to carry at all times, she dressed again in dry clothes. She chose her fleece pajama bottoms instead of her yoga pants.

Scrambling onto her seat and back through the sunroof, she slid down the back, keys in hand to let Houston out.

Kate had to get Houston to crawl under the vehicle to free up enough space for Kate to pull out the dog crate.

She collapsed and folded it with shaking hands, then stilled to listen.

Nothing.

Stowing the crate to the side out of her way, she called Houston back out.

Houston crawled backward—tail, then fur butt, then out.

The Iniquus emergency kit—enough food and water for 72 hours for each of them. There was a kit for Houston, too, stashed in the storage compartment under his crate. Emergency sleeping bags made of mylar. Flashlights… with the number of diapers she'd brought, Kate could survive and keep Zack and Houston alive for at least the initial 72 hours if she were trapped here. Longer when she dove into Ryan's bag as well. Survival from this situation was not an immediate weight. She needed to let that go.

The scariest thing? Cyn could come back.

All right, she needed to get out. Again, she went back in her mind to all the things she knew or had seen about trucks.

It wasn't a lot.

But she did know that the roof wouldn't hold an adult's weight. She'd seen that in a few movies. Though movies weren't at all reliable, Kate was going to at least test the hypothesis.

Because the locking system on the back door was sure to keep robbers out, and when she knocked on the walls, they seemed pretty solid, up seemed her only chance.

Kate examined the toolbox. It held mostly wrenches and screwdrivers, wire, duct tape. She pulled out the tire iron. Would that do the trick?

Kate had so much adrenaline running through her system right now, she thought she could probably rip the lid off this truck with her fingernails. She shut the hatch and dragged herself back up to the roof.

There, she whaled on the panel.

Flimsy as all get out, it wasn't nearly as hard as she thought it was going to be. But examining it, there was no way it would hold her weight.

She climbed down from the car roof to think.

Standing at the back of the car with a flashlight between her teeth, Kate moved through the things she had in her vehicle. No solution presented itself to her.

Even if she were to get onto the roof of the truck, could she get down to the ground? She hadn't seen a ladder attached, but then again, that wasn't where her attention was at the time.

If she got down, was the truck locked with a key and would Kate no longer have access and could no longer reach her son?

Would she abandon Zack to go find help with the potential for Cyn to come back and for Zack to disappear into the night?

When Kate was following Cyn's driving instructions, Kate saw nothing and no one. She had no idea where she could reach help.

If she got down and could find the jammer…

She was not going to leave her baby.

Not.

"All right, Houston. Here we go," she said, gathering three strobe flashlights into her coat pockets.

Kate looked at the top of her sleeping child's head, visbible over the seat. Turning her face toward the Heaven's she said, "Thank you for that much. His crying would be such a distraction."

Would this work?

She had no idea. They were pretty far from anything or anyone.

Was Cyn out there watching to see if Kate could get free? She had no idea.

But Kate had learned that sitting back and waiting for the magic "fix-this fairy" to show up was a bad strategy.

"Okay. This might be a little weird, but you've got lots of training. Maybe you can figure this out." Kate tried to lift Houston. And Houston was very gentle about it, holding herself passively as Kate lifted with a grunt.

There was no way Kate could get Houston past her shoulders.

Blowing out a gust of frustration, Kate paused and waited for an idea to come to her.

Her gaze alighted on Houston's training vest—a tactical vest. This was the kind of vest that Reaper used when he was attaching his work K9 to him as he fast roped into a situation. The clasps would hold Houston's weight. Kate tied a figure-eight knot through the handle.

Back up on the car roof, pressing her feet into the back of the truck for stability, she hoisted Houston from the truck's metal floor up to the car roof.

Panting, Kate hugged Houston to her. "I'm so glad you're here, my helper girl."

Awkwardly getting to her feet, keeping clear of the sunroof's opening, Kate tried again to lift and press Houston through the hole that she'd made with the displaced truck roof panel.

But even with her fear and anger giving her strength, she couldn't get Houston up high enough to make it out. Her vest-lifting strategy wouldn't work here.

Kate set Houston down and signaled her to sit and wait.

Such a good girl.

A miracle of a girl.

Houston was doing everything that Kate was asking of her.

Kate closed her eyes and pictured Houston training the obstacle course at Iniquus. And then, a possible solution occurred to her. Kate reached over her head and gripped the edge of the roof and stuck a feet out in plank position, making herself as much like the ramps Cerberus had going up to the ropes courses. Kate had no idea what the signal was for this move, so she just pictured it in her head as clearly as she could and said, "Climb, Houston! Climb."

With her claws digging into Kate's thigh and back, Houston scrambled up, but then seemed at a loss. "Keep going. Go, Houston! Up! Up!" Still clinging to the roof Kate wiggled herself a bit as some kind of encouragement. Houston seemed to understand because she hooked her paws over the roof and struggled up. With her back paw on Kate's head for the final thrust, Houston was out on the roof.

Panting, Kate told Houston to stand there.

Reaching for the emergency strobes set to ultra-high lumen, oscillating light, Kate set them on the roof.

And lastly, she signaled to Houston to bark.

Houston's call for help echoed out into the night sky.

Man, it was cold.

"Please, if there are any guardian angels out tonight, please hear Houston and come to our rescue."

Sobbing, she sat down to wait.

44

Cyn

Monday Night

Though the weather was way too cold for her get up, Cyn was hitting the stupid romance tropes, wearing strappy sandals and a white toga-styled dress that wasn't quite fingertip length.

Her hair draped over her shoulders in long wavy curls. Her makeup was light but flattering.

She looked beautiful.

She knew that Reaper thought so, too. He hadn't taken his eyes off her. They were dark with intensity. A wolfishness directed toward her that she hadn't experienced from him before. Feral energy. She liked it.

Her long legs were freezing cold as she, wrapped in a pashmina, accepted Harlow's hand climbing into the Omega SUV. She was grateful for the interior's warmth as the chauffer shut the door behind her.

Dressing like a damsel was both inconvenient and uncomfortable.

But what did Cyn care? She was ebullient.

This was the last night of her efforts.

After tonight, she would be Nike, and bask in her victory.

Cyn had arranged for a caterer to go into the house earlier and lay out a spread on the buffet. Those remote door opening apps were ridiculous, and she was oh so glad for them. They made her life that much easier.

With a heads up that the meal had been arranged, Harlow could act as if he were the host with the most as he flourished his arm to invite her in.

Harlow took Cyn's wrap while Reaper and Max inspected the house.

Allowing the K9 to run, nose chuffing, looking for the drugs that ClearSight insisted Harlow was using.

Of course, what ClearSight's CEO was really worried about was the file of pictures and documents that Cyn had showed him. Such a naughty boy. So many bad actions that would mean a long, long prison sentence.

Was it work to gather that together?

Sure.

Did it serve her?

Absolutely. Every time she needed corporate cover, ClearSight et al were ready and willing to help.

They'd never met Harlow. Hadn't even seen his picture.

Like good little soldiers, they were given their orders, and ClearSight was very happy to comply, calling Iniquus in a panic, signing and paying for the ludicrously expensive contract.

It was even more amusing to Cyn that many years back—before the CEO got a little too full of himself, before he was a piece of shit lawbreaker—that ClearSight had hired Iniquus to do close protection when they went in as do-gooders in Haiti. It made perfect sense for ClearSight to reach out to Iniquus to deal with their internal issues with "sex-deviant" Harlow.

Things were going to move fast here in a minute.

Cyn walked over to the buffet and picked up a plate.

Fuel canister flames licked at the bottom of the warming dishes. Cyn had chosen a catered menu consisting of things that she liked. So what if Harlow had digestive issues with the things on the menu? He wouldn't be hungry for long.

Last meals were overrated.

Reaper moved into the room, catching Harlow's gaze. "Clear. I'll be outside if you need me."

Cyn put the plate on the table. "In this weather?" Cyn asked, skating her hand down her bare leg and sliding off her high heels. "Wouldn't you rather be inside?" She gave a flip of her long blonde hair and peered provocatively past the wave that crossed over her face.

Reaper stared at her for a long moment.

Cyn read desire in his penetrating focus.

Penetrating. Thinking the word brought a smile to her face.

"No, ma'am. I'll be outside walking the perimeter."

Cyn hoped that wasn't too far to hear her screams. Well, the K9 would pick up on it, surely.

After the door shut, and she watched Reaper walk into the distance, Harlow said, "So what's the plan? Are we just going to eat and watch T.V.? I really wish you'd explain to me what the hell's going on."

"Later," Cyn said. "I'm hungry. The food looks good."

"You know I can't eat that. Did you pick this on purpose?"

"No," she lied as she shoveled up a forkful of shrimp scampi. "I said the caterer should pick fresh and light. You can't even eat the fruit?"

"Not when it's all mixed up in the bowl like that I can't."

"Okay, well make a plate and rub some sauce around to make

it look like you ate. We'll get you something later." She smiled at him. "While you're standing there, would you mind cutting a piece of the beef for me?" She canted her head. "You can't eat that either?"

"Not with this sauce. How long have we known each other? Years. You know this about me." He grabbed up the knife and sliced into the meat.

"I was pushed for time and my mind was elsewhere, I apologize, okay? I'll make it up to you, promise. How about dinner in Paris next week."

"Dinner in Paris, and I'll forgive you." He laid the beef onto her plate.

"Hey, how about you go into the bedroom to stage. Strip down to your boxers and get into bed. Maybe find something on the television to watch to pass the time."

Shaking his head, Harlow made his way to the back of the house.

Cyn picked up the knife, careful that Harlow's prints were on the handle and hers were only on the blade. She went to the bathroom and locked the door.

From her purse, hanging across her body, Cyn pulled a razor.

She began slashing at her skin. The thing that Cyn had discovered over time, was that razor cuts were a bleedfest, and they really didn't hurt that much. She sliced her forearms where they's take the brunt of slashes if she were protecting herself from an attack. She aimed to place other slashes in places that were easy to hide, lest they left a scar.

Once she was dripping blood, sCyn smeared the knife then moved out of the bathroom, her purse dangling from its thin golden chain.

Moving up and down the hall, leaving footprints and handprints, blood smears and puddles, Cyn stood back and admired her work.

And here we go.

Cyn ran into the bedroom, dropped the bloody knife onto the carpet, and leaped onto Harlow.

"What? What?"

They thrashed together on the bed. As soon as Harlow was covered in the blood, his grip prints and strikes bruising her body, she'd pull her gun from her purse.

A scream and a point-blank range series of shots to the heart, would get Reaper running to her side.

Off to Iniquus, she would go.

Bye Harlow, buh-bye now, bye.

45

Reaper

Monday Night

He wasn't supposed to use the phone for personal reasons while he was on guard duty, but Reaper decided that while he was back in the copse of woods that he'd take a second and check on Kate.

Ever since she left for Faith's there had been a low hum of concern buzzing his system.

Could be nothing, but that had been a fairly reliable indicator back in his operator days in the sandbox.

When he pressed the speed dial, he went right to voice mail.

Reaper stared at his phone.

Yeah, that didn't feel right.

He called Faith next. "Hey, have you heard from Kate?"

"No, but I'm just now leaving the hospital, reception is tricky inside. Is something wrong? You sound worried."

"I'm going to hang up with you. If you talk to Kate, please tell her to call me ASAP, would you?"

"Sure thing, Reaper."

Reaper dialed into Iniquus Control. "Reaper. Strike Force."

"Go for control."

"I need you to bring up my wife's car, would you? And tell me where it is."

"Searching for Kate Hamilton and she is not registering a GPS point on our control map."

"Is there a way to trace back to last known?"

"Certainly, sir." There was a pause. "I have her location. The car stopped sending signal on Deer Run Road."

"It just stopped? There was no distress signal with manual or mechanical?"

"We stopped receiving a signal on Deer Run Road. We have a Cerberus Tactical operator team ten minutes out. I'm sending a high-priority request that they get to that location and take a look around."

"I appreciate it. Can you get back with me?"

"Wilco."

"Thank you. Out."

Sweat slicked over Reaper's body. He tried to talk himself down. It could be anything. A loose sensor on the car's GPS maybe. If the car had been in a crash, the computer would have sent out a message, and Iniquus would have been on it.

He called Striker. "Reaper." Without waiting he dove in. "I need someone to come relieve me. Something's going on with Kate. I need to get out of here."

A few quick questions and Striker was up to date.

"Our team is already headed your way with Prescott and Finley. Not knowing if they might have a parabolic ear out near you, we'll catch you up when we get there. Five mic ETA."

"Five."

"Over and out."

Out.

Huh.

The entire team *and* the FBI?

The screams that came from the house raised the hair on Reaper's head. His skin covered with gooseflesh. As another scream cracked the night sky, he ran toward the house, Max at his heels

In his mind, memories flashed of women and children being crushed by shelling, their death cries swelling in the air.

Reaper's lungs caught and held, refusing to oxygenate his system.

When Max and he got to the house, the door was locked.

Reaper stepped back and with a running start lifted his leg, jamming his foot just below the knob.

Just as the door slammed into the wall, BANG! BANG! BANG! rose from the back.

Dragging his sidearm from its holster, Reaper put his shoulder to the wall and followed the sound back, taking a moment to stick his head into each room along the way.

Blood was smeared everywhere.

He stepped carefully over the puddles.

Back in the bedroom, Cyn knelt on the bed, her knees wide. The gun was pressed between her palms and rested between her thighs.

Her white dress, wet with her blood, plastered to her torso.

"Cyn!" he called, holstering his own gun and moving slowly toward her, his palms lifted.

He reached into her lap, and with his index finger and thumb removed her pistol and moved it to the dresser.

Harlow had three holes in his chest. His eyes wide, death had come as a surprise.

"Cyn, what happened?" he asked her gently.

She climbed from the bed. "I'm not safe. I need you to take

me back to your office right away. I can tell you everything once we get there."

"I'm calling 9-1-1 and getting you to a hospital."

"No! You have a clinic at Iniquus don't you?"

"Yes, but—"

"You have to take me there, now. I need to get there for safety's sake."

Reaper shook his head. "I can protect you at the hospital. There's no way that I can take you to Iniquus. That's against protocol. They'll refuse me entrance through the gate."

Suddenly, Cyn's expression changed from shell-shocked victim to fierce anger. "Ryan James Hamilton, you will take me to Iniquus now. You will find a way to get me through the gate, and you will protect me."

Reaper shook his head, watching the blood dripping from her wounds.

"Reaper, you *will* do this. I have your wife and kid. I even have your dog. If you want to see them again. You will do as I—"

Before she could finish her sentence, Reaper was on top of her.

She fought back. She was trained. Very trained. *This* was a fight.

Max barked behind Reaper waiting impatiently for the command to bite.

Reaper's phone was ringing in his pocket as he worked to gather Cyn's sticky-slick blood covered limbs under control.

He picked her up and threw her onto the bed. Leaping on top of her, his knees pressing her shoulders into the mattress, Reaper chambered a punch.

"I swear to god, I will torture you to hell and back until you tell me. Where is my family?"

Strike Force swarmed the room.

With big eyes, Cyn turned her head and screamed, "Help me!

He's gone crazy! The PTSD! He killed Harlow! He's trying to kill me!"

Striker and Blaze grabbed Reaper under the arms and dragged him off.

"She has Kate. She's got Zack!" Reaper yelled and tried to shake of their iron grips.

Lynx moved in front of Reaper and took his face, ferocious with pain, between her hands. "Look at me, Reaper. She's safe. Kate's safe. Zacks' safe. Houston's safe. They're with Ridge and Ryder from Cerberus. She's *safe*."

Reaper's legs wouldn't hold him; he collapsed to his knees.

"Cynthia Demitrova," Prescott said, dragging her to her feet beside the bed. "You are under arrest for the murder of Thomas Demitrova. The CIA has been looking for you." His gaze caught on Harlow. "It looks like we'll have a list of charges to add."

She shook her head. "I'm Cynthia Parker. You have me confused with someone else. I was attacked by your operator. He killed Harlow!"

"You might remember Margot from your time with the CIA. She recognized your photo. Your fingerprints are a match."

"How bad are those wounds?" Blaze asked.

"They look superficial" Prescott said. "Do you want to grab a blanket from somewhere, we'll wrap her up and take her to the hospital for a once over."

"Margot?" Reaper asked as he climbed back to his feet.

"Nutsbe was working on the photograph of Mary Wise," Lynx said. "Margot came in and saw what he was working on and IDed her from Margot's time at the CIA. Cyn had a psychotic break and went on a rampage. Her brother tried to stop her, and she shot him when they were in Istanbul. She disappeared and was blacklisted."

"I know you want to see your wife and baby. First, I'm going to need you to come with us to make a statement, Reaper."

Prescott pressed Cyn forward to get her moving toward their vehicle.

"Reaper is me!" Cyn screamed. "I am *the* Reaper. You," she spat toward Reaper, "are my scythe. Together, the world will bow and quiver. Fear *this* Reaper! Fear *me*!"

With Prescott and Finley on either side of a barefooted Cyn, they marched her toward the FBI SUV parked out front.

As they stepped off the brick stairs, Cyn collapsed straight down, turning into a puddle on the ground.

Finley turned her over and stared at the black hole between her eyes. "Sniper!" he yelled, and everyone ran for cover, leaving Cynthia Demitrova lying in the mud.

EPILOGUE

Kate and Reaper were cuddled on the couch, watching the news. An open box of pizza lay on the coffee table in front of them. "Oh look!" Kate called as Reaper leaned forward to add another couple of slices to his plate.

He lifted his head to see Julie and Nia walking side by side into the courthouse.

"Perp walk. To think I let that woman babysit Zack. That's it, I'm never leaving a child of mine without either you or me present ever again."

"Kind of extreme. I don't think your instincts were off. She's a good kid who had a terrible hand to play from what Lynx was reporting to us."

When Kate glowered, he added. "I get what you're saying. I was terrified when I found out she was in our home."

Silently, the two watched the women as they moved through the heavy doors, their hands cuffed. Berry Greg, with red splotches over his face that looked like a bad case of hives was reading off the charges that included conspiracy and being unregistered foreign agents.

"What's going to happen to their babies?" Kate asked.

"My guess? They'll be born in prison. Probably put up for adoption." Reaper turned to her. "You look so sad. What's going on, Kate?"

"Just…pregnancy should be a time of joy and happy expectations."

"That's not what it was for you when you were pregnant with Zack." He leaned in to kiss her hair. "I'll always be sorry for that."

"It was a busy time. I was fighting to keep our marriage intact and to help his father get well. I'm hopeful though that this time, we'll spend the entire time feeling nothing but joy, and maybe a little morning sickness."

Reaper caught her chin in his fingers. "This time?"

"Dr. Marquette says that our little girl should be arriving at the end of October."

"Little girl." He grabbed Kate's hand and pulled her into his lap where he full body wrapped her.

"Squishing me!" she gasped out.

"This time you're not alone, Kate." He tucked her under his chin and stroked her hair. "I'm there every single step of the way."

"I know." Kate tipped her chin up for a kiss.

"She's safe? You're okay?"

"I'm perfect." Kate smiled.

"That's the absolute truth. You are *perfect*." Reaper stared into her eyes, infusing her with all the love he could possibly convey, and that he felt so deeply. "I am a one *hell* of a lucky man."

The END

Thank you for reading, ***Fear The REAPER***. We hope you enjoyed getting to know the Hamilton's: Kate, Reaper, and little Jack. Their story will continue in future Iniquus Security world novels.

Reaper Hamilton's backstory as experienced through his wife Kate's point of view is available to read now in the ***Kate Hamilton Mysteries***.

If you are reading Iniquus Security in chronological order, up next is, ***Warrior's Instinct***, the first book in the **Cerberus Tactical K9 Team Bravo Series.**

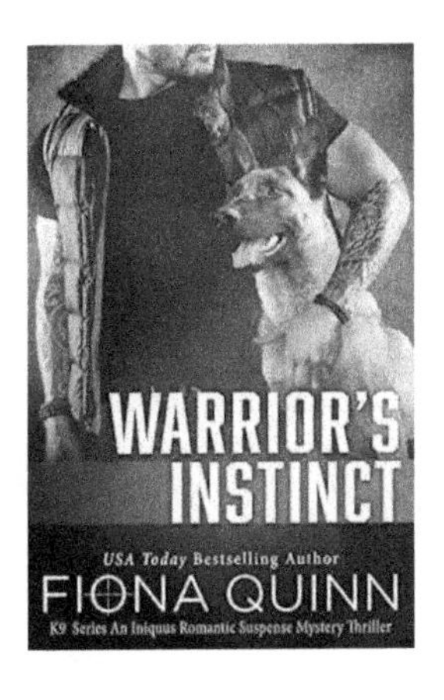

Readers, I hope you enjoyed getting to know Reaper, Kate, and Zack a little better.

If you had fun reading ***Fear the REAPER***, I'd appreciate it if you'd help others enjoy it too.

Recommend it: Just a few words to your friends, your book groups, and your social networks would be wonderful.

Review it: Please tell your fellow readers what you liked about my book by reviewing Fear the Reaper on Amazon and Goodreads. If you do write a review, please send me a note at FionaQuinnBooks@outlook.com so I can thank you with a personal e-mail. Or stop by my website: www.FionaQuinnBooks.com to keep up with my news and chat through my contact form.

I'd love to have you join me in my Facebook group: Fiona Quinn I do up dates, check ins, and parties there.

Please turn the page to find the World of Iniquus in chronological order.

THE WORLD of INIQUUS

Chronological Order

Ubicumque, Quoties. Quidquid

Weakest Lynx (Lynx Series)

Missing Lynx (Lynx Series)

Chain Lynx (Lynx Series)

Cuff Lynx (Lynx Series)

WASP (Uncommon Enemies)

In Too DEEP (Strike Force)

Relic (Uncommon Enemies)

Mine (Kate Hamilton Mystery)

Jack Be Quick (Strike Force)

Deadlock (Uncommon Enemies)

Instigator (Strike Force)

Yours (Kate Hamilton Mystery)

Gulf Lynx (Lynx Series)

Open Secret (FBI Joint Task Force)

Thorn (Uncommon Enemies)
Ours (Kate Hamilton Mysteries)
Cold Red (FBI Joint Task Force)
Even Odds (FBI Joint Task Force)
Survival Instinct - (Cerberus Tactical K9)
Protective Instinct - (Cerberus Tactical K9)
Defender's Instinct - (Cerberus Tactical K9)
Danger Signs - (Delta Force Echo)
Hyper Lynx - (Lynx Series)
Danger Zone - (Delta Force Echo)
Danger Close - (Delta Force Echo)
Fear the REAPER – (Strike Force)

Cerberus Tactical K9 Team Bravo
Warrior's Instinct
Rescue Instinct -2022
Hero Instinct - 2023

Coming soon, more great stories from the ex-special forces security team members who live, work, and love in a tightly knit family.

ACKNOWLEDGMENTS

My great appreciation ~

To my publicist, Margaret Daly who is my rock.

To my cover artist, Melody Simmons

To my editor, Kathleen Payne

To my Beta Force, who are always honest and kind at the same time, especially Elisa Hordon, Michele Carlon, and Kim Schup.

To my Street Force, who support me and my writing with such lovely enthusiasm.

Thank you to the real-world military and intelligence communities which serve to protect us.

To all the wonderful professionals whom I called on to get the details right, including Jonathan Kitchens and his expertise in getting K9 Houston to the top of the truck. Please note: This is a work of *fiction*, and while I always try my best to get all the details correct, there are times when it serves the story to go slightly to the left or right of perfection. Please understand that any mistakes or discrepancies are my authorial decision making alone and sit squarely on my shoulders.

Thank you to my family.

I send my love to my husband. Every day, I am content knowing that my life is better because of you. Thank you.

And of course, thank YOU for reading my stories. I'm smiling joyfully as I type this.

I so appreciate *you*!

ABOUT THE AUTHOR

Fiona Quinn is a USA Today bestselling author, a Kindle Scout winner, and an Amazon Top 100 author - Amazon All-Star.

Quinn writes smart, sexy suspense with a psychic twist in her Iniquus World of action-adventure stories including Lynx, Strike Force, Uncommon Enemies, Kate Hamilton Mysteries, FBI Joint Taskforce, Cerberus Tactical K9 Team Alpha, Delta Force Echo Series, and Cerberus Tactical K9 Team Alpha.

She writes urban fantasy as Fiona Angelica Quinn for her Elemental Witches Series.

And, just for fun, she writes the Badge Bunny Booze Mystery Collection with her dear friend, Tina Glasneck.

Quinn is rooted in the Old Dominion, where she lives with her husband. There, she pops chocolates, devours books, and taps continuously on her laptop.

Visit www.FionaQuinnBooks.com

COPYRIGHT

Chesterfield, VA
ISBN: 978-1-946661-53-1
Library of Congress Control Number: 2022905067

Fonts used with permission from Microsoft

CPSIA information can be obtained
at www.ICGtesting.com
Printed in the USA
BVHW081215111022
649158BV00002B/107